FOURTH OF JULY MURDER

Lucy was pretty sure Pru was home because her car, an aged but impeccably maintained Dodge Shadow, was parked in its usual spot.

Lucy knew the wisest course of action would simply be to leave. She could leave a note, she could call later. She could stop by on her way home from work. The one thing she shouldn't do was start poking around in the hopes of finding Pru perched high on a ladder cleaning out the gutters or out behind the chicken coop.

On the other hand, she was here right now and she wanted to get this thing off her chest. She wanted to get it over with. It certainly couldn't hurt to peek around the hosue, where Pru kept a clothesline.

Lucy squared her shoulders and continued a few more paces down the drive, until she reached the corner of the house. There she had an unobstructed view of the turning area, where the driveway widened and where Wesley and Calvin parked their trucks. There were no trucks, today, but there was a crumpled pile of something blue, maybe laundry that had dropped off the line where several pairs of jeans were hanging heavily in the humid air.

Lucy went to investigate and as she drew closer she realized it wasn't a pair of blue jeans that had fallen at all. It was Pru, herself, lying in a heap.

Reaching the fallen woman, Lucy instinctively reached out and touched her shoulder, as if to wake her up. But Pru wasn't going to wake up. Pru was dead. Definitely dead . . .

Books by Leslie Meier

Published by Kensington Publishing Corporation

A Lucy Stone Mystery

STAR SPANGLED MURDER

Leslie Meier

KENSINGTON BOOKS
KENSINGTON PUBLISHING CORP.
http://www.kensingtonbooks.com

KENSINGTON BOOKS are published by

Kensington Publishing Corp.
850 Third Avenue
New York, NY 10022

All Kensington titles, imprints and distributed lines are available at special quantity discounts for bulk purchases for sales promotion, premiums, fund-raising, educational or institutional use.

Special book excerpts or customized printings can also be created to fit specific needs. For details, write or phone the office of the Kensington Special Sales Manager: Kensington Publishing Corp., 850 Third Avenue, New York, NY 10022. Attn. Special Sales Department. Phone: 1-800-221-2647.

Kensington and the K logo Reg. U.S. Pat. & TM Off.

First Hardcover Printing: June 2004
First Mass Market Paperback Printing: June 2005
10 9 8 7 6 5 4 3 2

Printed in the United States of America

For Daddy

Who enlisted in November 1941 and served in the Army Air Corps for "three years, nine months and sixteen days" in England, North Africa, and Italy.

Prologue

He'd killed before and he would kill again. He couldn't help himself. It was more than an addiction; he was programmed to do it. It was in his DNA. He loved the rush of excitement when he spotted his victim and the sense of power he felt when he'd mastered his prey. They were so stupid. Going about their daily business unaware of the eyes watching them. His eyes. They thought they had it all under control, but they didn't. They would live or die as he willed. As he desired.

He sighed and rolled over on the sorry excuse for a bed that his captors gave him. There would be no killing today. He stared at the thick wire mesh that confined him. It was nothing more than a pen, really, but there was no way out. He'd tried, of course. It was his major occupation, considering the small amount of exercise his captors allowed him. He'd examined every corner, looking for a gap, a loose screw, a flaw in the concrete. So far, he hadn't found any.

So he'd just have to bide his time until they made a mistake. He could wait. He was used to it. He'd had to get used to it. But that didn't mean he'd given up. Oh, no. He was simply waiting for an opportunity. Hearing a door slam, he looked up. Maybe this was his big chance.

The woman was coming towards him carrying a bowl. His dinner. He got to his feet and watched as she opened the door and carefully slid the bowl towards him. "Hungry?" she asked, in a high squeaky voice. What did she think? Of course he was hungry. And bored. Eating was the high point of his day. Even the slop they gave him. He licked his chops, turning his attention to his meal.

And then he heard it. A shriek. "Mom! Come quick!"

She whirled around, slamming the heavy gate and ran for the house. He waited until she disappeared inside, then gave the gate an experimental push. It opened. This had happened before. She'd slammed it too hard and it had bounced back without latching. Stupid woman. Would she never learn? In a moment he was outside, sniffing the air, feeling the warmth of the sun on his back. It was a fine day, a fine day for killing.

He gave himself a good shake, then he was off, tail held high. His bowl of kibble remained untouched. Kudo was in the mood for chicken.

Chapter One

Lucy Stone wasn't usually a clock watcher. Time didn't pass slowly for her; it galloped ahead of her. As a part-time reporter—not to mention feature writer, listings editor and occasional photographer—for the *Pennysaver*, the weekly newspaper in Tinker's Cove, Maine, and the mother of four, her life sometimes seemed to her an endless chase after a spare minute. She was always late: late for meetings she was supposed to cover, late for doctor's appointments, late for picking up the kids. But not today.

Today her eyes were fixed on the old electric kitchen clock with the dangling cord that hung on the wall behind the receptionist's desk in the *Pennysaver* office. If only she could stop the minute hand from lurching forward, if only she could stop time, then she wouldn't have to go to the Board of Selectmen's meeting at five o'clock.

"Is there something the matter with my hair?" asked Phyllis, whose various job descriptions included receptionist, telephone operator and advertising manager. She gingerly patted her tightly-permed tangerine do. "You keep staring at it."

"Your hair's fine," said Lucy. "I'm looking at the clock."

Phyllis peered over her rhinestone-trimmed cat's-eye glasses and narrowed her eyes. "Have you got the hots for Howard White? Can't wait to see him," she paused and smoothed her openwork white cardigan over her ample bosom, "wield his gavel?"

Howard White was the extremely dignified chairman of the Board of Selectmen, a retired executive who was well on in years.

Lucy laughed. "Howard's not my type," she said.

Phyllis raised an eyebrow, actually a thinly penciled orange line drawn where her eyebrows used to be. "Why not? He's not bad looking for an old guy, and he's rich."

"He also has a wife," said Lucy. "And I have a husband."

"Details." Phyllis waved a plump, manicured hand, nails polished in a bright coral hue.

"I don't want to go to the meeting. I wish Ted would cover the Board of Selectmen until this dog hearing is over."

Ted was the owner, publisher and editor-in-chief of the *Pennysaver*.

"Did I hear my name?" he inquired, sticking his head out of the morgue where the back issues going all the way back to the *Courier & Advertiser*s printed in the 1800s were stored.

"Ted? Do me a favor and cover the selectmen's meeting? Please?"

"Trouble at home?"

"You could say that," said Lucy. "It's Kudo. He's been going after Prudence Pratt's chickens and I got a summons yesterday for a dog hearing. I just feel so awkward trying to cover the meeting with this thing hanging over me."

"Is the hearing tonight?"

"Next meeting."

"Sorry, Lucy, but I don't see a conflict of interest tonight. I'll cover the next hearing though."

"Do you have to?" asked Lucy, picturing her name in the headline. That darned dog was such an embarrassment. She felt like a criminal. "Couldn't we just skip that meeting? Pretend it never happened?"

"No," said Ted, flatly. "And if you don't get a move on, you're going to be late for today's meeting. It's five, you know."

Lucy checked the clock. It was five minutes to five.

"They never start on time," she said, slowly gathering up her things. "And town hall's just across the street. There's no hurry, really."

"You better get a move on."

Lucy hoisted the faded African basket she used as a purse on her shoulder and drifted towards the door.

"I'm not going to miss anything. Bud Collins is never on time and they always have to wait for him."

Ted yanked the door open, making the little bell jangle. "Go!"

"See you tomorrow," said Lucy, walking as slowly as a convict beginning the last mile.

The door slammed behind her.

Selectmen's meetings were held in the basement hearing room of the town hall. The walls were concrete block painted beige, the floor was covered in gray industrial tile, and the seating was plastic chairs in assorted colors of green, blue and orange. One end of the room was slightly elevated and that's where the board members sat behind a long bench, similar to the judge's bench in a courtroom.

What with the flags in the corner and a table and chairs for petitioners, the room was quite similar to the district court, thought Lucy. It wasn't a comforting idea and she tried to put it out of her mind as she took her usual seat, smiling at the scattering of regulars who never missed a meeting. Scratch Hallett, a gruff old fellow who had a plumbing and heating business and was active in veteran's affairs, was a particular favorite. She also recognized Jonathan Franke, the former environmental radical who was now the respected executive director of the Association for the Preservation of Tinker's Cove, and several members of that organization. They were exchanging friendly nods when Lucy's attention was drawn to a newcomer. Tall and gaunt, with her skimpy red hair pulled back into a straggly ponytail, it was none other than her neighbor Prudence Pratt, dressed in her customary summer outfit of baggy blue jeans and a free Blue Seal T-shirt from the feed store.

Lucy's heart sank. She hoped Pru hadn't gotten the date wrong, and thought the dog hearing was today. Or maybe she wanted to file an additional complaint. Kudo had gotten loose again the other day, and had come trotting home with a chicken feather stuck in his teeth. The memory made Lucy wince. She was at her wit's end; she'd tried everything she could think of to restrain the dog but he was some sort of escape artist. And whenever he got out, he went after her neighbor's chickens.

Lucy tried to catch Pru's eye, hoping to start

some kind of dialog. Maybe if she apologized for the dog's behavior, or offered to pay for the damages, they could work something out and avoid the hearing. But Mrs. Pratt stared straight ahead, pointedly ignoring her.

A little flurry of activity announced the arrival of the board members, who filed into the room accompanied by their secretary, Bev Schmidt, who kept the minutes. They always came in the same order, with IGA owner Joe Marzetti going first. He was a bundle of energy, tightly focused on the task at hand.

He was followed by newly elected member Ellie Sykes, a dollmaker and member of the Metinnicut Indian tribe whom Lucy had gotten to know when Indian rights activist Curt Nolan was murdered a few years before. Kudo had actually been Curt's dog and Lucy had taken him off Ellie's hands when he'd begun raising Cain with her flock of chickens. Ellie gave her a big smile as she sat down and arranged her papers.

Next came board veteran Pete Crowley, whose crumpled face and world-weary attitude seemed to imply he'd seen it all in the twenty years or so he'd sat on the board and nothing would surprise him.

Chairman Howard White always took the center seat, and was the only board member to wear a sport coat. He invariably shot his sleeves when he sat down, as if he were chairing a high-level meeting of movers and shakers instead of this oddly assorted group of public-minded citizens.

Bud Collins always brought up the rear. A retired physical education teacher and coach, he seemed to have used up all his energy urging Tinker's Cove High School students to run faster and jump higher.

He often dozed off during meetings. Lucy would have made a point of it in one of her stories, except for the fact that she sometimes dozed off too, especially during presentations by the long-winded town accountant, who tended to drone on endlessly in a monotone.

"The meeting is called to order," said White, with a tap of his gavel. "As usual, we'll begin with our public comment session. This is the time we invite citizens to voice any concerns they might have, keeping in mind that once we begin the advertised agenda discussion will be limited to the issues under consideration."

Pru's hand shot up.

Lucy swallowed hard and sat up straighter.

"You have the floor," said White, with a courteous bow of his head. "Please state your name and address for the minutes."

"You know perfectly well who I am," she snapped, "and so does Bev Schmidt. Gracious, we were in school together."

Howard White was normally a stickler for detail, but after glancing at Bev and receiving a nod in reply, he decided to allow this breach of procedure. "Please continue," he said.

"Well, as you know, my property on Red Top Road goes back all the way to Blueberry Pond, which is owned by the town. It's conservation land, open to the public for swimming and fishing, duck hunting in the fall, and up 'til now there's been no problem."

"But now there is?" inquired White.

"I'll say there is. They're naked back there. Butt naked! It's a disgrace!" Pru was clearly outraged: her mouth seemed to disappear as she sucked in her lips and her pale blue eyes bugged out.

Lucy fought the urge to giggle in relief, concentrating instead on the board member's reactions. They also seemed to be struggling to keep straight faces.

"I think there has always been a certain amount of skinny-dipping at the pond," said Bud Collins. "The kids like to go there after practices, especially the baseball team. To cool off with a swim."

"I don't know who they are and I don't care. I don't like it and I want it stopped! Isn't there a law against this sort of thing?" demanded Mrs. Pratt.

White looked to the other board members, who shook their heads.

"I am not aware of any town bylaw that forbids nudity," said White.

"And a good thing, too," offered Joe Marzetti. "There's nothing the matter with a hard-working man stopping by the pond for a quick dip on his way home on a hot summer day. Or at lunchtime, for that matter. There's nobody there most of the time. What's the harm?"

"What's the harm?" Pru's eyes bugged out in outrage. "It's immoral, that's what. It's time this town took a stand and stood up for public decency!"

"You're welcome to write up a proposal and put it on the town warrant for a vote at the town meeting," said White.

"Town meeting! That's not until next April!"

"We could call a special town meeting, but you'd have to get signatures for that." White paused. "Bev, how many signatures would she need?"

"Two hundred and fifty registered voters," said Bev.

"Bear in mind that a special town meeting costs

money," said Marzetti. "It's not generally popular with taxpayers."

"We'll see about that," said Pru. "I'll be back, you can count on it."

"We'll look forward to it," said White, casting a baleful glance at Ellie, who was struggling to suppress a giggling fit.

Lucy knew her duty as a reporter, so she followed Pru out of the room, catching up with her in the parking lot.

"Do you have a minute? I'd just like to get your reaction to the board's decision for the paper. . . ."

"My reaction isn't fit to print," snarled Pru. "That board's a bunch of godless, lily-livered, corrupt scoundrels. They'll rot in hell and so will you, Lucy Stone, you and that dog of yours." With that she climbed into her aged little Dodge compact and slammed the door.

"Can I quote you on that?" yelled Lucy, as she rolled out of the parking lot.

When Lucy returned to the meeting, Jonathan Franke was making a presentation with the help of a laser pointer and a flip chart. He had certainly adopted all the accessories of success, thought Lucy, who remembered the days when he was usually seen holding up a sign protesting government inaction or big business profiteering and sporting an enormous head of curly hair.

"As this chart shows," he said, indicating a bar graph, "Tinker's Cove is blessed with one of the few surviving communities of purple-spotted lichen in the entire state. Once abundant, this complex life form has fallen victim to a sustained loss of environment due to development and pollution. It is now considered endangered and is protected under the state's environmental protection act. I'm here tonight, with other members of the Association for the Preservation of Tinker's Cove, to request that the town take all appropriate steps to protect our priceless legacy of purple-spotted lichen."

Judging from their pleased expressions, Lucy understood the board members were congratulating themselves on their good judgement and wise management of a resource they hadn't actually known they had. Whatever they'd been doing, it had apparently been the right thing, at least for purple-spotted lichen.

"And how do you suggest we continue to care for this rare and wonderful little plant?" asked Ellie.

"That brings me to my next illustration," said Franke, flipping to the next page on his chart, a map of the town with prime lichen areas indicated by purple patches of color.

"As you can clearly see," he said, making the little red laser dot dance over the map, "one area of particular concern is out on Quisset Point. This is actually the town's largest community of purple-spotted lichen, thanks to the abundance of ferrous rock."

The board members nodded, indicating their high level of interest in an issue that was surely noncontroversial and certain to resonate positively with voters.

"That is why our organization, the Association for the Preservation of Tinker's Cove, is here tonight to request the cancellation of the upcoming July Fourth fireworks display."

All five board members were stunned, even Bud Collins, who had been nodding off. They had certainly not expected this.

"I'd like a clarification," said White. "Did you say you want us to cancel the fireworks?"

"You mean call them off?" demanded Marzetti.

"No fireworks at all?" exclaimed Crowley. "Isn't that un-American?"

"Believe me, we are not making this request lightly," said Franke, looking very serious. "We wouldn't consider it except for these facts." He lifted a finger. "A: The lichen is severely endangered throughout the state. B: The lichen is extremely fragile and easily damaged by foot traffic. And C: The lichen is highly flammable and one errant spark could wipe out the entire Quisset Point colony."

"I get you," said Crowley. "What say we move the fireworks off the point? Onto a barge or something?"

"Once again I believe there would be substantial risk from sparks."

Crowley scratched his head. "Okay, you say this is the best colony in the entire state, right? Well how come, if we've had the fireworks out there every year since who knows when? I mean, maybe this pinky-spotted moss likes fireworks! Have you thought of that, hey?"

"Actually, we have, and we've concluded that the continuing success of this particular colony of purple-spotted lichen is nothing less than miraculous. We've been lucky so far, but it's far too dangerous to continue endangering this highly-stressed species."

The board was silent, considering this.

"Can I say something?"

Lucy turned and saw Scratch Hallett was on his feet, his VFW cap in his hand.

"Please do," invited White, desperate for an alternative to calling off the fireworks.

"This just don't seem right to me," began Hallett. "A lot of folks have fought and some have even made the supreme sacrifice to keep America the land of the free and the home of the brave. We celebrate that freedom on the Fourth of July, always have, ever since 1776, and I don't see what this purple-spotted stuff has got to do with it. We didn't know we had it, none of us did except these here environmentalists. I never noticed it myself, and I don't care about it. We defeated the Germans and the Japanese and just lately the Iraqis so we could enjoy freedom, and you're telling me we have to stop because of an itty-bitty little plant?"

"Mr. Franke, would you care to reply?" said White. "I think this gentleman has made an important point."

"Yes, yes he has," said Franke, beginning diplomatically. "And I and the other members of the Association value our American values and freedoms as much as anyone, and the sacrifices made by members of the Armed Forces. I want to assure you of that. But," he continued, his voice taking on a certain edge, "I'd also like to remind you that the purple-spotted lichen is on the list of endangered species in this state and is therefore subject to all the protections provided by the state's environmental protection statute, which includes substantial penalties to any person or agency judged to have caused harm to said species."

The board members looked miserable. If she hadn't known better, Lucy would have suspected they were all coming down with an intestinal virus.

"As much as I hate to cancel the fireworks, it seems to me we have a responsibility to preserve our environment," said Ellie.

"I think we have to look at the APTC track record," said Crowley. "They've been active in our town for a good while now, and Tinker's Cove is a better place for it. We've preserved open space, we've maintained our community character, I think we've got to give them the benefit of the doubt on this one."

"I don't know what community character you're talking about. It's things like the Fourth of July parade and the fireworks that give our town character. I refuse to vote against the fireworks," declared Marzetti, who had grown hot around the collar.

"Well said," drawled Bud Collins.

"Is this a vote?" Howard White seemed uncharacteristically confused.

The others nodded.

"Two for and two against. I guess it's up to me."

The room was silent.

"My inclination is to hold the fireworks. It's been a tradition in this town for as long as I've been here and I hate to see it end." White sighed. "But I truly believe it would be irresponsible and futile to ignore the state regulation. It would set a bad precedent and it would cost us dearly in the end. It's with great sorrow that I vote to discontinue the fireworks display."

He had hardly finished speaking when Scratch

Hallett was on his feet, marching out of the room. He paused at the door. "This isn't the end of this," he declared, as he set his VFW hat on his head. "We may have lost the battle, but we haven't lost the war!"

Chapter Two

The buzz of the alarm woke Lucy and she squinted, trying to make out the time. Five-thirty. There must be some mistake. Then reality gradually dawned and she remembered it was Wednesday, deadline day. It was no mistake. She had to get up.

With a groan she sat up and groped with her feet for her slippers. Then she slipped on her lightweight summer robe and headed downstairs to the kitchen to make a pot of coffee. While it dripped she made a quick stop in the downstairs powder room, then went outside and down the driveway to get the morning paper. Kudo greeted her with a wagging tail and she stopped by the kennel to stroke the big, yellow dog's long nose, which he poked through the heavy-duty wire mesh fencing. Then she went back inside to drink her first cup of coffee and check her horoscope. It didn't look good: only two stars out of a possible five. Not that she really believed that stuff. Not at all.

At six she climbed back upstairs with a cup of coffee for Bill and to wake Elizabeth, who had to be at work at the Queen Victoria Inn by seven.

Elizabeth liked to cut it close and sacrificed break-fast in favor of an extra half-hour of sleep before starting work at her summer job as a chamber-maid. Lucy knew she was counting the days until she could go back to Chamberlain College in Boston to begin her sophomore year. Toby, the oldest, was already gone; he'd left the house well before four. He was working for Chuck Swift on his lobster boat this summer and had to be down at the harbor be-fore dawn.

While Bill enjoyed his coffee in bed, checking out the sports pages, Lucy got dressed. Since she'd be in the office all day and didn't have any inter-views, she opted for comfort in a pair of khaki shorts and a polo shirt. It was already warm and there was every sign it would be a scorcher of a day.

Elizabeth wasn't up yet, so she called her again. "You're going to be late," she warned. Elizabeth groaned in reply. Encouraged, Lucy went back downstairs and popped an English muffin in the toaster. She was sitting at the table, eating it, when Elizabeth sped through the kitchen, the apron strings of her uniform streaming behind her. Minutes later she was back.

"My car won't start."

"You probably flooded it. Give it a minute and try again."

"A minute!" she shrieked. "I haven't got a minute!"

"Shhh. You're going to wake up Sara and Zoe." The youngest girls were still asleep; Friends of Ani-mals day camp didn't start until eight-thirty. Since she had to be at the *Pennysaver* as early as possible, Bill would drop them off, starting a bit later than usual on his current project, restoring an old one-room schoolhouse that had been moved from New Hampshire to become a guest house for some wealthy summer people.

"Let me take your car, okay, Mom? Please?"

"But what if I can't start your car, either? Then I'll be stuck. Call and tell them you're running late. They'll understand."

"I've already been warned, Mom!" Elizabeth was close to hysterics. "They'll fire me."

"Well, whose fault is that?" grumbled Lucy. Maybe there was more to those horoscopes than she thought.

"I know. I know. I'll do better in the future I promise. If only you let me take the car this one time. Please. Pretty please."

Lucy knew she was making a big mistake.

"Okay," she said, handing over the keys. "But this is the last time."

"Thanks, Mom. You're the best."

When Lucy tried to start Elizabeth's car, the engine didn't sound right. "RRR," it droned. "RRR." After a few tries she gave up and went back into the house to get help from Bill.

"The battery's dead," said Bill, who had progressed to the breakfast table.

"Are you sure?" asked Lucy. "How can you tell?"

"I can tell," said Bill.

"Can't we jump it or something?"

"I doubt it'll hold a charge. You'd just stall out somewhere and get stuck," said Bill. "You'll have to ride with me."

"I'll be late," groaned Lucy. "On deadline day."

"Nothing you can do about it," said Bill, with a

shrug. "You might as well relax and have another cup of coffee."

At a quarter past eight, the girls were ready to go, but they didn't like the idea of cramming into the cab of the pickup truck along with their parents.

"Can't we ride in back?" asked Sara.

"Mom'll squish me," observed Zoe, smoothing her new summer outfit.

"It's way too hot in the truck," whined Sara.

"Get a move on," snapped Bill. "Time's a wasting."

"Bill," asked Lucy, as she struggled to get the seat belt around herself and Zoe, who was sitting on her lap. "Will you pick up a battery?"

"I will not."

"We've got to get that car back on the road. What will Elizabeth do?"

"She can damn well take care of it herself. It'll be good for her. Teach her a valuable lesson." He paused. "You're way too soft on that girl."

"Right," said Lucy, wondering why she couldn't take the same hard line that Bill did.

"You're late," said Ted, when she finally arrived at the *Pennysaver*.

"I know," said Lucy. "Car trouble."

"I don't want excuses. . . ."

"Not again. I've already been through this with Bill." Lucy practically growled at him. "You'll have your story. On time."

"Okay, okay." Ted held up his hands and turned to Phyllis. "Must be that time of the month."

"I wouldn't go there if I were you," warned Phyllis.

"I have proofs to check," said Ted. "I'll be in the morgue."

Good place for him, thought Lucy, as she booted up her computer. If only he could stay there permanently. With Bill. They could sit and congratulate themselves on issuing tough lines and demands and ultimatums while the women of the world conciliated and compromised and kept things going.

"Anything much happen at the meeting?' asked Phyllis. The little fan she'd set up on her desk didn't even ruffle her hair-sprayed hair.

Lucy stared out the plate glass window, through the old-fashioned wood venetian blinds. A few early tourists were cruising Main Street, looking for breakfast. Mostly older couples, the men sporting captain's caps and the women with straw sun hats.

"They canceled the Fourth of July fireworks," said Lucy.

Phyllis choked on her coffee. "What?"

Ted stuck his head out of the morgue. "What?"

"You heard me. They canceled the fireworks. 'Cause of this purple-spotted lichen. It's endangered. At least that's what Jonathan Franke and the APTC people say."

"Lichen?"

"A flowerless plant composed of algae and fungi in a symbiotic relationship," said Lucy, quoting from the dictionary open on her desk. "It grows on rocks. And there's a major colony growing on the rocks out at Quisset Point."

"So why can't they move the fireworks?" asked Phyllis, looking quite perturbed.

"That was suggested, but they'd have to be in the cove so people could see them and there's a danger of falling sparks."

"The board actually voted to cancel the fireworks?" asked Ted, incredulous.

"They weren't happy about it," said Lucy. "But I think they figured it was that or face all kinds of penalties from the state. This lichen is on the endangered species list. And Franke as much as threatened to take them to court and they're terrified of spending taxpayer's money on legal fees."

"What does it look like?" asked Phyllis. "I never heard of it."

"It's that patchy stuff on rocks and trees."

"Like barnacles?"

"Kind of. It's softer. Sort of fuzzy."

"With purple spots?"

"I guess so. It's called purple-spotted lichen. It must have spots. Purple ones."

"We're going to need a picture," said Ted, reaching for his camera. "Quisset Point, you say?"

"Just look for the spotty stuff."

He left in a hurry, slamming the door behind him and making the little bell fastened to the top jangle.

"I wouldn't want to be one of those selectmen," said Phyllis. "This isn't going to be popular. Not at all."

"The VFW's already declared war," said Lucy.

"I'm not surprised."

It wasn't the VFW who fired the first salvo, however. It was the Chamber of Commerce. When Ted returned with his film he was accompanied by chamber president Corney Clark, who was toting a picnic basket. Corney operated a successful catering business out of her stylish home on Smith Heights Road.

"I know it's deadline day and you all work under so much pressure, so I brought you some relaxing herb tea and some fresh-baked corn muffins with my homemade lavender-lemon marmalade," she cooed. "Lavender is sooo relaxing."

In a matter of moments Corney had spread a blue and white checked cloth on the reception counter and topped it with an artful arrangement including a basket of muffins, a crock of marmalade and a cute vase of pansies. A thermos held the tea, which Corney was pouring into blue and white striped mugs.

"Sugar?" she asked.

"Sure," said Lucy, absolutely amazed.

"Ted, would you like a muffin? With marmalade?"

"M-m-muffin," stammered Ted. "Thanks."

"This lavender marmalade isn't half bad," said Phyllis, talking with her mouth full. "I wouldn't have thought it, but it's very good."

"I'm so glad you like it," said Corney, taking a chair, crossing her legs and getting down to business. "Now, Ted, I have a letter to the editor here from the Chamber about the fireworks. It's very timely and I hope you can get it in this week's paper."

Lucy knew the editorial page was already set, ready to go to the printer.

"Sorry, but that's impossible," mumbled Ted, biting into a second muffin.

"It's extremely important," continued Corney. "I think we're all in favor of protecting endangered species, but the local economy is also something of an endangered species, especially if this fireworks ban isn't lifted. The Fourth of July celebration with the fireworks is traditionally the beginning of our summer tourist season, and Ted, I'm sure you know how much many local businesses rely on the tourists."

She flourished the letter, making Lucy wonder where she'd had it stashed. Was the woman a magician?

"Of course, this is all stated much better in the letter," continued Corney. "Joe Marzetti and I and some of the chamber members got together first thing this morning. We decided it would be best to simply ask the selectmen to reconsider the probable impact of canceling the fireworks."

"Great letter," said Ted. "But I'll have to run it next week."

"Now, Ted, I don't mean to tell you your business, but you're missing the boat here. This is a hot issue. Everybody's going to be waiting for their *Pennysaver* this week, believe me. You don't want to let your readers down."

Lucy found herself agreeing with Corney. "She's got a point, Ted. Why not run it in a little box, a sidebar to my story."

"Old news is no news," said Phyllis.

Ted knew when he was beat.

"Okay," he said. "I could use a little more of that tea."

"My pleasure," said Corney, reaching for the thermos. She paused before pouring, holding it in mid air. "No fireworks, and now Pru Pratt wants an anti-skinny-dipping bylaw!" She giggled. "What's the town coming to?"

Corney was just packing up her picnic basket when the contingent from the VFW arrived, dressed in their parade uniforms, already wilted from the heat. Scratch Hallett had brought reinforcements; he was accompanied by the post commander, Bill Bridges, and the chaplain, Rev. Clive Macintosh. They stood in a line, hats in hands, and saluted Ted.

"Good morning, gentlemen. What can I do for you?" he inquired.

"It's about the fireworks," began Bridges, removing his cap and mopping his forehead with a large red bandanna.

"We want you to write an editorial condemning this un-American action by the Board of Selectmen," continued Scratch. "The fireworks are an expression of American freedom, the right to pursue happiness. It's in the constitution."

"Actually, it's in the Declaration of Independence," said Ted.

"Well, wherever it is, it's a fundamental American right and we want to protect it," added the chaplain, uncharacteristically bellicose. "We're ready to fight!"

"I haven't really had time to form an opinion myself," said Ted, hedging. "But I'll certainly bear your thoughts in mind. In the meantime, if you want to write a letter to the editor, I'll be happy to run it."

"How soon do you need it? We can get it to you by twelve hundred hours."

Ted sighed. "That's fine, as long as it's not too long."

"Just one more thing," said Scratch. "In addition to our fundamental American freedoms, which must be preserved, we also need to bear in mind that the post, as well as other local organizations, counts on the fireworks for part of its operating budgets.

We run the parking, you know, at two dollars a car. The Ladies Aid Society has a big bake sale, and the Hat and Mitten Committee sells popcorn and glow sticks."

"He's right," said Phyllis. "I promised to make four-dozen brownies. The kind with cream cheese swirls."

"Most delicious," said the chaplain. "And the Ladies Aid Society does a great deal to help our less fortunate residents."

"Thanks for reminding me," said Ted. "That's a good point."

"I just can't understand people who think a plant's more important than people," said Scratch. He winked at Lucy, who was clacking away on her keyboard. "Gosh, she's fast, and in this heat, too." He chuckled. "Better make sure you keep your shirt on! You don't want to get Pru all upset."

Then Bill barked an order and the three made a neat about-face, encountering Jonathan Franke and Ellie Sykes. No words were exchanged, but Franke politely held the door open for the departing veterans.

"Let me guess," said Ted. "You're here about the fireworks."

Jonathan and Ellie looked at each other.

"The opposition's beat us to it?" asked Jonathan.

"Representatives from the VFW and the Chamber have already stopped by," said Ted. "They're pretty upset that there won't be any Fourth of July fireworks."

"We anticipated that reaction," said Jonathan. "That's why we're launching a public relations campaign, and we'd like you to help."

"It's called 'I Like Lichen,'" said Ellie, producing

a fact sheet. "This explains why lichen is important, it's vital role in the ecosystem, and the special properties of our own purple-spotted lichen. Did you know that researchers think it may offer a cure for cancer and other diseases?"

"They say that about every endangered plant," sniffed Phyllis. "But even if they do find some fabulous cure, who do you think is going to be able to afford it with drug prices the way the are? If you ask me, this is getting out of hand. Lichen, shmiken. Who cares?"

"That's exactly the problem," said Jonathan, pulling himself up to his full height and adopting an earnest tone. "Lichen's not glamorous, like the bald eagle or the moose, but it's every bit as important to the ecosystem." He gestured grandly with his arms. "It's a whole wonderful super-organism, and every species has a vital role to play. Lichen is a valuable winter food source for moose, you know. If the lichen goes, it's possible the moose won't have enough to eat and they'll disappear, too. Did you ever think of that?"

"I'm not all that keen on moose, if you want to know the truth," grumbled Phyllis. "My cousin Elfrida hit one last year on the highway and her car was a complete loss. Moose, shmoose."

Jonathan Franke's face was reddening, but Ellie put a cautionary hand on his arm.

"All we're asking, Ted, is that you consider this informational material. We know that you have a reputation for including all sides of an issue, so people can make up their own minds."

"Maybe we can run the information sheet along with the letters from the VFW and the Chamber," suggested Lucy.

"That's a great idea," said Ellie.

"Will you be writing an editorial?" asked Jonathan.

"Not this week," said Ted, with a sigh. He glanced at the clock. "I hate to push you out the door, but we've got a paper to put together."

"Thanks for your time," said Jonathan, extending his hand to Ted for a parting handshake.

"I just want a word with Lucy," said Ellie, seating herself on the extra chair next to Lucy's desk. "I'll catch up with you back at the office."

"I'm really in a hurry here," said Lucy.

"This will only take a minute. I know you have that dog hearing coming up and I'm sure you're worried about it."

"Do we have to talk about this now?" groaned Lucy.

Ellie smiled at her. "I just wanted you to know that I think you've done a good job with Kudo."

This wasn't what Lucy had expected her to say.

"Really?"

"I was so grateful when you took him after Curt died," she continued. "He was a handful, more than I could manage, that's for sure. He was constantly after my chickens. Curt never trained him, he had this idea that he was some sort of American wild dog and that training him would kill his spirit or something."

"He was doing pretty well," said Lucy, "until he discovered Mrs. Pratt's chickens. I try to keep him confined, I really do, but he's an escape artist."

"I know. I had the same problem with him going after my chickens. No matter what I did, I couldn't stop him. Fences, loud noises, nothing worked. Believe me, I tried." Ellie stood up. "I just wanted you to know that no matter how the hearing goes, the board members all respect you. They know you're a good person."

Lucy was appalled to discover she felt weepy. "Thanks."

"Well, I'm off," said Ellie, a naughty sparkle in her eye. "It's a pretty hot day, you know. I think I might stop by the pond for a quick dip . . . *au naturel.* Just don't tell Pru!"

"I wish I could join you," said Lucy, glancing over her shoulder at Ted. "But you know how he is." She pointed at the sign that hung above her desk: "It's not a guideline—it's a deadline."

Ted cleared his throat. "I need that story, Lucy. NOW."

Ellie scooted out the door, and Lucy bent over her keyboard. The little bell on the door gave a jangle or two, and then the only sound in the office was the steady clicking of three sets of fingers striking computer keyboards.

Chapter Three

By the time Lucy typed the final period and sent her story to Ted for editing, the digital thermometer outside the bank read an unseasonable ninety-four degrees. It wasn't much cooler inside the *Pennysaver* office, where the aged air conditioner wheezed and dripped.

"If you don't need me for anything else, I'm going to beat it," said Lucy, fanning herself with a sheaf of paper. "I'm hoping I can catch a ride home with Toby. They ought to be coming in around now."

"See you tomorrow, Lucy," said Ted, nodding his assent.

"Keep cool," advised Phyllis, lifting her brightly-printed Hawaiian shirt away from her skin so the little fan she kept on her desk could cool her. "This is awfully warm for this time of year. Must be that global warming."

Her words echoed in Lucy's mind when she stepped outside and was hit by a blast of hot air. The bright sunlight bounced off the concrete sidewalk, radiating heat, and shimmers rose from the black asphalt road, which felt sticky on her feet when she crossed the street. It wasn't much cooler at the harbor, either, but there was a faint breeze off the water. Chuck's boat hadn't come in yet, so Lucy found a shady spot and sat down to wait.

She didn't have to wait long. Pretty soon she heard the steady chug of an engine and spotted the distinctive red hull of the Carrie Ann, named after Chuck's wife, rounding Quisset Point. Lucy got up and slowly walked down to the floating dock to greet them.

"Hot enough for you?" she asked, watching as Toby tied the boat fast. Sweat was dripping down his face.

"Boy, it's a lot hotter here than it was out on the water."

"Phyllis thinks it's global warming."

"Maybe that explains it," said Chuck, hoisting a fish box onto the pier. He was already tanned from working outdoors and his hair was bleached by the sun. "I never saw such a small catch. This is pitiful."

"Maybe the bugs are going deeper, to cooler water?" speculated Toby, using lobsterman's slang. "Or maybe it's that virus."

"Or maybe somebody's getting to the traps ahead of us," said Chuck.

"Poaching?" asked Lucy, unhappy at the idea. There hadn't been any poaching for some time, but she remembered the violence that rocked the waterfront years earlier, when Toby was just a baby. Accusations and suspicions had flown, and the body of a suspected poacher had been found floating face down, tangled in gear that didn't belong to him. He hadn't drowned; he'd been killed by a shotgun blast. "I hope not."

"Me, too," said Chuck, loading only two partly-filled boxes onto a barrow. "But I never saw so many traps come up absolutely empty. Usually there's females with eggs and undersized juveniles that you've got to throw back. Not this time."

"They're even taking the illegal lobsters?" Lucy was shocked.

"If they're stealing in the first place, Mom, they're not going to worry about breaking the rules," said Toby, who was hosing off the deck.

"I guess not," admitted Lucy, wiping her forehead with the back of her hand. "I need to ride home with you, and we have to get a battery for Elizabeth's car. Give me the keys and I'll open up your car, see if I can cool it off."

Toby tossed her the keys. "I'm almost through here." He laughed. "Promise you won't complain about the way I smell?"

"Wouldn't dream of it," said Lucy, reeling as she caught a heady whiff of lobster bait and honest sweat.

Bill was already home when they arrived, having quit early because of the heat. He was sitting on the back porch, freshly showered, drinking a beer.

"Too hot to work," he said, lifting the brown bottle that was beaded with moisture.

"You can say that again," agreed Lucy, collapsing onto the wicker settee beside him. Toby's rattle-trap Jeep wasn't air conditioned, and she'd spent a hot half-hour at the service station buying the battery. And then there was the matter of the way Toby smelled.

"I hope you're headed directly for the shower," said Lucy.

"You can't say I didn't warn you," said Toby. "It's too hot for a shower. I'm going for a swim at the pond."

"Good idea," said Bill. "Why don't we all go? In fact, why don't we have supper down there? It would save heating up the kitchen."

"I don't know," said Lucy, "maybe we should go to the beach instead. Mrs. Pratt was at the selectmen's meeting complaining about people misbehaving at the pond."

"Misbehaving?" Bill's eyebrows went up. "How?"

"Rowdiness, I guess." Lucy paused. "Skinny-dipping."

"Aw, Mom, everybody skinny-dips down there once in a while," protested Toby. "What's the big deal?"

"Not a big deal to me," said Lucy, looking up as Elizabeth whipped into the driveway in the Subaru wagon, with Zoe and Elizabeth in the back seat. "Since you're a filthy mess anyway, why don't you help your sister install that new battery?"

Once again Bill's eyebrows rose, but he didn't say anything.

"I'm going to change into my swimsuit," said Lucy. "Maybe you could start packing the cooler?"

"Can't I watch you change?" asked Bill, following her inside.

Lucy rolled her eyes. The man was impossible, she thought, smiling to herself.

An hour later the whole family had piled into Bill's truck and was bouncing down the old logging trail that led to the pond. The kids were all piled in the back, along with beach chairs, towels, a cooler and a portable grill. Lucy and Bill were in front, with the windows open. The radio was blaring out an oldies station and they were all singing along to "She Wore an Itsy Bitsy Teeny Weeny Yellow Polka Dot Bikini." Zoe was singing loudest of all, delighted at this change in the usual routine.

When they came to the makeshift parking area in a clearing near the pond, they found it was packed with cars. It was full to overflowing and there wasn't room for the truck, so Bill had to drive into the underbrush in order to leave the road clear.

"Good thing it's old and has a few dings," said Lucy. "I guess a lot of people had the same idea we did."

"This heat's bringing 'em all out," grumbled Bill, busying himself handing out all the picnic paraphernalia. Toby and Elizabeth had run ahead with the towels and chairs. "I'll take the grill, Lucy, if you and Sara can tote the cooler. Zoe, is this bag of charcoal too heavy for you?"

Zoe was offended. "I'm a big girl, Daddy."

"Do you think it's a church picnic or something?" wondered Lucy. "I mean, only local people know about the pond, and I can't believe the whole town is here. I've never seen it this crowded before."

"High school reunion, maybe? Something like that?" mused Bill.

"Could be. It's the right time of year."

Indeed, when they approached the pond they saw that the large granite boulders surrounding it were covered with people. Quite a few swimmers were in the water, too. Music from portable radios filled the air, and the inevitable cries of "Marco Polo" could be heard.

"Wow," said Bill. "The population boom is out of control."

"It's people like us," said Lucy. "We broke the zero population growth pledge. We have two extra children."

"Okay. We'll keep Sara and Zoe and eliminate the other two."

"Bill!" protested Lucy. "We can't do that! And we don't have to. Look, nobody's on our rock."

For as long as any of the Stones could remember, the family had always spread out their blanket and chairs on the same enormous rock.

The family formed a little procession, almost like a caravan, with Elizabeth and Toby leading the way. Toby was balancing a stack of folding aluminum beach chairs and Elizabeth had a canvas bag full of towels and sun lotion. Bill was next, toting the portable grill, followed by Zoe who was carrying the charcoal and a string bag containing some balls and frisbees. Lucy and Sara brought up the end, carrying the big red-and-white plastic cooler between them. It was heavy and Lucy was feeling a bit out of breath.

"Do you want to rest a minute, Mom?" asked Sara.

"Nnnnnh," said Lucy, distracted by Toby and Elizabeth's odd behavior.

They'd reached the rock and started putting down their stuff when they suddenly began laughing hysterically and bolted back down the trail to the rest of the family.

"Those people are tanning all over!" exclaimed Elizabeth.

"They're butt naked," added Toby.

"All of them?" asked Lucy, shading her eyes with her hand and taking a closer look.

Her chin dropped. It was true. Every single one of the people sunbathing at the pond was stark naked. Not a single person was wearing a stitch: not the babies, not the grandmothers, not the mommies and the daddies. Not even the very pink, corpulent man who was standing up and stretching.

Lucy dropped her side of the cooler and clapped her hands over Zoe's eyes.

"Back to the truck!" she barked.

"C'mon, Lucy, be a sport," teased Bill. "I'm game if you are."

"Well I'm not," said Lucy, dragging Zoe down the path.

"Mom!" protested Elizabeth. "I want to stay! Just think—no tan lines!"

"Me, too," agreed Toby. "There were some cute girls back there."

"And some really icky fat people," added Sara.

"You shouldn't have looked," said Lucy, primly. "We're not staying. We're going to the town beach, where they have regulations against this sort of thing. Chop-chop! In the truck, everybody."

Giggling, the kids obeyed and soon they were ready to leave.

"I can't believe it," mused Lucy, as Bill backed out and made a three-point turn. "This is Maine, for Pete's sake. Not the French Riviera."

"Don't you think maybe you're overreacting?" asked Bill.

"I don't think so," protested Lucy, but deep down she wondered if he didn't have a point. Even worse, she had to admit to herself that Pru Pratt was right. These were not casual skinny-dippers. The pond had been taken over by nudists.

Chapter Four

"Naked?"

The voice on the other end of the telephone line was incredulous. Sue Finch, Lucy's best friend, had never heard of anything so ridiculous.

"You mean without any clothes at all?"

"Not a stitch," said Lucy.

"But the swimsuits are so cute this year," said Sue, who had a lifetime subscription to *Vogue* magazine. "Little boy shorts, triangle top bikinis, though those aren't for me. I splurged on a wet-look halter number in black."

"You go swimming?" This was news to Lucy.

"It's not likely I'd actually get in the water," admitted Sue. "But I like to sunbathe on my deck. With plenty of sunscreen, of course."

"You don't get a tan that way," said Lucy.

"If you keep at it long enough, you do," said Sue. "You have to *work* at it."

"I thought the idea was to relax," said Lucy, who occasionally rolled her pants up to her knees in hope of tanning her legs when she was sprawled on a chaise lounge in the backyard. She usually fell asleep. And her legs usually kept that fish-belly look well into August, her tan developing just around the time the temperature started to drop and she had to start wearing long pants again.

"Well, within limits. I keep an eye on the time and turn over every ten minutes, and I make sure to drink a lot of water so I stay hydrated. And I'm aware of shadows and things like that. It makes a difference, it really does.

"And you don't worry about tan lines?"

"Not a problem. I wear the same suit all season."

"I'll suggest that to Elizabeth. She can't wait to join the crowd down at the pond. Says she doesn't want to have tan lines."

"Right." Sue sounded skeptical.

"Well, I can't imagine she's interested in anybody down there. They all seemed a bit the worse for wear, if you know what I mean." Lucy paused. "From what I saw, most of them could've benefitted from an article of clothing or two or ten."

Sue laughed.

The next caller was Pam Stillings, the wife of Lucy's boss, Ted, and the mother of Toby's friend Adam, who had a summer job mowing lawns and trimming hedges.

"Wow, news travels fast in this town," said Lucy, who hadn't been back from the beach for an hour.

"It's the heat. A lot of people had the same idea you did to go down to the pond for a swim. It's funny, but most of the folks around here don't like swimming in salt water. Anyway, I heard all about it from Adam. He went for a quick dip after work and got an eyeful."

"You can say that again."

"Oh, Lucy. You're so prim and proper. Didn't you go skinny-dipping when you were a kid. I did, all the time." She lowered her voice. "I even have photos of the whole gang."

"Photos? I'd get rid of them if I were you."

"No way. They bring back happy memories of the days before I had cellulite," said Pam. "But, you know, I grew up in North Carolina. It was a lot warmer there. I can't imagine why these folks think Tinker's Cove is such a great place that they put it on their Web site."

"What?"

"Yeah. They're an organized group. The American Naturist Society. Not nudist, *naturist*. That's what they want to be called. And they have a list of the ten best places for 'enjoying the natural world *au naturel*.' Their phrase, not mine. And little Blueberry Pond is number one."

"Well, I guess that explains why all those people were down there. There must've been at least a hundred."

"And this isn't the weekend, you know."

"Ohmigod," said Lucy. "There could be thousands."

"Not if this heat wave breaks," said Pam. "Don't forget the average high around here in June is something like fifty-eight degrees."

"We can only hope."

"And don't forget the black flies," said Pam, giggling. "This hot, still weather will bring them out. Reinforcements are on the way!"

* * *

Rachel Goodman didn't see anything funny about the black flies.

"Those poor people!" she exclaimed. "They don't have any idea what they're exposing themselves to."

"I think they know," said Lucy.

"They couldn't, or they wouldn't do it," said Rachel, who was a firm believer in the value of education. "The black flies are just the beginning. There's mosquitoes—they carry that West Nile virus. And I'm not at all convinced bug spray is safe for people. You have to figure that if it kills insects it must be full of toxins. And don't forget the wild animals—raccoons and all use that pond, too—and when they're rabid they lose their fear of people. And I know people like to swim there but I certainly wouldn't do it because I don't think that water is all that clean, what with the wildlife and all."

"I wonder what all those people are doing for toilets," mused Lucy.

"You know what they're doing—and it's filthy. You wouldn't catch me anywhere near the place."

"There were a lot of people. Children, too."

"Not children!" Rachel was outraged. "I hope they were wearing sunscreen!"

"Oh, I'm sure they were," said Lucy, not meaning to sound sarcastic at all.

"Oh, those poor babies," moaned Rachel. "They'll all get cancer and die. And their parents, too."

"Maybe before the weekend, if we're lucky."

"Lucy!"

When Lucy got to work Thursday morning there was no sign of Ted. But Phyllis, who was looking cool and comfortable in a brightly-printed green and blue muumuu, handed her a packet of print-outs from the American Naturist Society Web site.

"His Lordship wants you to look these over and then interview some of these naturists at Blueberry Pond. Find out if they've got a leader or something and talk to him," said Phyllis. Seeing Lucy's shocked expression she added, "Or her."

"You're kidding, right? This is a joke."

Phyllis pursed her Frosted Apricot lips and fanned herself with her hand. "I don't think so, honey. He wants you to get reaction to that proposed public decency bylaw."

"But those people are naked. I can't talk to naked people."

Phyllis was bent over, rummaging in her bottom drawer. "He wants photos, too."

"What did you say?"

Phyllis sat up and held out a box of candy. "Want one? These are really good. I'd go for the square ones, if I were you. They're usually caramels."

She waited until Lucy's mouth was full of gooey candy, then she repeated Ted's request. "I'm pretty sure you heard me, but I'll say it again. Ted wants photos of the nudists."

"Mmmph," said Lucy, plunking herself down at her desk and chewing furiously. She swallowed. "Absolutely not. I am not talking to naked people. I am not photographing them. If Ted wants this story so much he can get it himself. I've got another story. A bigger story. Lobster poaching."

Phyllis's brows rose above her rhinestone-trimmed half glasses. "You don't say." She examined her nails, which were painted bright blue, to coordinate with the muumuu. "That could get nasty."

"Exactly. I want to get on it before somebody gets hurt," said Lucy, scanning the printouts.

The American Naturist Society, she discovered, was indeed a national organization with thousands of members. Their purpose was to "promote and encourage the practices of healthful living including freeing the human body from restrictive and harmful clothing." While they insisted that all clothing was detrimental because it "smothered the pores" they were especially concerned about anything that changed the shape of the body such as high heel shoes or support garments like girdles and bras. In particular, they believed pantyhose to be especially harmful.

Lucy found herself agreeing with them.

"So they're not so crazy after all?" inquired Phyllis.

"They're death on pantyhose."

"Sensible group."

"They don't think much of elastic, either. They say it cuts off circulation."

"They're wrong there. The happiest day of my life was the day I discovered elastic-waist pants."

Lucy smiled and resumed reading, wondering why she'd had such a strong reaction to the presence of the naturists at Blueberry Pond. Now that she was reading about the group, they seemed pretty reasonable. Just regular folks who happened to dislike wearing clothing. Come to think of it, clothing was pretty unnatural. She remembered how she'd had to struggle to keep the kids clothed when they were little. They hated wearing snowsuits and even on the coldest days pulled off their hats and mittens. She remembered watching one of Toby's little sneakers floating downstream, after he'd pushed it off when Bill was carrying him across a bridge in a backpack when they were hiking on a nature trail. In fact, it had been difficult to keep that child in diapers; whenever she changed him he'd attempt a bare-bottomed dash for freedom. And the girls hadn't been much different, struggling and squirming whenever she tried to get them into their snow boots and protesting loudly when she tried to get them to trade their comfy overalls and sneakers for starched party dresses and Mary Janes.

When she finished reading the last page, Lucy leaned forward over her desk and propped her chin in her hand, asking herself what she found so offensive about the presence of naked people at the pond. She wasn't prudish, really she wasn't. She enjoyed a healthy sex life, she faithfully made appointments for annual physicals and mammograms, she'd given birth four times. She wasn't ashamed of her own body, she just didn't want to look at other peoples'.

Not that she didn't enjoy watching a steamy love scene in a movie, or looking at nude paintings and sculptures in a museum. She'd made a point of taking the kids to museums and introducing them to great art, with or without fig leaves. And she'd never objected to Bill's collection of *Playboy* magazines, they were fine with her. So what was the problem? Why was she so uncomfortable about these naturists?

Maybe, she decided, it was because they were practically in her backyard. Maybe it was because she could choose to look at a movie or a magazine or a work of art, but she had no control over the naturists. Now that they were around, they could pop up anywhere. What if they came to the house, asking for a Band-Aid or something? How could she talk to them? Where would she look? Not to mention the fact that the nudes in movies and works of art and even in magazines were carefully edited. They were presented attractively, even glorified. Imperfections were air-brushed away or edited out. Not like the folks at Blueberry Pond who were happy to let it all hang out.

Most of all, she decided, was the feeling she had that these people were depriving her of something she enjoyed by their presence. If she didn't want to see them, she couldn't go to the pond. Her pond. Well, it wasn't as if she actually owned it. It was conservation land, owned by the town. But Blueberry Pond was so close to the house, and the family went there so frequently, that they all felt a bit proprietary about it. If she saw litter, she picked it up and so did the kids. If somebody had dumped an old appliance or couch there, as sometimes happened, she made sure the town sent workers to pick it up. She loved the pond and the naturists had seized it. They might as well have marched in with an army and raised a flag, claiming it for their cause.

The bell on the door jangled, announcing Ted's arrival.

"What are you doing here, Lucy? I wanted you to go down to the pond and see what the naturists think about Pru Pratt's proposed bylaw."

"I'm pretty sure they won't like it, Ted. In fact, I think it's a foregone conclusion. There's something else I want to work on. Are you aware that there's lobster poaching going on? Chuck Swift told me."

"I hadn't heard anything about that, Lucy." Ted scratched his chin. "Are you sure?"

"I told you. Chuck says his traps are being poached."

"Anybody else?"

"That's what I want to find out. So I'll get right on it, okay?"

"No. The naturist story is top priority. This is big and you can bet it's going to get some regional, maybe even national attention. TV even." He waggled a finger at Lucy. "And we want to be the ones who break it."

"Not me," said Lucy. "I'm not interested. If you're interested, I think you should cover it yourself. I could get some more reaction to the fireworks cancellation. Or get a head start on the listings—there's a lot of holiday activities next week. We ought to play up the parade, for example, since there aren't going to be any fireworks."

"I would Lucy, except that's what I'm paying you to do. I'm the editor. I'm the one who makes the assignments. You're the reporter. You're the one who does the assignments." He gave her a hard look. "Do you understand?"

Lucy nodded and got to her feet. "If you're going to put it like that. . . ."

"I am."

She picked up her bag and checked to make sure she had her camera and a notebook.

"Well, I'm on my way." She stopped at Phyllis's desk. "If I die of embarrassment, let my family know that it was all Ted's fault. Promise?"

"If you ask me, honey, you're not the one who should be embarrassed."

* * *

Lucy tried to remember that as she approached the pond, camera in hand. She hoped to get some discreet long-distance shots first, before attempting any interviews. That was the plan, anyway. She really wasn't sure if she was going to be able to work up the courage to talk to any of the naturists.

But first she had to get to the pond, which was quite a hike. Recalling the lack of parking the previous day, she'd decided to leave the Subaru at home and walk. She wasn't going to risk having to park in the underbrush and scratching the finish on her relatively new station wagon. Walking also had the benefit of buying her some time, time to figure out a way of conducting the interviews.

She wasn't exactly marching along. She was dawdling her way down the trail, actually playing a little game of seeing how quietly she could walk. It was something she used to do when she was a little girl, pretending to be Lewis and Clark's famous Indian guide, Sacajawea. She was walking so quietly, in fact, that she surprised Calvin Pratt, Pru's husband, who was installing a wire fence along his property line.

"That's a good idea, Calvin," she said.

Calvin jumped a mile, dropping his hammer.

"I didn't mean to startle you," she said, smiling in a friendly manner.

Calvin looked like a deer caught in the headlights. He didn't say anything. He just stood there, a skinny fellow with a gaunt face sporting a stubble of beard in a pair of oversized farmer's overalls. He wasn't wearing a shirt and Lucy could see the ropey muscles in his arms and a tuft of gray hair sprouting from his hollow chest.

"Say, Calvin, I'm supposed to write a story for the *Pennysaver* about these naturists at the pond. Would you mind giving me a quote? How do you feel about having all these naked people so close to your property?"

Calvin didn't answer her. He bent down and picked up his hammer and, next thing Lucy knew, he was gone. He had vanished into the woods.

Lucy shrugged and continued down the path, wishing it would go on forever. It didn't, of course. It ended and she found herself in the cleared space bordering the pond. The rocks were once again full of people. It was still morning so there weren't quite as many people as there were the day before, but there were still quite a few naturists stretched out on blankets or sitting in beach chairs, enjoying the sunshine. It was a peaceful scene. Only one radio was playing and a few kids were splashing in the water. One serious swimmer was crossing the pond in a neat Australian crawl.

Lucy snapped a few shots of the general scene, figuring she was far enough away that the figures in the photo would be an indistinct jumble of arms and legs. No faces. No breasts. Maybe a round bottom or two, but no sex organs.

The thought froze her in her tracks. She wanted to flee, like Calvin. If only she could. But unlike Calvin, who had probably been forbidden by Pru to even glance at the pond, she was under orders to see everything she could.

Nothing ventured, nothing gained, she told herself, putting on her sunglasses. They would give her a bit of privacy, which she valued even if her subjects didn't. She took a few steps forward, scoping out the situation. Not so bad. The rock closest to her was occupied by a young woman, an attractive girl who reminded her of Elizabeth. She ought to be able to handle this, she told herself. Just pretend she was talking to her daughter.

Lucy took a few more steps. She looked closer. It *was* her daughter.

"Elizabeth!"

"Mom!"

"What are you doing here?"

"Getting a tan! It's great, Mom. You should try it."

"Put something on!"

"Relax, Mom. It's no big deal. Everybody's naked. It's cool."

Lucy didn't know what to say. Like Calvin, she was standing transfixed, with her mouth open. Like Calvin, she turned and ran for home. She was running pell-mell down the path, panting heavily, when she ran smack into somebody very solid. A naked somebody.

"I'm so sorry," she stammered, recognizing another neighbor, Mel Dunwoodie, who owned a nearby campground.

"Take it easy, Lucy," he said.

"I will," she said, continuing on her way at a brisk clip.

Thank goodness Mr. Dunwoodie had brought something to read.

Chapter Five

Ted was not amused when Lucy returned to the office empty-handed. He stared at her, incredulous. "You mean to tell me you didn't get any interviews? Any photos?"

"Sorry," said Lucy, slinking into her chair.

"Why the hell not?" he demanded, standing over her.

Lucy shrank into the chair, making herself as small as possible. "I got scared and ran away."

Ted scratched his chin. "Didn't you see any familiar faces down there? Wasn't there anybody you knew?"

Lucy spoke in a very small voice. "That was the problem."

Phyllis was intrigued. "Who? Who did you recognize?"

"Mel Dunwoodie, for one."

Phyllis let out a hoot. "Mel Dunwoodie! He must weigh two hundred and fifty pounds!"

"At least," agreed Lucy, who was trying to erase the image of all that naked flesh from her mind. She had an awful feeling the memory was going to stay with her for a long time.

"Anybody else?" asked Phyllis.

"Well, yes. In fact that's why I exposed my film."

"Who was it?"

"Elizabeth."

"No!"

"As much as it pains me to admit it, my own daughter was sunning herself in her birthday suit."

"I wish you hadn't done that, Lucy," muttered Ted, adding up potential sales that would not now be realized. "A nice, discreet shot of Elizabeth would have been perfect for the front page. Just think what it would have done for newsstand sales."

"That's exactly what I was thinking of, Ted," snapped Lucy, looking at him through a red haze. "There's no way my naked daughter's photo is going to appear in this paper. Not while I have breath in my body. No way."

"Well, I can understand that," he admitted, checking the film in his camera. "I guess I'll go down and see what I can do. You can make some phone calls."

Lucy was on her feet, shaking a finger angrily. "Ted, I'm warning you: Absolutely no photos of my daughter. Got it?" She paused. "I'll tell Pam."

"Don't worry," he grumbled as he left. "I won't even look at your daughter."

"I wish I believed him," said Lucy.

"Well, you don't honestly believe the little hussy's out there in broad daylight without a stitch on because she doesn't want people to look at her," said Phyllis.

"No, I don't," wailed Lucy, collapsing back into the chair. "That's the worst part. My daughter's an exhibitionist!"

* * *

Lucy was on the phone talking to Myra Dunwoodie—she'd caught her just as she was going out the door, on her way to join Mel at the pond—when the bell on the door jangled and she looked up to see Beetle Bickham entering the office with a piece of white paper in his huge hand.

"So how long have you and your husband been naturists?" asked Lucy.

She was having a tough time keeping her mind on the interview. She was curious about what had brought Beetle, who was head of the Lobstermen's Association, to the *Pennysaver*.

"Oh, forever," said Myra. "In fact, that's how we met. At a naturist camp in Pennsylvania. I fell in love with him during a game of volleyball. He had a fantastic spike, and his serve wasn't bad, either."

"Right," said Lucy. "Great spike."

"On second thought, don't put that in the paper," said Myra, giggling. "Someone might take it wrong."

"Right," said Lucy, who was dying to talk to Beetle. "Well, I shouldn't keep you any longer. I'm sure you don't want to miss this beautiful weather."

Hanging up the phone, she turned to Beetle, who was leaning on the counter and chatting with Phyllis. He was a terrific flirt, speaking with a faint hint of a Quebec accent, and Phyllis was all smiles, responding to his flattery.

"Anything I can do for you?" asked Lucy.

"Well, yes, Lucy, since you mention it." Beetle unfolded the paper and handed it to her. "This here's a letter to the editor I'd like you to print."

"What's it about?"

"Well," said Beetle, hitching up his waterproof yellow oilskin pants. "Some of the fellas are saying they think somebody's poaching their traps." He shrugged. "It's hard to tell seeing that the catch has been down lately and all. But there's signs. Some people, and I'm not naming names, seem to be doing better than others. A lot better than you'd expect, considering the amount of time they're putting in. Not to mention their history as kind of shiftless and not exactly hard workers."

"Could be luck," suggested Lucy. "Maybe they found a hot spot."

"Could be," admitted Beetle, sounding doubtful. "And that's why I worded this letter very carefully. It's just kind of a general plea to play fair, if you get my meaning."

"I get it," said Lucy, quickly perusing the letter. "But do you think the poachers will read it? And if they do, will they take it to heart?"

"I hope so, Lucy," said Beetle. "It'd be in their best interest, that's for sure. Lobstermen don't take kindly to poachers. Folks who mess with a man's livelihood have a way of turning up dead. It's happened before, and I don't want to see it happen again."

"Me, either," said Lucy. "I'll make sure Ted gets the letter."

"Thank you kindly, Lucy," he said, flashing her an irresistibly lopsided smile, "and have a nice day." He paused on his way out the door and winked at Phyllis. *"Au revoir, madame."*

Ted read the letter thoughtfully when he returned, but didn't say anything.

"I think we've really got to look into this," said Lucy. "Maybe we can help defuse the situation before there's any violence."

"We only report the news, Lucy," said Ted. "We can't change it."

"That's not exactly true, Ted. Take the school budget increase. That would never have passed except for our coverage, showing how Tinker's Cove students were doing worse on standardized exams than kids in towns with bigger budgets."

He read the letter again.

"Okay," he said, with a sigh. "I'll run the letter and budget space for a story in next week's issue. Okay?"

"Okay," said Lucy. She chewed her lip nervously. "So, did you get any good photos at the pond?"

"Sure did." Ted sounded awfully pleased with himself. "And interviews, too."

Lucy swallowed hard. "Elizabeth?"

"She wasn't there. She must've left."

Lucy gave a huge sigh of relief, but she knew it was only temporary. She wanted to stop Elizabeth's nude sunbathing but she wasn't sure how to do it. She couldn't lock her in the house, after all.

One of the things Lucy liked most about working at the *Pennysaver* was the flexible hours. Today, for example, she was finished by two o'clock which give her time to stop by the library to return her books. While she was there, she decided, she'd see if there were any books offering expert advice to parents of young adults. She could certainly use some help.

The library was only a few blocks down Main Street

so she decided to walk. She hadn't gotten very far, however, before she noticed a crowd of people gathered in front of town hall, where several tables had been set up. She was wondering what it was all about when a clipboard was shoved into her face.

"Would you like to sign our petition?"

"What's it for?" she asked the ponytailed girl holding the clipboard.

She was one of several college students dashing up and down the sidewalk accosting everyone. They were all wearing T-shirts printed with the APTC logo.

"It simply requests that the town take all necessary steps to protect the endangered purple-spotted lichen."

"Don't sign it, Lucy," yelled Scratch Hallett. He was seated at a flag-draped table with a couple of cronies from the VFW. "Sign ours, instead. We want to bring back the fireworks."

Lucy smiled and waved. "As a member of the press I have to remain impartial," she said.

"You can't avoid the day of judgement," warned a man with a familiar face whom Lucy couldn't identify. He was sitting at a third table with members of the Revelation Congregation, a fundamentalist Christian church that had grown steadily since its founding a few years ago. "Choose decency and godliness and support the anti-nudity bylaw."

Thinking of Elizabeth, Lucy was tempted.

"Sorry," she shrugged.

"Come on, Lucy," urged Jonathan Franke, who was supervising the APTC volunteers. "You're entitled to have opinions, especially since you live so close to Blueberry Pond."

"What's Blueberry Pond got to do with lichen?" she asked.

"It's a prime lichen environment and we're worried the increased use by naturists may have a negative impact."

Lucy reached for her notebook. "Does this mean APTC is supporting the anti-nudity bylaw?"

"Oh, no," he said, holding up his hands. "We're not *against* nudity, we're *for* lichen. Putting Blueberry Pond on the Web site has attracted large numbers of people, and people can be quite destructive to lichen. It's so small and blends into the rock so well that they may not even realize it's a life form."

"That's right," agreed the girl. "So will you sign?"

"I'll think about it," said Lucy. But what she was really thinking about as she continued on her way was how very strange it was that APTC was finding common ground with the Revelation Congregation.

Once inside the library, she shoved her books through the return slot and went to check out the new arrivals. There wasn't anything new about parenting, but there was a Family Medical Guide that had photographs illustrating skin cancer. Just the thing to put on Elizabeth's bedside table.

When Lucy pulled into the driveway, she noticed the kennel gate was swinging open once again. Kudo was gone and she had a good idea where she'd find him. She grabbed the leash and set off on foot along Red Top Road to her neighbors, the Pratts.

In contrast to her own yard, where the weeds and flowers and pea vines and lettuces all grew exuberantly and where bicycles and badminton rac-

quets and volleyballs tended to sprout on the over-
grown lawn, the Pratts' yard was extremely neat. A
few clumps of hostas promised some pale and fee-
ble blooms later in the summer, but nothing was
flowering now, in late June, when almost every garden in town had at least one rambler rose in ri-
otous bloom. The grass had been clipped to an
inch of its life and was already turning brown in
spots. Unless it rained soon, it would be entirely
brown in a week or two, giving the yard a sere and
dry look. Not that it was exactly lush and vibrant
now. It was also empty; there was no sign of Kudo.

The house was a stark set of geometric shapes, a
tall rectangle dotted with awkwardly placed square
windows and topped with a rectangular roof. There
was no chimney, no porch, no bushes to soften the
harsh lines and angles.

Lucy knocked on the door and when she received no answer she went around back to check
on the chickens. They were clucking and pecking
at the ground in their run attached to the coop
and seemed contented enough. There was no sign
of any intrusion, no break in the fence. Even though
she was relieved he hadn't attacked the chickens,
Lucy was anxious about the dog's whereabouts.
Where could he be? She decided to try the pond
by following the path that wandered from the rear
of the Pratts' yard and through their woods. Once
behind their barn, however, her attention was
drawn by the large amount of lobster gear that was
haphazardly stacked there. It was funny to see traps
stacked up this time of year, when they should be
in the water. Lucy was taking a closer look when
she was startled by Pru Pratt's voice.

"What do you think you're doing, Lucy Stone?"

Lucy jumped. "Hi," she said, forcing her mouth into a friendly smile. At least she hoped it was friendly and disarming. "I was just looking for my dog. You haven't seen him, have you?"

"No I haven't and I don't believe you, either. A pile of lobster traps is a mighty funny place to look for a dog."

"I thought he might've picked up the scent of the bait, you know," said Lucy, knowing it sounded lame. "Actually, I was on my way down to the pond. I thought he might have been attracted by all the activity there. I was just headed for the path."

"I'm not aware that my path has become a public right-of-way," said Pru, planting her feet firmly on her property and blocking Lucy's way.

"Ma! What's going on?"

It was the Pratt's son, Wesley. He was about Toby's age but the similarity ended there. Where Toby was relaxed, even lazy, Wesley seemed to be looking for a fight. He bounced on the balls of his feet and alternately flexed his fingers and balled them into a fist as if he were dying to take a punch at something, anything. He had inherited his mother's lean and wiry look; he even wore his dirty-blond hair long and pulled back in a ratty ponytail.

Lucy sensed it was time to beat a hasty retreat. "No problem. I'll go back along the road."

"And don't come back," snarled Wesley, as she trotted down the driveway.

Lucy wasted no time in getting back to the security of her own property, where she was relieved to see Toby's Jeep parked in the driveway.

"Those Pratts are something else!" she exclaimed when she found him in the kitchen, peering into the refrigerator. "I went over there looking for Kudo and they kicked me off their property! Like I was a bum or something."

"What do you expect? They've never exactly been friendly," said Toby, popping open a can of cola.

"I'm not trying to be best friends," said Lucy. "I'm just trying to be a good neighbor. A little co-operation wouldn't hurt, you know. I'm doing my best to control the dog and I could use a little help."

"I'll help," said Toby. "Do you want me to see if he's down at the pond?"

"That's awfully nice of you," said Lucy.

"No problem, Mom."

"I'll go, too," said Lucy. "Sometimes he comes if he hears my voice."

That wasn't the real reason. This was a rare opportunity to spend some time alone with her only son and she didn't want to miss it.

"You don't have to, Mom. I can handle it."

Lucy fingered the leash thoughtfully. "I get it. You want to check out the action down at the pond, and you don't want me along to cramp your style?"

Toby blushed. "That's not it. . . ."

"Okay then, let's go," said Lucy, resisting the urge to grab his hand as she used to do when he was small. Somehow it had never gone away, even though he now towered over her at six feet plus. "I just hope Elizabeth's not there."

"Elizabeth!" Toby was appalled. "What's she doing down there?"

"I don't know if she is or not, but I saw her there

this morning. It was really awkward, seeing her like that." Lucy sighed philosophically. "But if she's not going to wear clothes, I guess she doesn't mind people seeing her naked."

"It's not what she minds, it's what I mind. I don't want to see my sister naked."

"So it's okay to leer at other people, but not Elizabeth?"

"Yeah!"

"I see your point," said Lucy, as they walked past the garden and took the path through the woods. "Say, do you know anything about this lobster poaching? Beetle Bickham wrote a letter to the editor."

"Nah."

"But Chuck said he thought his traps had been poached, didn't he?"

"I guess."

"It's not just him. It's a lot of lobstermen, according to Beetle."

"Hmmm."

"Well, what are they saying down at the docks? People must be talking about it."

"Not really."

"Okay, okay. You obviously don't want to talk about it, so I won't ask you anymore," said Lucy. "But when I was over at the Pratts I noticed there was a lot of lobster gear piled up behind the barn. Isn't that odd, for this time of year?"

"Maybe he's got extra."

"Is that common?" asked Lucy.

"Sure," said Toby. "Like a spare tire, you know."

"Yeah," said Lucy. "But if it's all his gear, wouldn't it all have the same identification on it. The same license number?"

"Of course," said Toby, suddenly taking an interest. "Did his gear have a lot of different numbers?"

"I didn't really notice," lied Lucy, as they approached the pond. She sure didn't need any more trouble with the Pratts. "Do you see the dog?"

Toby scanned the sea of naked flesh stretched out before them. He shook his head.

"Damn," said Lucy, looking in vain for any sign of the dog. "We might as well go home. It's getting on for supper time and he never misses a meal. He'll probably show up soon."

"You go on back," said Toby. "I think I'll go for a dip myself."

"You, too?" She put her hands on her hips. "Where did I go wrong? Have you no shame?"

"Guess not," said Toby, pulling his T-shirt over his head.

Lucy turned around and headed for home as fast as she could.

Chapter Six

Kudo was back in his kennel, crouched on all fours with his chin resting on his front paws and a mournful expression on his face, when Lucy left for work on Friday morning. He'd come wandering into the yard after supper, when the girls were kicking a soccer ball around, and Lucy had coaxed him into the kennel with his bowl of kibble. He'd looked at her reproachfully when she slammed the gate shut, as if she'd played a dirty trick on him, and she was still battling a lingering sense of guilt as she drove off with Sara and Zoe in the back seat, ready to be dropped off at Friends of Animals day camp.

"Mom, Kudo looks so sad. Do we always have to keep him locked up?" asked Sara.

"It's like he's in jail or something," added Zoe, who had a flair for the dramatic. "A life sentence."

"I don't like it either," said Lucy, as she backed the Subaru wagon around in a three-point turn, "but he keeps getting in trouble. If we can't control him, the selectmen might decide to have him destroyed. That's a lot worse than a life sentence."

"You mean they could kill him?" asked Sara.

"No!" exclaimed Zoe.

"Yes. They could," said Lucy, as they tooled down Red Top Road. "That's why it's so important that you all help make sure he doesn't get out. If he kills any more of Mrs. Pratt's chickens we could lose him forever."

"That's not fair," whined Sara, resorting to the middle-school battle cry.

"It's not fair that he kills Mrs. Pratt's chickens either," said Lucy.

"Mrs. Pratt's a poop," said Zoe.

"Watch your tongue," admonished Lucy, as she turned into the camp driveway. "I don't want to hear any more of this talk. It's our responsibility to take care of Kudo and to make sure he doesn't do any harm." Under her breath, she added, "I only wish he'd make it a little bit easier."

Curious about the large flat-bed trailer that was taking up most of the parking lot, Lucy decided to have a chat with the camp director, Melanie Flowers, who was welcoming the kids as they arrived. Melanie was a petite woman with short, dark hair and a big, friendly smile.

"Hi, girls. Are you ready for a busy day?"

Sara and Zoe gave her the traditional camp high five and ran off to join their friends, leaving Lucy alone with Melanie.

"So what's with the rig?" she asked. "Are you going into the trucking business?"

"It's for the parade," said Melanie. "I know it doesn't look like much now, but it's going to be beautiful when we finish decorating it. The theme this year is 'With liberty and justice for all' and we think that includes animals."

"Are the kids going to be in the parade, too?"

"Sure thing. We're counting on their adorable little faces to win over the judges. Competition is especially keen this year. Since there are no fireworks the parade is going to be the centerpiece of the celebration. Everybody's entering floats: the Lions, Boy Scouts, Girl Scouts, the town band, the lumber yard, just about anybody you can think of." She lowered her voice. "Just between you and me, it's the garden center I'm most worried about. I think they'll give us a real run for the money."

"So what have you got planned?"

"Well, we're covering the base with a carpet of red, white and blue crepe paper flowers, you know the kind I mean. And then we're going to artistically arrange some small trees and flowers to make a sort of park-like setting, complete with a fire hydrant. Cute, don't you think? And there'll be the kids and some well-behaved pets . . . Zoe offered Kudo but I didn't think . . ."

"Understood," said Lucy. "He'd probably eat the other animals."

Melanie's eyes widened. "Well, anyway, the kids will wear Friends of Animals T-shirts with information lettered on the back: how many kittens a cat can produce if it isn't fixed, how many puppies are destroyed in shelters every year. Stuff like that. We'll also distribute flyers and cat and dog treats."

"Sounds like a winner to me."

"I hope so, but we have a long way to go." She turned to Lucy and placed a hand on her arm. "Say, Lucy. Do you think you and the girls could help out by making some of those crepe paper flowers? You know, while you're watching TV or something. We need an awful lot of them."

"How many?"

"I figure three or four thousand ought to do it."

"F-f-four thousand?" sputtered Lucy.

"Oh, goodness. I didn't mean for you to make all of them. Could you do, say, five hundred?"

"How soon do you need them?"

Melanie's voice was an apologetic squeak. "By Monday."

"We can try," said Lucy.

"Great. I'll send the crepe paper and pipe cleaners home with the girls."

"Thanks," said Lucy, wondering why she was saying it. Shouldn't Melanie be thanking her? No matter, Melanie was already on her knees, consoling a little boy who had tripped over his own feet, shod in brand-new sneakers with room to grow, and scraped his chin.

Next stop was the IGA, where Lucy had promised to pick up coffee and other supplies for the office. But when she tried to make the turn onto Main Street, her usual route, she encountered a police barrier. The yellow saw- horse was manned by Officer Barney Culpepper.

"What's going on?" she asked Barney.

Lucy and Barney were old friends, who had first met when they both served on the Cub Scout Pack Committee many years earlier when Toby and Barney's son, Eddie, were still in elementary school.

"Look for yourself, Lucy. It's them nudists. They're having a big demonstration against that public decency bylaw." Barney resembled a big old St. Bernard dog, and his jowls quivered as he pointed out the crowd of people gathered around the town hall steps.

"Do I dare?" asked Lucy, peeking through her fingers.

Barney roared with laughter. "You can relax. They're wearing clothes today."

Lucy dropped her hand and surveyed the crowd that was rapidly spilling out into the street in front of the town hall. There seemed to be hundreds of them, all decently covered and listening quietly to their leader, a middle-aged man with a pot belly and a bald spot.

"Where did all the Calvin Klein models go?" she asked Barney. "Do they all have to be middle-aged and paunchy?"

"They do seem to be a pretty well-upholstered bunch," said Barney, hitching his utility belt a bit higher on his pot belly. "Not that I'm much better, but at least I keep my clothes on, except when I'm showering. Their leader there, Mike Gold's his name, is a case in point. I can't see why he'd be in any hurry to strip down. Most guys his size would be happy to hide themselves inside a big old Hawaiian shirt."

The idea made Lucy grin. "Listen, you think it would be okay if I drove behind the plumbing supply place and through the bank parking lot to get to the IGA?"

"Fine with me," said Barney, holding up his huge hand to stop an oncoming VW and giving Lucy room to make her turn.

After she parked her car in the nearly empty lot in front of the IGA, Lucy paused to survey the scene. The naturists seemed extremely well-organized; this was no impromptu demonstration. They were carrying professionally printed signs, some of which had clever illustrations and sayings. "If people were meant to wear clothes, they'd be born that way!" proclaimed one placard. Another said: "Naturists have nothing to hide." "Wear a smile!," "Clothing is optional" and "Nudity is Natural" declared others, but the one that made her smile said, "Fig leaves belong on trees."

Most of the protesters were also wearing official American Naturist Society T-shirts. Lucy suspected that ANS headquarters had sent out a call for volunteers and this demonstration was the result. If they'd gone to all that trouble, she figured, they'd probably also alerted the media. After all, you didn't have a demonstration unless you wanted to get some attention.

Lucy considered pulling out her camera and getting a few photos for the *Pennysaver,* and some quotes, too, but changed her mind when she saw Ted working his way through the crowd, notebook in hand. He seemed to be the only reporter working the crowd, but Lucy figured it was just a matter of time before other media showed up. This was a story that TV news directors wouldn't be able to resist.

She turned and went inside the IGA, where a few locals were standing in front of the plate-glass windows, watching the show outside.

"My word," fumed one elderly lady, whose hair was shellacked into a permanent sixties-era flip. "I can't imagine wanting to go around with no clothes."

"I thought it was shocking when women stopped wearing girdles," confided her companion, wearing a tightly-buttoned twinset topped with a three-strand pearl necklace. "Mother always warned about girls who jiggled when they walked."

Amused by this exchange, Lucy was smiling to herself as she got a cart and headed for the paper goods aisle. There she bought jumbo packages of paper towels and toilet paper, which she balanced precariously on top of each other. She picked up a few basic cleaning supplies, then went on to the coffee aisle where she picked up a dozen cans of this week's special as well as a few jars of nondairy creamer. She never used the stuff herself but Phyllis loathed black coffee. A five-pound bag of sugar completed her purchases and she headed for the checkout where she found Miss Tilley and Rachel waiting in line.

Julia Ward Howe Tilley was the town's oldest resident and had reluctantly agreed to retire from her position as town librarian only a few years earlier. She was as strong-minded as ever and although a few telemarketers made the mistake of calling her by her first name, no one in town dreamed of doing so. She had always been Miss Tilley and always would be, even to Rachel, who helped her with daily tasks like shopping and preparing meals. Rachel's influence only went so far, however. Today Miss Tilley was wearing a track suit with racing stripes down the legs and the latest in high-tech athletic footwear.

Lucy greeted them with a smile. "What do you think of all these goings-on?" she asked.

"Not much," said Rachel. "I don't know how we're going to get out of the parking lot and home in time for lunch."

"Lunch can wait," said Miss Tilley, a naughty gleam in her bright blue eyes. "I'm hoping one of these protesters will strip—while it's still legal."

"She's been like this ever since she heard about Pru Pratt's proposed bylaw," said Rachel, clucking her tongue in disapproval.

"I'll never understand why people who claim to worship the good Lord and all his works find the human body so objectionable," said Miss Tilley, as Rachel began unloading their groceries onto the conveyor belt.

"You have a point," said Lucy. "What do you think about the fireworks?"

"I think Jonathan Franke is running out of projects. APTC got the town to set up a recycling center, they got that real estate surtax for buying up open space land, they've put up bluebird houses and poles for osprey nests all over town. Worthy projects all but not very exciting so he decided to make a big deal about the lichen, which seems to be doing fine without his help and despite the annual fireworks show." Miss Tilley snorted. "It's a lot of fuss over nothing, if you ask me."

"That'll be forty-seven dollars and fifty-six cents," said Dot Kirwan, the cashier.

They all waited patiently while Miss Tilley got out her rusty black purse and counted out the amount to the penny, then took her receipt and carefully folded it before tucking it into her purse. Then she and Rachel proceeded out to the parking lot at a stately pace, her silver sneakers giving off flashes of light with every step.

"Hi, Lucy," said Dot. "Big doings in town today."

"It all seems peaceful enough," said Lucy, unloading her cart onto the conveyor belt. "They're very well-organized."

"I haven't got any problem with them, as long as they stay out by the pond and don't go wandering around town in their birthday suits," said Dot, waving a can of coffee over the scanner. "And business has been up since they started coming. Joe says there's been a big jump in deli sales over last year. A lot of them take picnics out to the pond. Not to mention bug spray and suntan lotion." She raised an eyebrow. "Well, it figures, doesn't it? After all, some parts are more sensitive than others, if you get my drift."

"Are they mostly day-trippers, or do they stay around here?" asked Lucy.

"A lot of 'em are staying at Mel Dunwoodie's campground," volunteered Marge Culpepper, Barney's wife, who had taken the place behind Lucy in the check-out aisle. "He's got a big banner up that says, 'Nude is Not Lewd.' I almost went off the road when I saw it."

"I heard he's thinking of turning the campground into a nudist colony," said Dot. "That's what Jack Kimble said. He's in real estate, you know, and he said he's worried about property values."

"That's right in your neighborhood, Lucy," observed Marge. "You and the Pratts would be most directly affected. Are you worried?"

"I'm worried," admitted Lucy, thinking of Elizabeth. "But not about property values."

"I suppose you want this on account, like usual?" asked Dot.

"Righto," said Lucy, pushing her cart towards the exit. "Take care, now."

"Keep your clothes on!" said Dot, laughing. She leaned across the counter to Marge. "I used to say 'Have a nice day' but now I say 'Keep your clothes on'. The customers love it."

* * *

Outside in the parking lot, Lucy was interested to see that an impromptu counter-demonstration had formed. Members of the Revelation Congregation were out in force, making up for their lack of organization with righteous indignation. Their hand-lettered signs quoted Bible scripture, especially God's command to Adam and Eve to "cover their nakedness" when they were expelled from the Garden of Eden. The group's numbers were small, but they were doing their best to shout down the naturist speakers. One of the loudest was Pru Pratt.

"Sinners repent!" she shrieked, over and over, sounding like a crow.

Her husband, Calvin, was standing beside her. In contrast to his wife, Calvin looked abashed to be involved in a public display, and was practically hiding behind the sign he was holding. "Avoid the occasion for sin!" it proclaimed, in drippy red paint.

Not bad advice, thought Lucy, again thinking of Elizabeth as she wheeled the cart over to her car and unlatched the hatch. She tossed the giant package of paper towels into the back of the Subaru, then paused as she reached for the toilet paper. What was she thinking? She was once again agreeing with the Pratts. She needed her head examined.

Lucy was in the driver's seat, planning a route back to the paper that avoided Main Street, when she saw trouble looming on the horizon. A group of fishermen leaving the Bilge, their favorite hangout, had spotted the group from the Revelation Congregation. At first they were content to toss out a few ribald comments, and to laugh at the shocked reactions of the Revelation Congregation members.

They probably would have gotten bored and gone on their way soon enough, except for the fact that one of the more zealous demonstrators raised his sign and threatened the fishermen with it. That was all it took for them to charge into the crowd, seizing the signs and knocking several demonstrators to their knees.

Lucy grabbed her cell phone, intending to dial 911, but someone had beaten her to it. The wail of a siren was heard approaching and the fishermen quickly scattered. It was all over when the squad car came careening into the parking lot. Not far behind was a white van with a satellite dish on top. Tinker's Cove would make the TV evening news.

Chapter Seven

"This town's going to hell in a handbasket," announced Lucy, as she wrestled the giant package of paper towels through the back door at the *Pennysaver*. Traffic was still not allowed on Main Street and she'd had to wind her way through back streets and driveways to the grungy parking area behind the office. It was shared with other stores and businesses on Main Street and was primarily used for deliveries and as a place to store garbage cans and dumpsters.

"Want some help with those bundles?" asked Phyllis.

"No, I can manage," said Lucy.

She was out the door and back in a minute with the toilet paper. A third trip to get the bags of cleaning supplies and coffee completed her mission. Phyllis helped her unpack everything into the storage closet.

"Store-brand creamer?"

"You sound like my kids," said Lucy. "I don't think you appreciate what I went through to get this stuff. It's like a war zone out there, with the boys from the Bilge attacking the pious folk from the Revelation Congregation."

"Is that what happened? I heard the sirens and wondered what was going on." Phyllis was arranging cans of coffee on the shelf. "Anybody hurt?"

"I hope not." Lucy was picturing the encounter in her mind, wondering at the violence exhibited by the fishermen.

Phyllis voiced the same thought. "What do they have against the Revelation Congregation anyway?"

"I don't know," said Lucy. "Frankly, I'm kind of amazed that nudity is turning out to be so controversial. It's sure turned this town upside down."

"I wouldn't read too much into it," said Phyllis, with a knowing nod. "After a few boilermakers, those boys'll punch anything that moves."

"You've got a point," agreed Lucy, heading for the door. "See you Monday."

The hot weather held during the weekend and there was more traffic than usual on Red Top Road as naturists driving cars with license plates from all over New England and beyond gathered at the pond. Elizabeth spent every spare minute there, ignoring her parents' objections.

"You're asking for trouble," warned Bill, passing a platter of corn on the cob, the first of the season. They were all gathered around the picnic table for a barbecue dinner.

"Don't be ridiculous, Dad," replied Elizabeth. "The naturists are all polite and respectful."

"It's not the naturists I'm worried about," said Bill.

"Dad does have a point," said Toby. "A lot of the guys are going down to the pond to check on the action there."

"Well, I can't be responsible if they're pathetic and immature, can I?" countered Elizabeth.

"I hope you're using sunscreen," fretted Lucy. "Take it from me, sun can really damage your skin."

"You could get cancer," said Zoe.

"It's not fair," grumbled Sara, wiping her brow with a paper napkin. "Because of these nudists, we can't go swimming at the pond."

"Naturists," corrected Elizabeth. "And it isn't their fault. It's Mom's and Dad's. They're the ones who won't let you go."

"Well, maybe I don't want to go," snapped Sara, who was self-conscious about her developing body. "Maybe I'm not a show-off like you."

"That's enough, girls," said Lucy, determined to keep peace at the dinner table.

But keeping peace was no easy task, at the table or anywhere else for that matter, as the temperature soared and the humidity climbed. Frustrated by the unusual amount of traffic when he made his usual Sunday morning dump run, Bill finally slammed his hand on the horn and pulled into the road in front of a line of cars, prompting a flurry of honks in return. Toby made himself scarce, and when Lucy casually asked him what his plans were on Saturday night he was unusually evasive. There was no question about what Elizabeth was doing— she continued to go down to the pond and was so defensive about it that no one dared to say a word to her because she'd snap their heads off.

Finally, on Sunday afternoon, Lucy and the younger girls settled in the gazebo to make the crepe paper flowers. They occasionally caught a slight breeze off the ocean out there, and Lucy kept the lemonade pitcher filled as the piles of red, white and blue "carnations" grew around them. When they'd used up all the crepe paper they bundled the flowers into plastic garbage bags and stuffed them into the back of the Subaru to deliver on Monday morning.

Melanie was in her usual spot, greeting the campers, when Lucy pulled up. The girls hopped out of the car and unloaded the flowers, eager to show her how much they'd accomplished. While she oohed and aahed, Lucy went and parked the car. Today she was covering Officer Barney Culpepper's annual fireworks safety lesson. As community outreach officer, he was responsible for educating town children about the rules of the road for bicyclists, Halloween safety and the danger of fireworks. Lucy always looked forward to covering these events because she got cute quotes from the kids and adorable photographs.

Barney was just beginning his presentation when she arrived at the covered pavilion, positioning herself on the outside of the circle of children gathered around him.

"Who knows what this is?" he asked, holding up a sparkler.

Almost all the children raised their hands. He pointed to a little boy with red hair and a freckled nose.

"A sparkler," said the boy. "My dad gets 'em every year for the Fourth of July."

"Does your dad let you hold them?" asked Barney.

"Sure. It's fun."

"It's fun, but it's also dangerous," said Barney, lighting the sparkler he was holding and receiving a chorus of ohhhs. "Do you know how hot this is right now?"

The kids didn't know, but a few raised their hands anyway. Barney chose Zoe.

"Five hundred degrees," she said, making an educated guess. "That's the hottest the oven gets."

"More than one thousand degrees," said Barney, carefully inserting the spent sparkler into a large coffee can filled with sand.

The kids were impressed.

"If you were to touch a lighted sparkler, you'd get a very bad burn. It could also set your clothes on fire. Who can think of some safety rules for sparklers?"

"Don't have them," offered a little girl with glasses.

"That's the safest thing, absolutely," said Barney. "But what if you do have them?"

"When they're done, put them in sand like you did," suggested a serious looking little boy.

"That's excellent. Anything else?"

The group was stymied.

"Well, if you're holding a sparkler be very careful. Watch it. Keep it away from other people. Don't run with it. Hold it out, away from your clothes. Don't let it get near your face, and don't keep holding it after it burns out because the wire stays very hot. And always have a bucket of water nearby, just in case of fire. Okay?" Barney held up a string of firecrackers. "Who can tell me what these are?"

"Firecrackers!" chorused the kids.

"Anybody here ever set off any firecrackers?"

If they had, nobody was going to admit it.

Barney chuckled and winked at Lucy.

"Firecrackers make a lot of noise, right?" Barney had everyone step back and lit the string, which popped and crackled and banged and danced about on the ground. "They don't seem too dangerous, do they?"

"If you put one in a can it will make the can bounce," offered the boy with freckles.

"What do you do if you put a firecracker under a can and it doesn't go off?"

"You look and see if it's gone out."

"NO YOU DON'T!" yelled Barney. "If it goes off when you're looking, you could hurt your eyes. Even go blind."

Barney's expression became very serious. "Do you know how many people are injured by fireworks every year?"

"Millions?" guessed the boy with freckles. He looked so serious that Lucy couldn't resist snapping his photo.

"Not millions, thank goodness," said Barney. "It's around nine thousand, which is a lot of people. That's why firecrackers and most other fireworks are illegal in our state. They can get you in big trouble."

The children had grown very quiet. Lucy guessed some were probably thinking guiltily of the supplies of fireworks their families had at home, ready for the holiday. After all, they were sold legally in neighboring New Hampshire and Canada, too.

"Anybody here hungry? Anybody want some watermelon?" asked Barney, sensing it was time to liven things up.

He lifted a small, round watermelon out of a

box and held it up, prompting an enthusiastic reaction. The kids shrieked and clapped until he
held up his hand for silence.

"Before we eat the watermelon, I want to try a
little experiment. What do you think will happen if
I put a little cherry bomb inside the melon and set
it off?" He held up the little device. "It's pretty
small, isn't it? It can't do much damage, can it?"

Lucy was surprised to see Zoe had her hand
raised. She waited until Barney gave her a nod before posing her question.

"Officer Barney, isn't that cherry bomb illegal?
You said only sparklers are legal, didn't you?"

"That's a very good question, Zoe," said Barney,
adding a big humph. "This cherry bomb was con-
fiscated from somebody who was trying to bring it
into the country illegally from Canada. It was given
to our department for demonstration purposes
only." He paused, letting this information sink in,
then pointed to a little girl with long braids. "I see
we have another question."

"Will it make the watermelon taste funny?" she
asked.

"It might," agreed Barney. "But we won't know
unless we try. Everybody move back."

Once he had everyone gathered at one end of
the pavilion, he took the melon to the other end,
where he set it on a concrete block. Then he donned
safety glasses before he dropped the cherry bomb
into the melon and awkwardly scampered away. A
minute later, the fireworks started popping and
the melon exploded, spraying chunks of rind everywhere.

"Sorry, kids. I didn't expect that to happen. I

guess these firecrackers are more powerful than we thought, hunh?"

There were nods all round, as well as a few pouts.

"I want you to remember what happened to this watermelon if somebody asks you to play with fireworks on the Fourth of July, okay? They may look pretty, and you might think it would be fun to play with them, but they can be very dangerous They can really hurt you, and I don't want to visit you in the hospital."

The kids were clearly impressed, sitting silently with somber expressions.

"Well, lucky for you, I brought two watermelons." Barney bent over and hoisted an even larger melon out of the box.

The kids cheered.

Afterwards, when they were sitting side by side, chewing on half-moons of ripe, red watermelon, Lucy asked Barney about the scuffle on Friday afternoon.

"Just between you and me," he said, wiping his chin with his huge hand, "that whole brouhaha had nothing at all to do with the church. Those guys were after Calvin Pratt."

"Calvin?"

"Yeah. It's no secret that a lot of the fishermen suspect him and his son Wesley there of poaching their traps. He hasn't been very popular on the waterfront for some time."

"Really? I didn't know that."

Barney smiled slyly. "You should read those police logs you pick up every week."

"I would if I had time," said Lucy, defending herself. "Phyllis scans them into the computer."

Barney took a bite of watermelon. "We've saved his butt a coupla times, breaking up fights."

"No wonder he looked so miserable," said Lucy. "Pru probably dragged him there."

"I'll bet. He knew he was in big trouble if he was spotted."

"Did they hurt him?"

"Nah, he ran for his truck as soon as he saw them coming. A couple of the naturists got in the way, there were some bruises. No broken bones."

Lucy nodded. "You know, there's an awful lot of lobster gear on the Pratts' property, behind their barn. I went over there when the dog got out last week and it made me wonder because I figured they'd have all their pots in the water. But when I looked closer it seemed as if the stuff had a whole lot of different registration numbers on it. I think it was stolen." She paused. "Wouldn't that be evidence that they're poaching?"

"Not really. Fishing gear breaks off all the time. They could just say they found it floating around."

"Well shouldn't they return it?"

"They could say they've been too busy." Barney spit out a seed. "It's high season, you know."

"So a search is no good?"

"Gotta catch 'em in the act."

"How are you going to do that?" asked Lucy, who knew the town police department had limited manpower, stretched even thinner by the presence of the naturists in addition to the usual influx of summer visitors.

"We can't, but we've asked for help from the state natural resources people."

Lucy also knew the state was having budget problems, and had cut back many departments. Natural resources had been one of the hardest hit.

"You don't expect them anytime soon, do you?"

"Nope," said Barney, tossing his rind into the trash. "No I don't."

"Mind posing for some pictures?"

Barney grimaced. "I might break the camera."

She studied his homely, jowly face as he knelt down to show his portable radio to a little boy.

"I'll risk it. Handsome is as handsome does, Barney."

"Aw, Lucy." It was going to be a great photo, the big bear-like policeman and the adorable little boy, heads together over the radio. She snapped a couple of shots, just to be on the safe side.

"You'll look great on page one."

"Sales will drop, I'm warning you."

"Never fear. Ted's putting the naturists above the fold."

Chapter Eight

Back at the *Pennysaver*, deadline was approaching and Lucy could no longer ignore the pile of press releases that had been growing on her desk all week. A roast beef dinner at the VFW, a square dance in the Community Church basement, a meeting of the Ladies Aid Society, story hour at the library, bingo at the senior center, all these and more had to be added to the community calendar. Some, like the Drama Guild's upcoming production of "Our Town" merited more attention than a listing and Lucy had to write three or four inches of copy for a brief announcement.

"What can I write about 'Our Town'?" she wondered aloud. "Talk about an old chestnut."

"Don't you mean 'classic'?" corrected Ted, sounding a bit sarcastic. As deadline drew nearer he tended to grow increasingly caustic.

"If you say so, but that old thing has been performed by every amateur theatrical group on the coast," said Lucy. "The entire population must know it by heart."

"Okay, smarty-pants, do you know it by heart?"

"No, Ted, I don't. But that's only because I keep

my brain clear and uncluttered, so I can better concentrate on the intricate details of the bird club's walks. It's the conservation area on Sunday and Quisset Point on Tuesday and I wouldn't want to get them switched."

"Oh, I don't know," sighed Phyllis. "They've had the same schedule for years. You'd think anybody who's interested would know it by now."

"What about visitors? Or new residents?" snapped Ted. "Don't they deserve to know what's going on in Tinker's Cove?"

"Doesn't take long to figure that out," said Phyllis. "Not much."

The office scanner cackled just then, contradicting her observation. Something was indeed happening in town, something that required a response from the police or fire department. They all listened intently, but the only word they could make out was "waterfront," combined with a lot of garbled numbers, police codes for classifying incidents.

"Did you catch that?" asked Ted, screwing up his face.

"Funny, isn't it? When some old guy has difficulty breathing and needs an ambulance it's clear as a bell."

Ted was on his feet, checking his camera and making sure he had extra film.

"Do you get the feeling they don't want us there?" he asked, heading for the door.

"That would be my guess," said Lucy, slinging her bag over her shoulder and hurrying to catch up with him.

"I'll stay here and take the messages," said Phyllis, feeling sorry for herself. But nobody was there to listen.

* * *

The waterfront was only a couple of blocks from the *Pennysaver* office but Ted got in his car and started the engine. Lucy hopped into the passenger seat and they were off, chasing a police cruiser that was racing down Main Street with its siren blaring and its lights flashing.

The scanner in Ted's car was also cackling as the dispatcher reeled off numbers and called in units from the far ends of town. The sound of approaching sirens filled the air.

"I don't like this," said Lucy, who was growing nervous. "Fishing's so dangerous. I hope nobody's in trouble."

But when they careened into the harbor parking lot it was clear that this was no tragedy at sea. Instead, police officers were busy breaking up a brawl. And as they got closer and had a clearer view of things they discovered that Toby was in the center of the fray, locked in fisticuffs with Wesley Pratt. Lucy was shocked to see her normally peace-loving son grappling with Wesley, his face red and twisted with rage.

She winced as two burly police officers administered a liberal dose of pepper spray before grabbing the young men by their shirt collars and yanking them apart. Toby's eyes were tearing and he was coughing and sneezing but the officers ignored his distress as they clapped his wrists into handcuffs and bundled him into the back of a cruiser.

"He needs a doctor!" exclaimed Lucy, frantic with concern.

"He needs a lawyer," said Ted, busy snapping pictures of Wesley getting the same treatment.

"Where are they taking them?"

"The station for now. Court's in session today so they'll probably arraign them this afternoon."

"Arraignment?" Lucy was shocked.

"This is serious, Lucy. Toby's not going to get off easily. I meant what I said about getting a lawyer. Come on, I'll take you back to the office so you can make some calls." He paused. "You better let Bill know what's happened."

"I can't," said Lucy, as they climbed up the hill to the car. "He's over on the other side of the state, picking up some salvaged doors and windows."

"That's too bad." Ted was starting the car.

"Yeah," said Lucy, fastening her seatbelt. But she wasn't altogether convinced. It was probably better that Bill would learn about Toby's arrest after the fact, when things had settled down a bit.

When they got to the office Lucy immediately put in a call to Bob Goodman, her friend Rachel's husband, who was a lawyer. He promised to meet Lucy at the courthouse for the afternoon session which began at two o'clock.

The district court was located in Gilead, a good half-hour drive from Tinker's Cove and Lucy left early so she wouldn't miss anything. That meant she had to wait. She was too nervous to sit on the benches provided in the lobby, so she paced. A few other worried-looking people were also waiting, some sitting with slumped shoulders and grim expressions. Others could be seen through the glass doors, standing outside and puffing on cigarettes. Lucy had never smoked a cigarette in her life but she suddenly wanted one.

A bailiff opened the doors to the courtroom and people started to drift in. Lucy took a seat right up front. She wanted to know everything that happened. But where was Bob? Minutes ticked by, a few lawyers gathered in the front of the courtroom, chatting casually, but there was no sign of the judge. Or Toby. Where was he? What were they doing to him?

Bob Goodman slipped into the seat beside her and Lucy threw her arms around him. "I'm so glad you're here."

Bob made a reassuring figure, with his graying hair and rumpled suit. His shoes needed polishing and his briefcase was overflowing with papers, all evidence of his heavy caseload. He was one of the hardest working lawyers in the district with a reputation for fairness that attracted clients from his better-tailored competitors.

"Take it easy Lucy," he said, seeing her worried expression. "This is just routine. I'll ask for bail and we'll get it. Have you got cash?"

Lucy nodded. "I stopped at the bank."

"Here they come," said Bob, squeezing her hand. "I better get down front."

Lucy watched as the court officers led a straggly line of miscreants into the courtroom. Toby was there, along with Wesley and a few other fishermen. There were also faces she didn't recognize: an older man, a couple of young girls. They were all in handcuffs and looked disheveled and miserable. None of them made eye contact with anyone and a few attempted to cover their faces.

"All rise!" thundered the bailiff and the robed judge hurried in and took his place at the bench.

He pounded his gavel and announced that court was in session. The fishermen were the first item of business.

"These young men engaged in a brawl this morning on the docks at Tinker's Cove," began the assistant district attorney.

He was a clean-cut youth, apparently fresh out of law school, crisply dressed in a spotless summer suit. His sturdy black wingtips were polished until they gleamed and he wore a large, gold signet ring on his pinky finger. Lucy hated him. He'd probably never, ever done anything bad. Never made a mistake. Never got himself into trouble.

"Testimony from police officers who were called to the scene . . ." continued the prosecutor, "one Tobias Stone is charged with assault with a dangerous weapon: a shod foot . . . other charges include disorderly conduct, resisting arrest . . ."

"He didn't resist!" exclaimed Lucy, jumping to her feet. "He was pepper-sprayed. I was there. I saw it."

Everyone in the courtroom was looking at her, including the judge, who had a very stern expression on his face.

"You are out of order," he warned her. "If this happens again I will have you removed from the court." He leaned forward. "Do you understand?"

Abashed, Lucy nodded. "I'm sorry, your honor."

The judge turned to the prosecutor. "Do you have any objection to bail?"

"None, your honor."

"We'll set the pretrial conference for July 30 and schedule the trial for August 15. Is that agreeable to everyone?"

Both the prosecutor and Bob Goodman nodded.

"Bail is fifty dollars." The judge banged his gavel, then leveled his gaze at Toby.

"Young man, release on bail is conditional upon your continued good behavior. Bail can and will be revoked if there are any further problems. Do you understand?"

Toby nodded and mumbled something which Lucy didn't hear. A court officer removed his handcuffs and sent him over to the cashier, where Lucy joined him. She handed over the money, the cashier gave her a couple of sheets of paper. Silently, they left the courtroom, only to encounter Pru Pratt in the lobby.

For once, Lucy sympathized with her neighbor. After all, they were in the same position. They were both mothers intent on the defense of their sons. She greeted Pru with a little smile and a nod.

"Don't you smirk at me, Lucy Stone!" exclaimed Pru, obviously offended. "From what I hear it was your son who started the whole thing!"

Toby didn't linger, much to Lucy's relief, but went outside to wait for her.

"I guess the judge will have to sort that out," replied Lucy. "From what I saw, there's plenty of blame to go around."

Pru's eyes bulged and her face reddened. "You'd like that wouldn't you? Pin it all on somebody else while your kid goes scot-free. Well, your family's not so perfect as you think." She waved a long, bony finger in Lucy's face, practically spitting out the words. "And keep your kids and your dog off my property! This is the last time I'm warning you."

Pru brushed past her, marching straight for the courtroom, and Lucy ran after her.

"What do you mean?" she asked, breathlessly. "My kids?"

Pru whirled around to face her. "You know perfectly well. You sent those girls over to spy on me and don't pretend you didn't."

"My girls? On your property?" Lucy was stunned.

"Yes indeedy and they've got no right to be there. I won't be responsible for what might happen if Wesley. . . ." This was one thought Pru decided she'd better not voice. "Well, anything could happen."

"I'm very sorry. It won't happen again," promised Lucy. "I'll talk to the girls the minute I get home."

"I've heard that before," said Pru, stalking off.

Lucy was wild with worry when she joined Toby in the car.

"Whatever were you thinking?" she demanded, when she slid behind the steering wheel. "You're in big trouble. And I don't even want to think about your father's reaction." She pounded the steering wheel. "I can't believe it. What did I do wrong? Did I raise you to beat up other people? To get in fights? Did I? Did I ever tell you that the best way to settle differences was with your fists? Did I?"

Toby hung his head.

"This is absolutely disgraceful. And it's going to be expensive. We're going to have to pay Bob to defend you, you know. I am so ashamed. So embarrassed I have to involve friends in this." A horrible thought struck her. "Your name will be in the newspaper! In the court report! I'm never going to be able to show my face in town. It's absolutely outrageous." She glared at him, and waggled a finger. "You're going to have to come up with the dough, buddy. There's no way your father is going to pay for this."

"I'll pay it, Mom. Every penny."

"What if you go to jail? Do you know you could be going to jail? Did you think of that? My son a convict! A criminal. Ohmigod. Jail!"

"Mr. Goodman said it would probably be a year's probation."

"He can't be sure of that. What if the judge decides to make an example of you? What if Wesley Pratt is his favorite nephew or something? You could be in really big trouble."

"I don't think Wesley Pratt is anybody's favorite anything," muttered Toby.

"Don't get wise with me!" snapped Lucy. "You're in no position to start getting cocky."

"Well, your position isn't so hot, either, is it?" exclaimed Toby, finally exploding. "I mean, you've got a court date, too, don't you? With the dog?"

Chagrined, Lucy bit her lip. "You're right. Who am I to scold you? I'm in trouble, too." She chewed her lip. "It's even worse than that. Mrs. Pratt said she caught the girls on her property. What is going on? When did we turn into a family of criminals?"

"We're not criminals, Mom. We're good people. Circumstances have been against us, that's all, and we ended up on the wrong side of the law."

"I know," said Lucy, wondering as she started the car how something like this could happen to such nice, decent people. And even worse, how was she going to tell Bill?

* * *

Lucy made sure Toby was out of the house and the girls were upstairs, out of the way, when Bill finally came home towards eight o'clock. She warmed up his dinner in the microwave while he settled himself at the round golden oak kitchen table with a cold beer.

"How was your day?" she asked brightly, setting the plate of meatloaf and mashed potatoes in front of him and taking a seat.

"Good."

"Traffic bad?"

"Not really."

"Did you get what you wanted?"

"Pretty much."

"Did you get a good deal?"

Bill put down his fork. "Is something the matter, Lucy?"

"Why do you say that?"

"You seem unusually interested in my day. Plus, there's no sign of the kids. What's going on?"

"Brace yourself. I've got bad news."

Bill took a swallow of beer and carefully set the glass back down on the table.

"We're not at the hospital, so it can't be that bad. What is it?"

"Toby got in a fight and got arrested. He's out on bail but he has a trial in August. He's charged with disorderly conduct, resisting arrest and assault with a deadly weapon."

"Deadly weapon?"

"A shod foot."

"Oh," said Bill, spearing a piece of lettuce and chewing it slowly. "Who was he fighting with?"

"Wesley Pratt."

"Somehow I'm not surprised."

"It's not about the dog, if that's what you're thinking." Lucy sighed. "Not that Toby's saying much about it, but I think it's about poaching. Wesley and Calvin are the prime suspects."

"It would be a Pratt, wouldn't it?"

"Why do you say that?"

"I got a call from Mrs. Pratt the other day, when you were out. Apparently Sara and Zoe were over in her yard. She says if they come back she won't be responsible for what happens to them."

"Why didn't you tell me? I saw Pru at the courthouse and she lit into me." Lucy took a sip of Bill's beer. "What were they doing over there, anyway?"

Bill scraped his plate with his fork, getting the last bit of gravy and mashed potato. "They told me they're upset about the dog hearing and they wanted to get evidence that she mistreats her chickens." He chuckled. "They're their mother's daughters, that's for sure."

"And Toby's your son," replied Lucy.

"That's what you keep saying," said Bill, reaching into the refrigerator for another beer. "But personally, I have my doubts."

Chapter Nine

B ill was in a foul mood next morning and barely touched the bacon and eggs Lucy cooked up for him as a treat. Toby wasn't around and Lucy thought his early hours were one bright spot in a day that didn't look very promising.

"Don't forget we have the dog hearing tonight," she told him.

"It never rains but it pours," he said, adding a big sigh for emphasis.

"Oh, cheer up," said Lucy, who was consulting the horoscopes. "You've got a five-star day."

"What's mine?" asked Elizabeth, breezing into the kitchen and pouring herself a cup of coffee.

"Four. It says, 'Your adventurous nature can lead you in new and rewarding directions if you will trust yourself.' "

"I think she's been quite adventurous enough," said Bill, draining his coffee and standing up.

"What's that supposed to mean?" demanded Elizabeth, who was always ready to defend herself.

"You know very well what I mean, young lady," said Bill. "You've had your fling with this nudism but now it's time to stop, especially considering your brother's situation."

Elizabeth glared at him. "Are you saying I can't sun myself because *Toby* got himself in trouble? That makes no sense at all!"

"It makes plenty of sense," said Bill. "You've got to think about your reputation, and what your brother does affects that."

"What is this? A time warp?" Elizabeth rolled her eyes. "This isn't the fifties, Dad."

"Your father has a point," said Lucy. "This is a small town and people talk. They're going to start wondering what's going on with the Stone family." She looked out the window towards the kennel, where Kudo was stretched out with his chin on his paws. "We all need to keep a low profile for a while, until we drop off people's radar screens."

"This is nuts," said Elizabeth, throwing her hands up in exasperation. "I'm out of here. At least they're sane at the Queen Vic." She paused at the door. "And don't count on me for supper—I've got plans."

"What plans?" demanded Bill, but Elizabeth was out the door.

"You've got to do something about that girl," he said, picking up his lunch cooler. "She's out of control."

"Right. I'll do what I can," said Lucy, standing on tiptoe to give him a peck on the cheek. She stroked his arm. "Everything will be okay."

"I hope so," he said.

Lucy watched through the screen door as he trudged out to his truck, looking as if he had the weight of the world on his shoulders. She went back to the table and picked up the paper to check her horoscope—one star.

* * *

Like many other mothers, Lucy had discovered that the time she spent chauffeuring the kids was a good time to broach difficult subjects, so she decided to tackle Zoe and Sara about their trespassing on the Pratts' property when she drove them to day camp.

"You girls know better than to do something like that," she said. "What were you thinking?"

"Mrs. Pratt's mean," said Zoe.

"The whole family is mean," added Sara. "I'm glad Toby punched Wesley. And you know what? I bet if they hadn't broken up the fight he would have beat up Wesley."

Lucy couldn't believe her ears. "Sara! That's no way to talk. What Toby did was very wrong. There's no excuse for fighting. It doesn't solve anything. It just causes more problems."

"Well, I don't care," said Sara, stubbornly. "If I'd been there I would've helped him."

"Me, too," said Zoe.

"Well, I understand that you love Toby, but that doesn't mean he's perfect. He made a big mistake and he's going to have to pay for it."

"Will he go to jail, Mom?" Sara's voice was very small.

Lucy felt as if she'd been stabbed right in the heart. She pulled the car over and braked, turning so she could face both girls.

"I wish I could tell you that won't happen, but the truth is that there's a possibility, a very tiny one, that he might be sent to jail." She reached out and held their hands. "Remember when Melissa Knight had meningitis and they sent that letter home from school saying we had to watch for the symptoms? It's kind of like that. There was a chance that somebody else might have gotten sick, but nobody did, did they?" She smiled in what she hoped was a reassuring manner. "Well, Toby's not going to go to jail, either. He's going to be fine."

She turned around and restarted the car. "He's going to be fine," she told herself, repeating it like a mantra. "He's going to be fine."

By the time she got to work, Lucy felt as if she'd already completed a full day of hard labor. She had no energy for the pile of press releases that was waiting on her desk, no desire to check her phone messages and e-mails. All she wanted to do was crawl into a hole somewhere.

"Lucy, did you pick up the police log?" asked Phyllis. "I can't find it anywhere."

"I forgot," said Lucy, dropping her head onto her hand and shaking it.

Talk about a Freudian slip: she'd forgotten because she didn't want to see Toby's name included with the drunken drivers and wife beaters and marijuana smokers that filled the roster each week. Now she'd have to take time she didn't have to go over to the police station to get it. Leaving it out was unthinkable; the police log was one of the paper's most popular features. Or was it? Ted was just coming through the door. She might as well try.

"Ted," she began, greeting him with a big smile. "What's the space situation this week? Tight?"

"You bet," said Ted. "I'm considering adding some

extra pages, but I don't really have enough ads to justify it."

"Well, since there are so many big stories this week, what do you think about cutting some of the listings and notices, stuff like the gas prices and mortgage rates and maybe even the police log?"

"You forgot to get it, didn't you?" Ted seemed amused.

"Well, actually I did, and I have so much work to do. . . ."

"No problem," he said, and Lucy's hopes rose only to be dashed. "I'll go."

"That's not like him," observed Phyllis, after Ted had gone. "Do you think he's coming down with something?"

"Maybe," said Lucy, sounding so hopeful that Phyllis gave her a sharp look.

The day dragged on as Lucy struggled to concentrate on her work. Her mind kept wandering, going over and over the same worries, like one of those mule trains that went down into the Grand Canyon day after day, wearing a winding trail into the rocky soil. Once started she couldn't seem to stop and her anxiety about the dog hearing led to her worry about Toby and her disappointment with Elizabeth which brought her around to the younger girls' disturbing behavior and finally Bill's blood pressure which she thought he really should have checked because it was the "silent killer."

The clock alternately lurched forward and stopped in its tracks while Lucy struggled with her emotions. She wanted the day to end and she wanted it to last forever; she wanted to get the dog hearing over with and she wished it could be postponed.

That night she cooked a family favorite, spaghetti, but nobody seemed to enjoy it. There was little conversation and they all ate mechanically, going through the familiar rituals of passing the basket of Italian bread and grating the Parmesan cheese without quite realizing what they were doing, each lost in their own thoughts.

Finally, leaving the dirty dishes for the kids to wash, Lucy and Bill left for the dog hearing. But not before Lucy finished one last chore. She fixed Kudo's bowl of kibble, adding a leftover meatball, and carried it out to him. She shoved it through the gate and stood watching him eat, wolfing down his meal in a matter of seconds and licking the bowl clean. He then came to the gate, tail wagging, expecting his evening exercise.

"Sorry," she said, rubbing his nose. "Not tonight."

Chapter Ten

Lucy found it felt very strange to go to a meeting of the Board of Selectmen without her notebook and camera, and accompanied by Bill. They could hear voices as they descended the stairs to the basement hearing room, which didn't surprise Lucy. Between the naturists and the spotted lichen, plenty of people would want to voice their opinions. Worse luck for her and Bill that Kudo's fate would be decided on a night when so many people were at the meeting.

When they entered the crowded hall, Lucy was struck once again with how much the room resembled a courtroom. Just the other day she had been in court with Toby; now it was the dog. She was spending entirely too much time these days on uncomfortable seats in the halls of justice.

She picked up an agenda from the table at the back of the room and they made their way down front, where the rows of seats hadn't filled up yet. Once they were settled, she checked the schedule and discovered what she had feared had happened— they were the first item, after the public comment period. There were only a few other official items—

accepting the gift of a new flag from the VFW, granting family leave to a DPW worker, and a presentation by the Fourth of July parade committee—which meant that everybody was there for the public comment period.

"Do this many people usually come?" asked Bill, shifting uneasily in his chair.

"No," said Lucy. "Usually there's just a handful of interested citizens. Regulars."

She twisted in her seat, to see who else had showed up, and spotted Ted standing in the back, looking for a seat. There were still a few vacancies in their row, but she didn't wave to him. He was supposed to be impartial and inviting him to sit next to her didn't seem quite right. Ted apparently agreed, because she saw him making his way down the other side of the room. Her heart sank when she noticed Cathy Anderson, the dog officer, sitting nearby. Lucy had been harboring a faint hope that somehow the whole matter might be canceled or postponed, but that seemed a pipe dream now. When Pru Pratt arrived, looking as sour as ever, she knew she and Bill would finally have to face the music.

They watched glumly as the selectmen entered and took their seats. When Howard White called the meeting to order with a bang of his gavel, Bill placed his hand over Lucy's.

"We'll begin tonight as always with the public comment period, when the floor is open to one and all. Does anybody want to speak?"

A middle-aged gentleman in the Tinker's Cove summer uniform of khaki pants and a polo shirt raised his hand.

"Mr. Weatherby," said the chairman. "Please state your name and address for the record and tell us what's on your mind."

"Thank you. My name's Horace Weatherby and I have a summer home on Wequaquet Lane. The reason I'm here is that I'm very upset that the fireworks have been canceled and so are my neighbors."

A sizeable contingent had accompanied him to the meeting and they all nodded and murmured in support.

"In fact, I have a petition here with over one hundred signatures asking the board to reconsider the matter."

The contingent grew a little louder, joined by many others in the room.

"Hear! Hear!" boomed Scratch Hallett, waving a fist in the air.

Chairman Howard White banged his gavel and called for order.

"We'll have no more of that," he said, as if scolding a classroom of rowdy kindergarteners. "You'll all get to express your views, but you have to wait to be recognized by the chair, that's me." He pointed the gavel. "Reverend Macintosh."

"Clive Macintosh, I'm the chaplain for the VFW, and I want to express support for Mr. Weatherby's petition."

Heads nodded and hands shot up throughout the room.

"Am I correct in assuming you're all here because you want the fireworks restored?" asked Howard. "Just raise your hands."

Almost everyone in the room raised their hands.

Howard White sighed, and the other board members looked pained.

"Perhaps if I explain our vote," said Howard. "The problem is that this plant is protected by state law and the town could face an expensive court battle if the lichen is harmed. We really had no choice but to cancel the fireworks this year. But I'm willing to appoint a committee to look into alternatives for next year."

The other board members nodded in agreement.

"We don't want a committee!" yelled a shrill female voice. "We want fireworks!"

This was greeted with enthusiastic applause, prompting Howard to bang his gavel furiously.

"I don't want to have to clear the room," he warned. "We have a consensus, however, and the committee proposal will be put on the agenda for the next meeting."

This was met with grumbles and somebody called out, "We don't want a committee! We want fireworks!"

"That's not the way business is conducted in this town," said Howard, setting his jaw firmly. "Now, does anyone have any other matter to discuss beside the fireworks?"

"Hold on, Howard," said Joe Marzetti. "Maybe we should take another vote."

"That's impossible," snapped Howard, "and you know it. We can't vote on a matter unless it's placed on the agenda and duly advertised."

"Well, then, let's add it to next week's agenda," said Joe, speaking through clenched teeth.

"We can add it, but it will be too late. The next meeting is after July Fourth."

Joe's face was red with embarrassment at his mistake and fury at Howard's high-handed manner. He sat silently, drumming his fingers on the table.

Lucy was so caught up in the drama of the situation that she'd forgotten all about Kudo until Bill tapped her thigh a few times with his knee. "How long is this going to go on?" he whispered.

"I don't know," she said, looking around the room. Nobody seemed ready to leave and Howard was looking increasingly uncomfortable with the situation.

"Discussion on the fireworks issue is hereby closed," he said, adding a smack of the gavel for emphasis. "Does anyone wish to bring any other issue to the board's attention?"

If he had expected the crowd to pack up and leave, he was going to be disappointed, thought Lucy. Hands had shot up throughout the room. Howard gave the floor to Millicent Blood, a patrician woman who happened to be one of his neighbors. If he'd been seeking a conciliator, however, he'd made the wrong choice. Millicent's comments only fanned the flames of controversy.

"I would just like to say that I applaud the efforts of the Society for the Preservation of Tinker's Cove to preserve our natural heritage. . . ."

Millicent was drowned out by a chorus of boos. Seeking to restore order, Howard pointed his gavel at the first person he happened to see: Mike Gold.

The portly, frizzy-haired representative of the American Naturist Society had dressed for the meeting, albeit in sandals, rather short shorts and a tank-style T-shirt. Definitely not the sort of thing people wore in Tinker's Cove, thought Lucy, but at least he was decently, if minimally, covered.

"My name is Mike Gold and I'm here on behalf of the naturist community . . ."

If only she'd had a camera, thought Lucy, to capture Howard's horrified expression.

". . . and I'd like to express our appreciation to the people of Tinker's Cove for their tolerance and hospitality," continued Mike. "We'd like to apologize for any disruption we may have caused and ask for your patience. We understand naturism is controversial, not everyone approves, but we believe that if you get to know us, you'll find we're a pretty responsible group and we're eager to work out any problems that may come up in a constructive way. Thank you."

The next speaker, Mel Dunwoodie, wasn't quite as tactful. "Whether or not you like it, naturists have rights, too, and we intend to exercise our right to 'life, liberty and the pursuit of happiness' to the utmost," he said, turning to glare at Prudence Pratt. "I'd also like to add that this proposed bylaw against nudity is a bad idea for our town and urge everyone to vote against it."

The crowd was divided on this issue: some applauded while others grumbled. Hands shot up and Howard scanned the crowd until he found someone who was certain to say the right thing, whatever the occasion: Corney Clark.

Corney got to her feet gracefully and gave a little toss of her head, causing her blond hair to fall into place. Trust Corney to find a fabulous stylist, a genius with the shears.

"I just want to say," she began, in her well-modulated finishing school voice, "that in all the years I've lived here in Tinker's Cove I've never seen the town so divided. These are challenging times and we're faced with many difficult issues, but I want to remind everyone that we're all members of the same community and we all want what's best for our town. The days ahead will be much more pleasant if we treat each other as we would wish to be treated ourselves: with tolerance and respect."

For once, the crowd was silent. Howard White seized the moment, closed the public discussion period and moved the meeting forward onto the first item of business. He slumped in his chair, mopping his brow with his handkerchief, while dog officer Cathy Anderson came forward and arranged her papers.

Lucy, who'd been enjoying the meeting so much that she almost forgot about Kudo, clasped Bill's hand.

"I have received several complaints about Kudo, a mixed-breed dog owned by Lucy and Bill Stone, who live on Red Top Road. The dog has on several occasions attacked chickens, and I myself have witnessed him running loose in violation of the town's leash law. On at least two occasions these sightings have coincided with complaints about knocked-over garbage bins. When I contacted the owners, they were exceptionally cooperative, they even built a kennel to specifications I recommended, incurring considerable expense. Unfortunately, the dog continues to defy their best efforts and keeps getting out."

"Are the owners here tonight?" asked White.

"Yes," said Lucy, rasing her hand.

"Ah, Mrs. Stone, I didn't see you there. You're

not in your usual seat." He surveyed the audience. "Are any of the complainants here?"

"Yup. Right here," Prudence Pratt spoke out loudly.

"Well, I guess we better hear what you have to say, Mrs. Pratt."

Lucy found herself sinking lower in her chair as Pru strode to the front of the room, taking her place beside Cathy Anderson. Pru was much taller than Cathy, and in contrast to the dog officer's womanly figure, she looked mannish from behind. Her T-shirt and jeans hung loosely from her bony body. Cathy's blond hair was clean and shiny while Pru's was scraped back and clumped into a sticky-looking ponytail.

"Well," began Pru, "I've got a flock of about forty Rhode Island Reds. These are chickens I breed myself, and they regularly take the blue ribbon at the county fair. They're also good layers, I get a lot of double yolks. And when they stop laying they make a very tasty stew, if I say so myself. The problem is that this dog, here, keeps coming over and gets 'em all in a panic and, well, being chickens, eventually one of 'em will manage to flap its way over the fence and right into the beast's mouth. And then there's blood and gore and feathers all over the place." She snorted. "He doesn't even eat 'em, mind, just shakes 'em 'til they come apart."

There were a few groans from the audience and Lucy found herself wincing.

"You're saying he doesn't dig under the fence, or break it in some way?' asked Joe Marzetti.

"No, he's a crafty devil. He just keeps worrying

'em and worrying 'em until he gets one in a panic. He's a master at it."

"Have you asked the Stones to repay you for the lost chickens?" asked Ellie Sykes.

"Sure. They always pay, but what's the good of that? I can't replace the chickens. They're breeding stock, see. Last week he got one of my prize-winners, one I was planning to breed."

"Do we have any other witnesses?" asked White.

No one came forward, and Lucy had a little surge of hope. Then she was called to the front of the room. Bill squeezed her hand as she rose from her seat.

"All I can say," she began, looking each board member in the eye in turn, "is that we have done our very best to restrain the dog. As Cathy mentioned we built him a very sturdy kennel, but he is something of an escape artist. I would like to mention that he is not a vicious dog, except for chickens, and he's a much-loved family pet. My two youngest girls, especially, are very fond of him."

Again, she tried to make eye contact with the board members, but only Ellie Sykes met her gaze. The others looked away. Not a good sign.

Lucy went back to her seat when Howard White asked Cathy for her recommendation.

"This is a very difficult situation," she began in a tight voice, pausing to consult her notes. "As I mentioned, the Stones are responsible pet owners who have followed all my suggestions and recommendations. Unfortunately, they have been unable to control the dog and his problem behavior continues. This doesn't leave the board with too many options. You could banish the dog, which es-

sentially means passing the problem on to someone else, or you could vote to . . . ," she paused
and swallowed hard, "destroy the dog."

Lucy actually felt her stomach drop.

"Is the dog a danger to people? To children?"
inquired Ellie Sykes.

"I don't believe so," said Cathy.

From her seat, Pru Pratt snorted. "I wouldn't
want to get between that dog and a chicken, that's
for sure."

"That's definitely a factor to consider," said Joe
Marzetti.

"I don't think we should concern ourselves with
speculation," said Howard. "We should base this
decision on the facts, on the dog's past history."

"The dog was before us a few years ago?" asked
Marzetti, who was leafing through his information
packet.

"Yes, when he was owned by Curt Nolan," said
Cathy. "It was a similar complaint."

"I actually brought that complaint," said Ellie. "I
keep chickens, too, and he did quite a lot of damage
to my flock."

"I had a dog like that once," said Pete Crowley,
"only he chased cats. He was always treeing the
neighbor's cats."

"Do we have a motion?" asked Howard, cutting
off Pete's reminiscences.

"I move we give the Stones one more chance,"
said Ellie. "We can continue the order that the dog
be confined to their property with the condition
that it will be destroyed if it gets loose again."

"Second," said Bud Collins, who Lucy had thought
was asleep.

"All in favor?"

The vote was unanimous.

"Whew." Bill let out a huge sigh. "A reprieve."

"But he's still on death row," said Lucy, wondering how they were ever going to manage to keep Kudo confined, considering he'd overcome their best efforts to date.

Pru wasn't pleased with the decision. She was clearly in a huff as she went back to her seat.

"Our next order of business is a request from the July Fourth parade committee," said Howard. "Who speaks for the committee?"

"I do."

Lucy turned around and saw the speaker was Marge Culpepper, Barney's wife. She was a tall, plump woman who looked older than her years due to the curly, gray hair she refused to touch up with color. Lucy gave her an encouraging smile; she knew that Marge was terrified of speaking publicly.

"I'm here on behalf of the entire committee," stammered Marge, indicating four other people seated in the same row with her. They all raised their hands, to identify themselves. Marge stood up a bit straighter and swallowed hard. "We're here to request that the board cancel the Fourth of July parade."

There was a shocked silence in the room. Even the group from the VFW was too stunned to protest.

"What is the reason for this unusual request?" asked Howard.

"The problem is that the American Naturist

Society has applied for permission to march in the parade."

"So what?' asked Pete Crowley, scratching his chin.

"We're not confident they will be appropriately attired," said Marge, blushing furiously.

"You mean they might march naked?" asked Crowley.

"That's ridiculous . . ." protested Mike Gold, only to be silenced by a bang of the gavel. He and Mel Dunwoodie both raised their hands, but Howard ignored them.

"It's a concern," said Marge, nodding.

"So deny the application," said Marzetti.

"It's not that simple. Marching in the parade is an exercise of First Amendment rights. Free speech and all that. The application is just a formality, really. We can't turn away anybody who wants to march, unless they're breaking some law. It's a violation of their right to free speech."

"That's why we need a public decency bylaw," yelled Pru, from the audience.

"We'll open this up for public comment later," admonished Howard. "After the board has finished questioning Mrs. Culpepper."

"It sure doesn't make much sense to me to cancel the whole parade because of one group," said Joe. "Besides, the parade's a big tourist attraction."

"Folks with kids are going to leave town fast and never come back if we have naked people in the parade," said Pete.

"Have you expressed your concern to the naturists?" asked Ellie. "Perhaps you could get some sort of agreement from them in advance."

"We considered doing that, but when we checked

with town counsel he said we couldn't apply a restriction to one group that we didn't apply to all. And even if we did get some sort of informal promise, it wouldn't be binding. I don't think we can risk it."

"Whiskey?" Bud Collins opened one eye. "Where?"

"Not whiskey, risky," said Ellie.

Howard banged his gavel. "Any comment from the audience?"

Several hands shot up, joining Mike Gold's and Mel Dunwoodie's. Howard ignored them and chose the commander of the VFW post.

"Well, all I want to say is that Tinker's Cove doesn't seem to be interested in celebrating the Fourth of July anymore," asserted Bill Bridges, his dentures clicking furiously. "First it was the fireworks and now it's the parade. What next?"

"Yeah, I don't suppose you're even interested in this flag that we're giving you," said Scratch. "It flew over the Capitol, you know."

"I don't recall recognizing you," said Howard. "You only get the floor when I give it to you."

"Well, I don't want your floor," said Scratch, handing the flag to the commander. "I don't want anything to do with the lot of you. I think it's a sorry state of affairs when we can't even celebrate the founding of our country and I know who to blame, too." He pointed a finger, shaking with fury. "It's you, Pru Pratt. It's because of you and that stupid bylaw that these naturists want to be in the parade, instead of doing what they do over at the pond."

"Well, I never," said Pru, rising to her feet, ready to give Scratch a piece of her mind. But it was too late. He'd left the room.

Unwilling to court further controversy, Howard called for a vote and the board members agreed unanimously, albeit reluctantly, to cancel the parade. They had hardly completed the vote when people started leaving. Down in front, Ted was getting quotes from Gold and Dunwoodie, scribbling furiously into his notebook.

"Do you want to stay any longer?" asked Bill.

Lucy shook her head and they joined the throng leaving the room.

"It just doesn't seem right," she said. "No fireworks, no parade. It's not going to be much of a Fourth of July."

"You can say that again," agreed Bill.

"The parade's the least of it," muttered Mel. "Whatever happened to free speech in this town?"

Chapter Eleven

Lucy and Bill were both quiet on the ride home, thinking over the implications of the board's decision.

"It could have been worse," said Bill.

"How are we going to keep Kudo from getting loose?"

"I'm working on it," said Bill.

They fell silent.

It was almost midnight when they got to bed and Bill, unused to such late hours, fell asleep immediately. Lying beside him, Lucy's mind kept following the same worn track of worries, but now there were a few new twists. It seemed to her that the board hadn't really done them any favors—they'd already tried everything they could think of to keep the dog confined and he'd always managed to get loose. It was just a matter of time before they'd be back at another hearing, and this time the result was a foregone conclusion. What could they do?

It was an unanswerable question, but that didn't stop her from trying to think of something. She heard the grandfather clock in the hall downstairs chime two before she fell asleep and she didn't wake until Bill roused her an hour late in the morning.

"You shouldn't have let me sleep," she protested.

"I thought you could use the rest. Besides, you don't have to write up the meeting today."

"That's right," she said, relaxing back against the pillows. "No deadline for me today."

"I brought you some coffee."

"Thanks." She took the mug he held out to her and took a sip. "Coffee in bed—I could get used to this."

"Enjoy it while you can, Madame Pompadour. I'm off to work."

"Have a nice day," said Lucy, stretching luxuriously.

She had at least fifteen minutes before she had to wake the girls and she was determined to enjoy them. If only she could start every day like this, with time to organize her thoughts. She was glad she didn't have to make sense of last night's meeting for a story; she wouldn't know where to begin. She'd never had to cover such a divisive issue. People were angry enough about the fireworks and now the parade had been canceled, too. Once word got out, the selectmen could very well have a rebellion on their hands.

Lucy was thinking it was really time to get up when Sara and Zoe rushed into her room in their pajamas and climbed into bed with her.

"What happened at the meeting?" asked Sara.

"Can we keep Kudo?" asked Zoe.

"We can keep him as long as he doesn't get loose. If he gets loose, even once, they're going to put him to sleep."

"That's not fair!" protested Zoe, snuggling against her mother.

"He always gets out, no matter what we do," said Sara, who was sitting at the foot of the bed.

"I know, honey. We're going to have to try harder. That's all we can do." Seeing Sara's discouraged expression, she added, "Daddy's trying to think of something."

"Don't they understand he's an animal? He can't think like people can. He's just doing what his instincts tell him to do."

"I know." Lucy paused. "Maybe we should try obedience school."

"I know! We could send him to a trainer. There are people who specialize in difficult dogs. I can find out from Melanie."

"You can ask her for information, but I bet something like that is awfully expensive. I don't think we can afford it."

Zoe didn't want to hear it. "We have to save Kudo."

"We also have to pay college tuition for Elizabeth and the lawyer for Toby and groceries and taxes and the mortgage. . . ."

"But you said they'll put him to sleep."

Lucy looked down at Zoe's earnest little face and stroked her hair.

"We'll see what we can do," she said, deciding to change the subject. "So, tell me what you did in camp yesterday."

"We made T-shirts to wear in the parade," said Sara.

What a morning, thought Lucy. Was no subject safe?

"Mine's pink, with a kitty," said Zoe.

"Mine's blue, with a whale. A right whale because they're endangered. Did you know that whales are still hunted? For food?"

There was no point in letting them continue. She had to tell them.

"The shirts sound great, but I don't think you'll be wearing them in the parade."

"Why not?"

"The parade's been canceled."

For a moment the girls couldn't think of anything to say. This was something completely out of their experience. For as long as they could remember there'd always been a July Fourth parade.

"Are you joking?" asked Sara.

Zoe giggled with relief. "That's funny, Mom."

"It's no joke, it's the truth. They're afraid people will march naked," explained Lucy.

Zoe considered this. "I bet Elizabeth would."

Lucy couldn't help smiling. "Come on girls, we've got to start getting ready or you'll be late for camp."

By the time Lucy got herself dressed and the dog fed and the lunches made and got the girls into the car, she felt exhausted, as if she'd been swimming against the current. And resentful. Without the pressure of deadline, it was supposed to be a relaxed morning but it hadn't turned out that way. The car was hot, sweat was forming on her upper lip, and her clothes were sticking to her body. And it was going to get hotter: the sun was threatening to burn through the clouds.

"Turn on the AC, Mom," said Sara.

"It is on."

"I can't feel it back here. Can you feel it, Zoe?"

"It takes a while," said Lucy, turning onto Red Top Road. "Give it a chance."

She was beginning to pick up speed when she saw the unthinkable: Kudo was running through their yard heading straight for the Pratts' property. She immediately pulled to the side of the road and slammed on the brakes. Jumping out of the car, she called the dog.

He stopped, ears perked up and looked at her. Amazingly enough, he began to run towards her. Worried about a speeding car on the road, she began to cross, intending to meet the dog and grab him by the collar before he crossed the road.

This was really too much, she muttered to herself. That darned dog couldn't even stay out of trouble for twenty-four hours. What a nuisance. They would have to find another home for him, there was really nothing else to do. Not if they couldn't even keep him safe in his kennel for a single day.

Hearing the sound of an approaching engine, she turned her head and saw a pickup truck coming at high speed. She had no choice but to stop and wait for it to pass. To her horror, she saw that Kudo had a different idea. He was still coming, trying to outrace the truck.

"Stay! Stay!" she yelled.

But Kudo was intent on getting into the car and coming along for the ride. He kept on running straight into the path of the truck.

She watched, horrified, as the action unfolded in slow motion. The dog's happy, smiling face, tongue flapping in the breeze. The impact, and then his body flying into the air. A quick glimpse of the driver. The haze of smoke and the stink of rubber as Wesley Pratt slammed down the accelerator and sped off. The crumpled bundle of yellow fur lying in the grass by the side of the road.

Lucy ran to the dog and found he was breathing, just.

Sara was behind her, holding the blanket they kept in the back of the car.

"I know what to do, Mom. They taught us at camp. We'll slide the blanket under him and carry him to the car, okay? Zoe, open the back!"

Gently, trying to hurry because they knew moments counted, but afraid of hurting poor Kudo, they carried him to the Subaru wagon and placed him gently in the cargo area. Then Lucy drove as quickly as she dared to the veterinary hospital. Everybody there was nice as could be, rushing out to the car with a miniature stretcher and hurrying the dog into a examining room, but it was no good. The doctor was listening to his heartbeat and Lucy was gently stroking his head, whispering mindless words of encouragement when he breathed his last.

"I'm sorry," said the vet, removing his stethoscope.

To her horror, tears sprang to her eyes.

"It's just so sudden. I didn't expect this."

The vet handed her a tissue. "He didn't really suffer. He probably went into shock when he was hit."

"He was happy, he was smiling as he ran across the road." Lucy blew her nose. "I can't believe it."

"It takes time," said the vet. "Not to rush you, but how do you want to dispose of the body?"

Lucy didn't have a clue. "I guess we'll bury him in the backyard."

"Not advisable," said the vet. "He's a pretty big dog. I recommend cremation. Then you can bury the ashes."

"Oh," said Lucy. "I guess that would be better."

"We'll call you when the ashes are ready."

"Thanks." Lucy walked out to the waiting room, feeling like a robot.

The girls jumped up and ran to her. "Is he . . . ?"

She shook her head, and found herself bursting into uncontrollable sobs. The girls joined her. Together, holding hands, they went out to the car. Too upset to drive, Lucy sat behind the wheel, mopping her face and passing tissues to the girls.

"I don't know why I'm so upset," she wailed. "He was a terrible dog."

"I used to be afraid of him," admitted Zoe, "when I was little."

"He smelled pretty bad," said Sara.

"He was no end of trouble," said Lucy.

"I'm really going to miss him," said Zoe.

"Me, too."

"We all are."

Finally, automatically going through the motions without thinking, Lucy started the car and followed the familiar roads to Friends of Animals day camp. She drove slowly, wondering why driving faster seemed to take more energy. Whenever she was tired or upset, she found the car slowing, as if she couldn't summon the strength to press firmly on the gas pedal.

Melanie Flowers rushed out to meet them.

"I've been worried . . . I called the house but there was no answer. . . ."

"I'm sorry we're late," said Lucy. "We had to take our dog to the vet. He got hit by a car."

"Oh, how terrible." She held out her arms and embraced the girls, who were still a bit teary. "Did this happen just this morning? You must all still be in shock."

Seeing the girls' stricken expressions, Lucy wondered if she'd made a mistake bringing them to camp. "Maybe they'd be more comfortable at home. . . ." she began.

"Probably better to keep busy," advised Melanie. "Zoe's group is just about to go to arts and crafts." She gave the little girl a squeeze. "Maybe you'd like to make a drawing of your dog? Or a clay model?"

"That would be nice, Zoe," said Lucy, with an encouraging little smile.

"Okay," she said, giving a shaky little nod.

"Maybe you can walk her over," said Melanie, giving Sara a squeeze, too. "Janine's making dog biscuits with the Hummingbirds and I know she could use a hand. They're in the kitchen."

"Come on, Zoe," said Sara, taking her little sister by the hand.

Lucy watched as they walked off together.

"Sara was a big help," she told Melanie. "She knew just what to do."

"How did it happen?"

"The dog just ran in front of Wesley Pratt's truck. It wasn't his fault. There was nothing he could have done."

"That's a terrible feeling," said Melanie. "I hit a deer last fall—there was absolutely no way I could have avoided it. It just jumped from the side of the road right into my car. I was devastated."

"I can imagine." Lucy was remembering how

she'd seen Kudo heading for the road, but had been unable to stop him.

"And it made a terrible mess of my car, too." Melanie nodded solemnly. "It was in the body shop for weeks."

"Oh my gosh, I didn't think of that," said Lucy, wondering if Wesley's truck had been damaged.

"The insurance covered most of it, but I had a hefty deductible."

"Doesn't everybody," said Lucy, wondering what Wesley's deductible was, or if he even had insurance. "Well, I've got to get to work."

"Don't worry about the girls—I'll keep an eye on them."

"Thanks for everything," said Lucy, letting out a big sigh.

"Let me know if there's anything I can do," said Melanie.

"I might just take you up on that," said Lucy, "because I'm just about at the end of my rope."

Chapter Twelve

Back in the car, Lucy was alone with her emotions. She sat for a minute, trying to sort it all out. Shock and sadness, of course, but also a sense of relief. As much as she hated to admit it, a very difficult problem had been solved. She no longer had to worry about what to do about Kudo.

Of course, this wasn't the way she would have wished to solve it. It would have been better if their efforts to control the dog had worked. But the sad truth was, they hadn't. He'd been impossible. Nothing they tried seemed to work. Even Cathy Anderson had said they'd made every effort to restrain Kudo. No matter what they did, he continued to get loose, and once loose he generally went after Prudence Pratt's chickens.

He had truly been an awful dog, thought Lucy, feeling tears pricking her eyes. An awful, terrible, horrible dog, but she'd loved him. He was loyal, in his way. He always came home, eventually. And maybe she was fooling herself, but she thought Kudo had a special place in his doggy heart for her. When she was sad or depressed, he had a way of sensing it and would stay with her, often resting his chin on her knee.

Lucy sniffed and reached for her purse, she needed a tissue. How could she feel relieved that Kudo was gone? What kind of person was she? He'd been a good dog and here she was practically glad he was dead. She might as well start adding up how much she'd save on dog chow and anti-flea drops and annual checkups at the vet. Not to mention the additional coverage they'd had to get on their homeowner's insurance. They'd practically be millionaires now that the dog was gone, and they'd have better relations with their neighbors, too.

Or maybe not, thought Lucy, trying to remember if Wesley's truck had been damaged when it hit the dog. He had driven off so quickly, and she had been so concerned about the dog, that she hadn't really thought about it. But if there had been damage, she had to make it right. Things were tense enough with the Pratts, they certainly didn't need to give them any more grounds for grievance. She considered driving over to the Pratts and getting the matter resolved, but she was already late for work. It was true she didn't have to write the story about the Selectmen's meeting, but there were always a million last-minute tasks and Ted would want her to help with those. On the other hand, the noon deadline meant they always finished up early on Wednesdays. She could swing by the Pratts place after the paper was put to bed, in the early afternoon.

* * *

Ted was in a lather when she got to the office, struggling with the story about the meeting. He was hunched over his computer keyboard, alternately typing a few words and flipping through the pages of his notebook, looking for quotes. He was too involved in his work to notice that Lucy was nearly two hours late.

Phyllis gave her a conspiratorial wink. "I told him that he ought to appreciate you more, considering that you do this week after week," she said, fanning herself with a sheaf of papers. She was wearing a purple and green Mexican cotton dress today and was the brightest thing in the dingy office.

"It was a killer meeting," said Lucy. "Did he tell you about the parade?"

"He didn't have to. We've had a steady stream of irate citizens dropping off letters to the editor."

"Yeah, Lucy, could you edit them for me? We don't have room for them all, so pick a representative sample, okay?"

Lucy took the folder of letters from Phyllis, noticing with a shock that she'd polished her nails green to match her dress. She sat down at her desk and turned on the computer, waiting while it produced the usual clicks and groans. She felt the same way—it was hard to settle down to work.

"If you're writing about the dog part of the hearing I guess you ought to mention that Kudo's dead," she said.

Both Phyllis and Ted dropped what they were doing. It was as if she'd exploded a bombshell.

"Dead? How did that happen?" asked Ted.

"Wesley Pratt ran him over with his truck," said Lucy, surprised by the pricking in her eyes.

"I'm so sorry," said Phyllis, enveloping her in a huge billowing green and purple hug.

Now Lucy was really crying and furious with herself for losing control.

"It was horrible," she blubbered. "The girls were in the car."

"Oh, no!" Phyllis patted her hand.

"Did he do it on purpose?" asked Ted. "Was it some sort of retaliation for the fight?"

"Oh, no!" protested Lucy, eager to nip this misconception in the bud. "There was nothing he could do. The stupid dog ran right in front of his truck."

"Did he stop?" asked Ted.

"Well, no, but he's just a kid. I didn't really expect him to." Lucy dabbed at her eyes. "The truth is, I'm kind of worried that the impact may have damaged his truck."

"It doesn't take much," offered Phyllis. "My cousin Elfrida only grazed that moose and her car was a total loss. The insurance paid, of course, but they only paid the replacement value and considering she had a twelve-year-old Escort it wasn't much."

This was not encouraging news to Lucy.

"I guess I better follow up and let them know we'll take care of any damages," said Lucy.

Behind her, Ted's and Phyllis's eyes met.

"Oh, I don't know," said Ted, "from what I've seen of Pru she won't hesitate to let you know all about it."

"In fact," added Phyllis, "I'm surprised she hasn't called already."

"Maybe she's mellowing," said Lucy, opening the folder.

Phyllis snorted. "Mark my words, you'll hear from her before the day is out."

The rest of the morning passed uneventfully, however, with no word from Pru. A few people stopped in with letters to the editor about the parade or to buy last-minute classified ads and Mike Gold called to see if Ted needed any more information about the naturists, but that was all. They were able to wrap up the paper on time and Lucy was done for the day before one o'clock.

She decided to make good on her resolution to stop at the Pratts' on her way home. She didn't want to be worrying about this all day, she wanted to have it all settled before she told Bill and Toby about the dog's death. That way there would be no reason for them to have any contact with the Pratts, especially Wesley, and no chance that things would get out of control. Not that they would, she told herself, but it was better to be on the safe side.

As she drove, Lucy rehearsed what she would say. Keep it simple and direct, she told herself, the Pratts weren't much for small talk. It would be easier if Wesley was there because then she could just tell him there were no hard feelings about the dog and ask if there was any damage to the truck. If Wesley wasn't home, she'd have to explain the accident to his parents, and she'd have to make it very clear that she wasn't seeking redress. She understood full well that Wesley couldn't have avoided hitting the dog, and as for the fact that he left the scene of an accident, well, she herself was the mother of a twenty-one-year-old and she knew how irresponsible they could be. They tended to follow their first impulse, which was generally fight or flight, without taking time to think.

By the time she reached the Pratts' house Lucy was beginning to think that this might be an opportunity for some sort of reconciliation. She didn't like being at odds with her neighbors, and most of the animosity had been a direct result of Kudo's behavior. Now that he was gone, maybe things would be more relaxed and agreeable. She certainly hoped so.

She turned into the Pratts' driveway, struck once again with the bareness of their yard. Not even the weeds dared to sprout in the driveway, no bushes or flowers softened the stark angles of the house. Since she knew the Pratts didn't approve of trespassers she parked at the end of the drive and went straight for the back door, where she stood on the stoop and knocked.

When there was no answer, she called out, guessing that Pru might be out back, tending to her chickens, or her vegetable garden where the spinach and Swiss chard and onions all grew in straight lines with military precision. She was pretty sure Pru was home because her car, an aged but impeccably maintained Dodge Shadow, was parked in its usual spot.

Lucy knew the wisest course of action would simply be to leave. She could leave a note, she could call later. She could stop by on her way home from work. The one thing she shouldn't do was start poking around in hopes of finding Pru perched high on a ladder cleaning out the gutters or out behind the chicken coop wringing a chicken's neck.

On the other hand, however, she was here right now and she wanted to get this thing off her chest.

She didn't want it hanging over her, distracting her and causing her more worry. She wanted to get it over with. It certainly couldn't hurt to peek around behind the house, where Pru kept a clothesline. She wouldn't even have to step off the drive to do that. No reasonable person could call that trespassing. Not at all.

Lucy squared her shoulders and continued a few more paces down the drive, until she reached the corner of the house. There she had an unobstructed view of the turning area, where the driveway widened and where Wesley and Calvin parked their trucks. There were no trucks, today, but there was a crumpled pile of something blue, maybe laundry that had dropped off the line where several pairs of jeans were hanging heavily in the humid air.

Lucy went to investigate, and as she drew closer she realized it wasn't a pair of blue jeans that had fallen at all. It was Pru, herself, lying in a heap.

Reaching the fallen woman, Lucy instinctively reached out and touched her shoulder, as if to wake her. But Pru wasn't going to wake up. Pru was dead. Definitely dead.

Chapter Thirteen

Lucy's first reaction was utter disbelief. This was too much. First the dog, now Pru. Two deaths in one day. How could this happen? Especially to Pru. She had seemed invincible, a force to be reckoned with like the tides or the temperature. You couldn't change her, you had to deal with her. But now, it seemed, she had met a power greater than her own.

Recoiling, Lucy stood up and stepped back, studying the body. What could it have been, she wondered. What did she die of? From what she could see there was no sign of violence, no gunshot wound, no knife protruding from her body. Maybe it was a stroke or a heart attack. Something sudden and overwhelming like a burst aneurysm. Whatever it was, there was no clue in Pru's expression. Her eyes were slightly open, her jaw hung slack, her face was blank.

She hadn't been a beauty in life and death certainly didn't become her. The poor woman, thought Lucy, hurrying back to the car. She probably woke up this morning full of plans, never guessing what fate held in store for her. Reaching inside the car she pulled her cell phone from her shoulder bag and dialed 911 with trembling fingers.

It seemed to take a long time for help to arrive, and Lucy found herself going back to the body. She knew she hadn't imagined it but finding Pru dead like that seemed so incredible that she had to reassure herself that it had really happened. There was no doubt, however, when she rounded the corner of the house. You didn't have to be an expert to know that Pru was dead: her extremities were cold and she was beginning to stiffen up.

Lucy stood awkwardly a few feet from the body and looked around. As she had noticed earlier, Pru was lying in the turning area at the end of the driveway, behind the house. Her car was parked about ten feet away and was the only vehicle. The clothesline was next to the driveway and beyond that was the barn, a ramshackle affair that looked ready to fall down but didn't. It had been in pretty much the same condition for the twenty-plus years Lucy had lived next door, occasionally losing another cedar shingle or a pane of window glass. Beyond the barn Lucy could see the pointy tops of the dark green fir trees and she heard the distant caw of a crow. She felt very alone.

Where was everybody? The police, EMTs, somebody ought to be here by now. She listened, straining to hear the sound of sirens but all she heard was more crows, answering the first. She looked at the body once again, lying exactly as she'd found it. Of course it hadn't moved, what was she thinking? Dead bodies didn't move and they didn't see.

They didn't talk, either, so there was no way Pru could object if she looked around.

Shrugging off a guilty feeling that she was doing something she shouldn't, Lucy wandered across the yard, past the vegetable garden and the chicken house, where the sudden flapping of one of the hens startled her. She stared at the dozen or so hens in the pen and they stared back with reptilian yellow eyes, then resumed their pecking and scratching. Lucy continued on her way behind the barn, where she remembered seeing a jumbled pile of lobster traps, line and buoys that she suspected was evidence of Calvin and Wesley's poaching but it was gone. There was no sign of any of it, just a bare bit of dusty earth with a few clumps of crab grass.

Now, finally, she heard sirens, weak at first but growing stronger. She hurried across the yard and reached the driveway just as a small caravan of official vehicles arrived. She pointed out the body to the police officers and EMTs and waited for permission to leave. She was very hungry, she suddenly realized, and no wonder. She hadn't had anything to eat since breakfast.

Feeling a bit dizzy, she decided to sit in her car. She was digging in her purse for a mint or something, anything with a bit of sugar, when she remembered she hadn't called Ted. It was probably just as well, she decided. There was no way that Pru's death could be included in tomorrow's issue anyway and there was no sense in rushing to tell Ted the news because it would only make him miserable. Besides, it wasn't as if she'd been murdered or anything, it wasn't really a story. They'd probably just run an obituary.

"Mrs. Stone?"

Lucy looked up and met the serious eyes of a youthful police officer. She didn't recognize him, but she knew the department had hired additional help for the summer. A glance at his name tag told her she was speaking to Officer Blaine.

"Yes?"

"I understand you found the body?"

"Yes, I did. Can I go now? I'm not feeling very well."

"I'm sorry, but I have orders to keep you here. Lieutenant Horowitz wants to talk to you."

"Lieutenant Horowitz?" Lucy knew he was the state police officer who investigated serious crimes that were beyond the scope of the local department. "Why does he want to talk to me?"

The officer shrugged. "I'm just following orders, ma'am."

Lucy's stomach growled and she thought longingly of her well-stocked kitchen, just a few hundred feet down the road. What she'd like more than anything, she decided, was a peanut butter and jelly sandwich and a tall glass of milk. She had those things, they were all there, waiting for her.

"You know I just live in the next house. Couldn't the lieutenant talk to me there?"

"My orders are to keep you here," he said, squaring his shoulders and resting his hand on his holster.

"No problem," said Lucy, hoping she wouldn't die of hunger before the lieutenant arrived.

* * *

Lucy was feeling queasy and light-headed when Horowitz arrived in his state police cruiser, accompanied by the medical examiner's van and a couple of unmarked Suburbans from the state crime lab. They were emblazoned with the motto of the Maine State Police: "Integrity. Compassion. Fairness. Excellence." Quite a turnout, she thought, for an ordinary unattended death.

"Ah, Mrs. Stone," he said, approaching her car, "another body."

Lucy had investigated numerous crimes through the years and was well acquainted with Horowitz. He looked the same as ever, dressed in a lightweight gray suit that needed pressing. His pale hair was thinning, his eyes were gray and there was no sign of color in his face. Lucy doubted he got outdoors much. Something about his expression always reminded her of a rabbit. Not a scared bunny but a wise and wary old buck who'd learned to suspect everyone and everything.

"I'm afraid so."

"The victim's your neighbor, right?"

"Victim? What do you mean? This wasn't a crime, was it?"

"There's a definite possibility that Mrs. Pratt was murdered."

Lucy was glad she was sitting because she felt as if a rug had been pulled out from under her. Suddenly, everything was spinning and she was retching. Horowitz yanked her car door open and helped her turn and lower her head between her knees. When she felt better, she sat up.

"I'm sorry. I guess it's a delayed reaction."

"Quite understandable." He paused. "Although I am a little surprised that you, of all people, didn't suspect foul play."

"I thought she'd had a heart attack or something. How was she killed?"

"The medical examiner will determine the cause but we think she was run down by a car or truck."

Lucy didn't have time to absorb this information before he asked, "How long were you neighbors?"

The answer didn't come to her quickly. This upsetting news had confused her. "About twenty years. As long as we've lived here."

"Did you have any problems with her? Or her family?"

Lucy didn't like the direction Horowitz was taking.

"Everybody had problems with her."

"I didn't ask about everybody, I asked about you." There was a gleam in his eye. "You're the nearest neighbors. It's a legitimate question."

"We had a few problems. Our dog went after her chickens a few times, there was even a dog hearing. But the dog was hit by a car this morning. That's why I came over. I wanted to tell her there wouldn't be any more problems." Lucy knew she wasn't telling the whole story.

"Did you see the driver?"

Lucy sighed. "It was her son. Wesley."

Horowitz digested this information. "So you came over to have it out with her?"

"No! It was an accident. I saw the whole thing.

But the kid drove off and I was worried there might be some damage to his truck. I came to let her know there were no hard feelings and to offer to pay for any repairs." Lucy paused, watching the investigators gathered around Pru's body. "I was hoping to get on a better footing with her."

"So the dog was the problem?"

"Not exactly," said Lucy. She knew there was no sense trying to hide Toby's fight with Wesley because it was a matter of public record. "There was a fight down at the docks last week and my son took a swing at Wesley." Lucy felt her face reddening. "But he wasn't the only one. A lot of fishermen suspect Wesley and his father of poaching their lobster traps."

"So your son has an unruly conduct case pending in district court?"

Lucy's heart sank. "Actually, it's assault and battery."

Horowitz didn't show any reaction to this information. He stood in the driveway, getting the lay of the land. "There's a pond around here, isn't there?"

Lucy pointed to the woods behind the Pratts' barn. "Blueberry Pond."

"That's the one where the nudists like to gather?"

"Mrs. Pratt didn't like them much," offered Lucy. "She was trying to get an anti-nudity bylaw passed."

"Sounds like she had a real knack for riling people up," observed Horowitz. "I have a feeling we won't have too far to look for our murderer."

Lucy grimaced. If only she'd been convinced he'd been looking in the direction of the pond, instead of her property, when he said that.

"I don't think we need to keep you any longer, Mrs. Stone." Horowitz started to walk away, then turned to face Lucy. "After all, I know where you live."

Chapter Fourteen

Free to leave, Lucy had to exert every ounce of self-control she possessed to proceed at a sedate pace. All her instincts told her to floor the accelerator and get out of there as fast as she could. But that, she knew, would only make Horowitz wonder why she was in such a hurry to get home.

Home, that's where she wanted to be. It was a great relief when she turned into the driveway to the antique farmhouse, but her heart dropped when she saw the empty kennel. She firmly pushed thoughts of the dog from her mind and hurried up the porch steps and into the house. The slam of the screen door when she entered the kitchen seemed to assure her that everything bad was outside and she was safe inside. Her hands were shaking and she felt light-headed; she knew she had to get something into her stomach. She stood in front of the refrigerator and downed a glass of milk, then, feeling a little better she made herself the longed-for peanut butter and jelly sandwich and poured a second glass of milk. This was no time to count calories.

She wolfed down the sandwich and was considering making another when she remembered Ted. The fact that the police considered Pru's death a homicide changed everything. She had to let him know about it right away. Even if it was too late for the *Pennysaver,* he could sell it to the Portland and Boston papers as a stringer. She dialed his cell phone number, but he didn't answer and she had to leave a message. What was the point of the darn things, she wondered, if people left them lying about instead of keeping them with them?

She was rinsing out her glass when he called back.

"Pru Pratt was murdered," she told him. "The cops are there right now. Do you want me to go over?"

"Murdered? Are you sure?"

"Horowitz told me himself. I thought she'd had a heart attack or something."

"You thought?" Ted's voice was suspicious. "What do you have to do with it?"

"I found her body."

"Good grief."

"Do you want me to write it up? What should I do?"

"Hold on, Lucy. Don't do anything. I'll take care of it."

"Don't you want me to help? I was there, after all."

"That's the problem, Lucy. I think you may be a little too close to this one."

"What do you mean?"

"Just lay low, okay?"

"Okay."

Puzzled, Lucy ended the call. This had never happened before. Ted had never told her not to pursue a story. She couldn't figure it out. The story was right next door, for Pete's sake, and she wanted to follow it. It wasn't just a job, it was personal. She wanted to find out who had killed Pru. After all, maybe there was a homicidal maniac loose in the neighborhood. They had certainly been attracting a lot of attention lately, what with the arrival of the naturists. Could some wacko be on the loose? They lived right next door to Pru—were they in danger? If they were, what could they do to protect themselves, without even the dog to alert them.

Lucy was lost in thought when the screen door slammed, practically causing her to jump out of her skin. It was Bill, home from work a little early because of the heat.

"Ohmigod, you startled me," she said, sitting down and fanning herself with her hand.

"Sorry." He took a Coke out of the refrigerator. "What's going on next door?"

"You won't believe this. Pru Pratt is dead. The cops think she was run down in her own driveway. And that's not all. Kudo's dead, too. Wesley hit him with his truck this morning."

Bill sat down hard and popped the top on his soda, taking a long, long swallow that almost drained the can. "What did you say?"

"Kudo's dead. Wesley hit him with his truck. I don't think he did it on purpose. It was an accident. The dog ran in front of his truck. There was nothing he could do."

"Before that."

"Pru is also dead. I found her body when I went over after work to find out if there'd been any damage to the truck."

Bill finished the Coke and got up for another.

"And the cops say she was run over, too?" Bill sat down and opened the second can, taking a sip this time. "Doesn't that seem fishy to you?"

Lucy looked at him with wide, disbelieving eyes. "You think Wesley did it? He ran over his mother and was fleeing the scene when he hit Kudo?" Lucy fell silent, struggling with the idea. "His own mother? That's horrible."

"It happens," said Bill.

"I know," admitted Lucy. "But I don't like to think of it happening next door."

Bill stared at the table. "Well, I guess we won't be having any more trouble with the neighbors."

Lucy was appalled. "Is that all you can say?"

"Well, I am going to miss the dog," he continued.

"It's terrible, isn't it?" confessed Lucy. "I think I feel worse about the dog than I do about Pru."

"He was a big part of our lives."

"It's funny about dogs. The way they're just sort of there, all the time, but you don't really notice. If I was cooking, he was in the kitchen. When we sat down at the table, he was under it. A quiet evening in front of the TV, he'd be stretched out on the rug."

"He was a great companion."

"Not much of a talker. . . ."

"But a great listener."

"That's for sure. I really liked having him in the house if you were away for the night." Lucy shrugged.

"I know it's irrational but I'm always a little nervous when you're gone. But I knew I could count on Kudo to let me know if anything was amiss. If he was relaxed, I could relax."

Bill sighed. "I don't think there's going to be much relaxing until they figure out who killed Pru."

"I feel especially vulnerable without the dog," fretted Lucy. "With all the new people in town, all those naturists, how do we know one of them isn't a serial killer or something. We could be next."

"I don't think so, Lucy. People who get killed generally get killed for a reason." He stood up. "You know, from the back, Pru looked an awful lot like Wesley."

"I've noticed that," admitted Lucy.

"It could have something to do with the poaching. The killer could have mistaken Pru for Wesley."

Lucy looked out the window to the driveway. "I wonder where Toby is. Shouldn't he be home by now?"

Bill fingered his car keys. "It's time to get the girls, anyway. I'll pick them up. You've had enough excitement for one day."

Lucy watched as he went out the door. She would have bet the house that he'd detour past the harbor on his way to the camp, just to see if the Carrie Ann was in port.

She shook herself. She wasn't going to worry, she wasn't going to jump to conclusions. She was going to make supper. Something wholesome and comforting, that's what was called for. She began filling a pot with water and reached for a box of shells. If ever there was a night for pasta salad, this was it.

*   *   *

Despite the comforting food, Toby's absence cast a shadow of tension over the meal. Bill reported that the boat was sitting in its berth but he'd found no sign of Toby. He'd even checked the Bilge, where the fishermen hung out, but nobody there knew his whereabouts. Or if they did, they weren't telling.

Elizabeth took the news of the deaths coolly. She only considered things that directly affected her as real tragedies, like a late paycheck at the inn or getting her period early or discovering a big, ugly zit on her chin. Those were real disasters.

The younger girls, too, had little sympathy for the neighbor.

"Mrs. Pratt was mean to animals," said Zoe, spearing a noodle with her fork.

"She mistreated those chickens, you know," said Sara. "I think poor Kudo was only trying to liberate the chickens from their terrible conditions."

Lucy's and Bill's eyes met across the table.

"We all loved Kudo. . . ."

"Not me," insisted Elizabeth.

"As I was saying, I understand you want to remember the good things about Kudo, and there were lots of good things . . ."

Elizabeth snorted.

". . . but to him those chickens were an irresistible combination of fun and food," said Bill, finishing her sentence.

"Mrs. Pratt may have had her faults, but I think she took pretty good care of her chickens. She was always winning blue ribbons at the fair. She must have known what she was doing."

"That's not true!" exclaimed Sara. "You should have seen it. The chickens were in a little tiny space and there was tons of poop and they'd step right in it. It was disgusting! They'd even poop in their water dish."

"Well, that's chickens for you," said Bill.

"They're not the cleanest, or the brightest creatures on this good earth."

"That's no excuse to treat them badly!" exclaimed Sara.

"There were no toys, Mom," said Zoe. "Chickens can't read, they can't watch TV, so what are they supposed to do all day if they don't have any toys? Poor things. They must have been awfully bored."

Lucy was beginning to wonder if Zoe was getting the wrong idea about animals at Friends of Animals day camp. "As much as we love our pets, they're not people, you know. Animals are pretty much happy just being, they don't need to be entertained."

"Mrs. Pratt wasn't just mean to the chickens," said Sara. "She was mean to her own son."

Now this was interesting, thought Lucy. "How so?"

"We saw her yelling at him. Telling him he was a piece of . . . well, a lot of bad things. Worthless. Stupid. Lazy."

"You heard her say these things?" asked Bill.

"She was yelling. We couldn't help it," said Sara, self-righteously.

"You wouldn't have heard if you hadn't been snooping around," Lucy reminded her. "Mrs. Pratt didn't know she was being overheard."

"Mom, you always say we should be as polite to

each other at home as we'd be if we were visiting friends," said Zoe. "Mrs. Pratt was not polite to Wesley."

"Maybe he did something very wrong and that's why she was mad at him," said Lucy. "Sometimes that happens. Did Wesley yell back at his mother?"

"He did. He yelled some bad words at her and then he got in his truck and drove away very fast." Sara paused. "That's when Mrs. Pratt saw us, because we'd been hiding behind the truck."

"We ran as fast as we could," said Zoe. "She was chasing us."

"Let that be a lesson to you not to go trespassing," said Bill. "Just think what might have happened if you'd got caught."

"She might have put you in an oven and baked you, like in Hansel and Gretel," said Elizabeth.

Lucy was about to admonish her when Toby strode into the dining room and sat down at the table, reaching for the salad and piling it onto his plate.

"What is this?" demanded Bill. "No hello, no apologies for being late, you just march in and start eating?"

"Uh, sorry Dad. Great salad, Mom."

"Thanks," said Lucy. "What held you up?"

"Stuff."

"What stuff?" asked Bill.

"You know. Stuff."

"NO, I DON'T KNOW!" yelled Bill.

"We're all a little upset," said Lucy, hoping to lower the emotional temperature in the room. "Did you hear that Mrs. Pratt is dead?"

Toby was busy helping himself to seconds.

"Nah, I didn't hear that."

"And Wesley killed Kudo with his truck," said Sara, her voice trembling.

Toby stopped, holding the serving spoon in midair. "Wes Pratt killed the dog?"

"It was an accident," said Lucy. "I saw the whole thing."

Toby's face had hardened and Lucy could practically hear the gears grinding away in his head as he pushed the food on his plate around with his fork.

"We'd really feel a lot better if we knew what you were doing this afternoon," said Bill. "Considering your situation and all."

"What do you think?" Toby's face was crimson. "That I killed the old bag because of the dog? I didn't even care about that dog!" He threw down his fork and stood up, scraping his chair noisily on the wooden floor, and left the table.

The rest of the family sat at the table in a heavy silence. From outside they heard the engine in his Jeep roar to life, and the crunch of gravel as he sped down the driveway and took off down Red Top Road.

Chapter Fifteen

"He's up to something."

That had been Bill's final word on the subject, uttered just before he fell asleep. But while Bill slept, the sentence kept repeating in her mind like a mantra. Not soothing like a mantra was supposed to be, but a nagging reminder that these days she hardly seemed to know her son. He was constantly surprising her. She'd always thought he was a peaceable soul and she never would have expected him to get in a fight like he did with Wesley.

As she tossed and turned in bed she told herself that fundamentally he was a good person, she had to believe that. He'd been raised in a caring and loving home, he'd had plenty of advantages. But she had to admit to herself that he hadn't made the most of them—he'd dropped out of college after two years of miserable grades.

She certainly hadn't expected that. After all, he'd been one of the best students in his class at Tinker's Cove High School, ranking in the top ten percent. And he'd gotten a solid fourteen hundred on his SATs. What went wrong when he went to college?

And what was he involved in now? She agreed with Bill that he was up to something, and she prayed that it wasn't something that would get him into even more trouble. After all, he was in plenty of trouble already with an upcoming court date. And even if he seemed oblivious to his situation, Lucy was convinced that the police investigating Pru's death would be taking a long, hard look at Toby.

The thought made her heart race and she got out of bed and went downstairs, checking his room as she passed the door. He wasn't there, of course. Where was he? It was nearly one in the morning. She went downstairs and peeked out the window, hoping to see his headlights as he turned into the driveway, but there was only darkness.

She paced through the downstair's rooms, going from window to window. Realizing it was pointless, she poured herself a mug of milk, added a dash of vanilla extract and set it in the microwave to heat, then sat at the kitchen table sipping the warm liquid.

What could she do? Lecturing didn't work, neither did probing questions. Setting limits, demanding a certain level of behavior if he was to continue living in the house would only backfire because he'd move out. There were plenty of kids in town, living on their own in squalid, substandard housing. Old, worn-out trailers parked in the woods. Rooms above garages, storage sheds. She didn't like to think what went on in those places: unprotected sex, drug use, binge drinking. No, it was better to have him home, where she could at least keep an eye on him.

She didn't believe for one minute that he had anything to do with Pru's death, but she wasn't sure the police shared her view. They would be looking for a conviction and she knew that the court system was not infallible—thanks to DNA testing they were finding plenty of innocent people who'd been wrongly convicted and sent to jail.

That wasn't going to happen to Toby, she decided, setting down her empty mug. The best way, the only way she could protect him was by finding the real murderer. And starting first thing tomorrow, that was what she was going to do.

The hot and muggy weather continued the next morning, but that didn't faze Lucy. She was full of energy when she arrived at the *Pennysaver* office and eager to start working. Her job at the paper gave her an inside track, after all, and she wanted to find out everything she could about Pru's murder.

"Good morning," she sang, greeting Phyllis.

Phyllis, dressed in a dazzling shade of lime green, with eyeshadow to match, raised her finger to her lips in warning, tilting her head towards Ted.

Ted was hunched over his computer, pecking away at the keyboard.

"The *Globe* wants a firsthand account," said Phyllis.

"Great!" said Lucy, eagerly. "Anything I can do to help?"

"I've got it covered, Lucy," said Ted. "Phyllis needs help with the obits."

"Sure, I can do those," said Lucy, taking the sheaf of papers Phyllis handed her.

She sat down and turned on the computer, turning to Ted. "What's happening? Any new developments?"

"Still waiting for the ME's report," he said.

"So what angle are you taking? Community reaction? Small town stunned? Cantankerous neighbor gets a comeuppance?"

"I'm trying to work here, Lucy."

"Can I help? Can I make some phone calls for you? Just tell me what you want?"

"I want you to be quiet, okay?"

"Okay," said Lucy, sulking.

She looked to Phyllis for sympathy, but Phyllis was taking an uncharacteristically serious approach to her work this morning. Weird, thought Lucy. What was going on? The phone rang and she reached for it, but Ted beat her to it. That was odd. Ted hardly ever answered the phone.

Lucy looked over the announcements from the funeral home, but she wasn't really paying attention. She was listening to Ted's conversation.

"No comment, sorry. Wish I could help you," he said, quickly ending the call.

"You were kind of brusque, weren't you? Who was that?" she asked.

"TV news. They've been calling all morning. Too lazy to do their own footwork."

"TV?"

Phyllis nodded and the phone rang again. This time she grabbed it. "I wish I could help you," she said, "but we're very short-staffed. I'm sure you understand." There was a pause; the voice on the other end was apparently quite persuasive. "I'll check."

Phyllis looked at Ted. "It's 'Inside Edition,' Ted. They want to interview you."

Lucy's jaw dropped.

"I'll take it," he said. "Lucy, be a doll and run over to the Shack for me. I want a coupla plain donuts, get some for you and Phyllis, too." He picked up the receiver. "Take some money from petty cash."

Lucy took the five dollar bill Phyllis handed her and walked towards the door, uncomfortably aware that Ted was waiting for her to leave before he started talking. What was going on? Was she paranoid? Or was there some sort of conspiracy to keep her out of the loop?

She was walking down Main Street when she noticed a TV truck, a white van with the call letters of a Portland station painted on its side. It was parked in front of the police station.

There would probably be more, she decided, as she walked along. Big city media seemed to find crime in small towns irresistible, maybe they thought it went to prove that violence wasn't confined to urban areas. And thanks to the naturists, the media were already familiar with the town.

At Jake's Donut Shack she picked up a rumpled copy of the *Boston Globe* to read while she waited in line to place her order. The story, written by contributing writer Edward J. Stillings, was on the New England region section front. Good for Ted, she thought.

But when she started reading she could hardly believe what he'd written.

"Investigators are looking into the possibility that Pratt's strained relationship with her Red Top Road neighbors, may have played a part in her death. There had been disagreement about a dog owned by the Stone family which was apparently killed by Pratt's son, Wesley. Investigators

*were also planning to question Toby Stone, 21, who has
been charged with assault and battery against Wesley Pratt."*

"Can I help you?" The kid behind the counter
was clearly impatient.

"A half-dozen," she stammered. "Two plain and
the rest assorted."

The kid rolled his eyes. "What do you mean assorted? Do you want cinnamon? Apple? You tell
me."

"Make 'em all plain," gasped Lucy, feeling rather
short of breath.

All she wanted to do was get out of there. She
felt as if everyone in the place was looking at her.
Suddenly she was the head of a criminal family,
like Ma Barker or somebody. She felt like a marked
woman.

When the kid handed her the bag of donuts she
threw the five dollar bill at him and bolted for the
door.

"Hey, lady! Don't you want your change?"

Lucy didn't want her change. She wanted to
hide under a rock, or pull a paper bag over her
head. She dashed across Main Street without looking and jumped back when somebody blasted a
horn at her. Looking up, she was dismayed to see it
was another TV truck. She waited for it to pass and
ran straight for the *Pennysaver* office.

"I can't believe you did this!" she yelled at Ted,
throwing the bag of donuts at him. "Is it true? Is
Toby a suspect?"

Ted looked up from his desk with an expression
of terrible sadness.

Lucy swallowed hard and struggled to hold back
tears.

He stood up and put his arms around her and she started sobbing. Phyllis grabbed a box of tissues and hurried over.

"I'm sorry. I didn't have any choice," said Ted.

"Toby's really in trouble?" she asked, dabbing at her eyes.

"Not just him. They're looking at lots of people. Even Wesley and Calvin."

Lucy sniffed. "I guess that should make me feel better, but it doesn't." She straightened her shoulders and attempted a smile. "Well, let's get to work. We've got to keep the cops honest, right? Make sure they nail the real killer. Remind the DA that it's 'innocent until proven guilty.' "

There was an awkward pause.

"Lucy," Ted finally began, "I think it would be better if you didn't work on this story."

Lucy was stunned. "What?"

"I'd like you to help Phyllis with the listings and obits and classified. I'll handle the reporting."

"Why?"

"Because you're too close. How can you possibly remain objective?"

"You're kicking me off the story? To do obits?"

Ted nodded, and Phyllis put her hand on Lucy's shoulder. Furious with them both, Lucy shrugged it off.

"Well, no thanks." She spit out the words. "I quit."

"Lucy, don't . . ." began Ted, but Lucy didn't wait to hear the rest.

She was out of there as fast as her legs could carry her, making sure to give the door a good slam. The little bell jangled furiously, ringing in her ears as she marched down the sidewalk to her car. Her heart was pounding and her hands were trembling as she yanked open the door and sat behind the steering wheel. Automatically she started the car, then sat holding on to the steering wheel for dear life, wondering what on earth she was going to do next.

She could only think of one thing: she was going to find Bill.

It seemed to take forever, but finally she spotted the bell tower on the old schoolhouse poking up through the trees. She was almost there, she only had to cross the bridge and climb the hill and then she would be there. She was signaling, preparing to turn into the drive when she had to slam on the brakes to allow a police cruiser to clear the narrow track that was only wide enough for one vehicle. She studied the officer's face as he passed, but his expression revealed nothing.

She bounced down the drive, going as fast as she dared, driving right up to the steps of the old schoolhouse. Bill was standing in the doorway, a hammer in his hand.

"Why were the cops here?" she asked, afraid to know the answer.

Bill took one look at her and put the hammer down, enfolding her in his strong arms. She felt his bristly beard against her forehead and smelled his good, sweaty smell. He stroked her hair with his rough, calloused hand.

"Don't worry," he said. "It was all pretty routine. They wanted to know where I was yesterday."

"What did you say?"

"The truth. I don't have anything to hide. I was

here, working." He gave her a squeeze. "I expected it, really. We're her closest neighbors and there were problems, there's no use pretending there weren't."

"It was in the *Globe*. Ted wrote that the police are investigating the neighbors—that means us—and especially Toby. Because of that fight with Wesley."

Bill stepped back and looked at her. Then he spoke, slowly. "I was here alone, you know. The cop asked me if I saw anybody or talked to anybody and I had to say no. I can't prove that I was here."

"You don't have to," said Lucy. "They have to prove you weren't. That's how it works."

"Well, that's a relief," said Bill, sarcastically. "Now I feel a whole lot better."

"I'm really worried about Toby."

"If they questioned me, they're definitely going to talk to him." Bill looked at his watch. "He's on the boat with Chuck. I don't think they'll be back for an hour or so. I could call and warn him that the cops are likely to be waiting for him."

"He's innocent so he shouldn't have anything to worry about, right?"

"Right." Bill's voice was firm. "I think I'm going to head down to the harbor. I'd like to be there when Toby gets back."

Lucy watched Bill go, then started picking up his tools and putting them away in his toolbox. She knew he wouldn't want to leave his valuable tools lying about in the open. Then she found the broom and began sweeping up the sawdust and bits of wood that littered the wide old floorboards. She loved the smell of clean, new wood and sheet-rock and the sense of emptiness in the nearly fin-ished building. Soon enough it would be filled with rugs and furniture and all the owner's stuff, but now it was bare and fresh.

She remembered Toby as a little baby with un-blemished, creamy skin and fine, curly hair and sweet round cheeks and tiny, tiny little toenails. He'd been an easygoing, bouncy baby who nursed enthusiastically and slept deeply. Full of energy, he'd walked and talked early. He'd been a delight and she'd been unprepared when colicky, cranky Elizabeth arrived on the scene.

Lucy brushed the floor sweepings into a dust-pan and emptied it into a trash barrel, then propped the broom into the corner, tucking the dustpan behind it as she always did. She stood up. Toby hadn't killed Pru Pratt, she was sure of it. She wasn't sure what he was up to these days, there was a lot about him that she didn't know, but she knew in her heart that her sweet baby boy would never kill anybody. The problem was making sure the police believed it, too.

Chapter Sixteen

When Lucy got home, she found Elizabeth in the family room, watching TV and having a late lunch of diet soda and baby carrots.

"What are you doing here? I thought you'd be working on your tan."

"It's not so nice down there anymore, Mom," said Elizabeth, wrinkling her nose. "There's a lot of black flies and mosquitoes and there's litter. It's kind of icky."

"I'm surprised," said Lucy. "I thought the naturists were more responsible than that."

"I think Mike's organizing a clean-up party this weekend." Elizabeth chewed a carrot. "It's not just that, Mom. I've got a rash."

"It's probably a heat rash"

"No." Elizabeth held out her arm. "Look. It's gross." Her voice tightened. "Do you think it's skin cancer?"

Lucy felt a stab of guilt. Maybe she shouldn't have put that library book on Elizabeth's night table. She took a look at Elizabeth's arm and immediately recognized the honey-colored scabs. "Impetigo."

"What's that?" Elizabeth grimaced. "Is it bad?"

"It's stubborn, like you. You have to keep after it with antibiotic cream. It'll go away, but it'll take a while." Lucy couldn't resist adding, "You probably picked it up at the pond."

"Don't worry. I'm not going back there. Some of those people were kind of creepy."

Lucy didn't like the sound of this. "What do you mean?"

Elizabeth shrugged. "They weren't cool, you know. They'd stare."

"Sightseers?"

"You could say that."

Lucy went into the kitchen to make herself a sandwich. She felt better than she had all morning. At least something was working out, even if it took a dose of impetigo to convince Elizabeth to keep her clothes on. While she didn't like the idea of unsavory characters hanging around so close to her house their presence did open a promising avenue worth investigating. She was humming to herself and spreading mustard on a piece of bread when she heard Elizabeth shriek.

"Mom! Come here!"

Lucy ran into the family room, where Elizabeth was pointing at the TV. "It's Mrs. Pratt, Mom. On TV."

"Police are investigating whether a family feud in a small Maine town led to the death of a woman there," said Brad Hicks, the New England Cable News anchorman.

Lucy's jaw dropped as she watched the story unfold in pictures. First there was a shot of Pru, accepting a blue ribbon for her chickens at the county fair. It was the only time Lucy had ever seen her in a skirt and she looked rather attractive.

She'd even tied a bit of ribbon around her pony tail. Then there was rolling video of the Pratts' house with the driveway filled with police cars.

"Long-standing feud with neighbors Bill and Lucy Stone . . ." was illustrated with a shot of their house, ". . . culminated earlier this week in a dog hearing. Responding to complaints that the Stones' dog attacked the dead woman's chickens, town officials voted to destroy the dog if there were any further attacks."

"I can't believe this," muttered Elizabeth.

Lucy watched in horror as the screen filled with a familiar action shot of Toby playing lacrosse taken from his high school yearbook. His hair was matted with sweat, he had a streak of mud across his face and was grimacing with exertion. He was also attempting to whack the opposing player with his lacrosse stick. "The Stones' son Toby is currently under indictment for assault and battery against Prudence Pratt's son, Wesley."

Then Wesley's yearbook photo, picturing him in a shirt and tie with neatly combed hair, filled the screen. Lucy knew enough about public relations to know this was a disaster. Wesley was a neatly groomed "good" boy and her son was an aggressive hooligan.

That photo was replaced with a live shot of Brad Hicks, announcing breaking news in Tinker's Cove. She and Elizabeth watched, fascinated, as the camera panned the harbor parking lot, which was crowded with reporters, photographers and TV cameramen. The camera then settled on a young blond woman in a blue suit.

"Stacy Blake, reporting live from Tinker's Cove where police are awaiting the arrival of Toby Stone, a suspect in the murder of Prudence Pratt. Stone is believed to be aboard a lobster boat now approaching the dock."

The camera focused on Quisset Point, where the Carrie Ann could be seen steaming steadily towards its birth. A uniformed officer and a plainclothes detective were stationed on the gangway, where they were soon joined by Bill and Bob Goodman.

"Are they going to arrest Toby?" asked Elizabeth.

Lucy was perched on the sofa, wringing her hands. "I hope not." She could hardly believe what she was seeing: people and places she knew were actually on TV. Somehow it made everything seem unreal.

"As you can see," the reporter continued, "the lobster boat carrying suspect Toby Stone has now docked and police are boarding it. They appear to be questioning the two men on the boat, one of whom we believe is Toby Stone, but we cannot hear what they are saying."

"Tell me, Stacy," came Brad Hicks's voice, "can you tell our viewers why Toby Stone is considered a suspect."

"Yes, Brad, I can. Stone was arraigned in district court last week and charged with assault and battery against Wesley Pratt, the victim's son. The two apparently had some sort of altercation right here on the docks."

"Was Stone the only one charged?"

"No, Brad. As it happens, several other men were charged in connection with that altercation, including Wesley Pratt, the victim's son."

"Well, that is certainly interesting information Stacy. Can you tell us what's happening now?"

"The police appear to be continuing to question the men aboard the fishing boat, the Carrie Ann." Behind the reporter the police could be seen leaving the boat and climbing up the gangway. "No, I stand corrected. The officers appear to have completed their questioning and are now leaving the boat."

The scene at the harbor erupted into chaos as the pack of reporters surged in two directions. Some followed the police officers and others headed for the gangway. The camera wobbled, then settled on Bob Goodman. He stood patiently while microphones were thrust into his face.

"We have no statement at this time," he said.

"Who are you?" called out several reporters.

"I'm an attorney. Robert Goodman. I have offices here in town."

"Who are you representing?"

"I represent a lot of people in this town," said Bob. "Now I'm warning you that you're obstructing the right of these fishermen to conduct their business."

The feed from Tinker's Cove was abruptly disconnected and Brad Hicks was back on the screen. "In other news . . . ," he began.

Lucy and Elizabeth remained in place on the couch, in shock.

"This is crazy," said Elizabeth.

"I have a feeling it's going to get a whole lot crazier," said Lucy, as the phone began ringing.

She picked up the receiver, expecting it to be one of her girlfriends: Sue Finch or Rachel Goodman or Pam Stillings. It was NECN and she slammed the receiver down.

"Don't pick up unless it's somebody you know,"

she told Elizabeth. "We can use the answering machine to screen our calls."

Lucy grew increasingly nervous as the afternoon wore on and there was no sign of Toby or Bill. The constant ringing of the phone was an added irritation, especially since the callers were all reporters. The worst part, she decided, was that she really had no right to get indignant at this invasion of her privacy. How many times had she done the same thing, calling some troubled person for a reaction? How many times had she exposed someone to shame and censure, all in the cause of truth? And had she really discovered the truth or had she found a few facts and crafted them into a sensational story, just as the NECN reporters had done. Oh, it was all true, but it added up to a big lie. There was no family feud, or if there had been it had been on the Pratts' side. Finally, she heard Bob Goodman's familiar voice.

"Lucy, it's me, Bob," he said. "Pick up if you're there."

Lucy grabbed the receiver.

"What's happening? I saw it on TV. I've been so worried."

"That's why I called. Everything's okay. We went to the police station and I stayed with Toby when they questioned him and it turns out he's got a good alibi. He was out on the boat all day yesterday and Chuck can vouch for him."

"That's a relief," said Lucy. "Do they have a time of death?"

"Between ten and two, when you found her."

"Not earlier than ten?" asked Lucy.

"Nothing's definite, yet, but they seem to think that's the outside limit. Listen, Lucy, this is important. If you were watching TV you know the media is all over this case, the town is full of TV trucks. They're going to be after you, the kids, too. Don't talk to them. Don't let the kids talk to them. Try to ignore them, try to keep your expressions pleasantly neutral, if you can."

Lucy was getting the picture. "In case we're photographed?"

"Right. Try not to look guilty, okay?"

"That shouldn't be hard," said Lucy. "We're not guilty!"

"If only it were that easy," said Bob, with a sigh.

That evening Lucy and Bill held a family conference to clue the kids in on the situation. It soon became clear that Bob was right; it wasn't going to be easy at all. There was a lot of grumbling as they pulled the kids away from their various occupations but eventually everyone was gathered in the family room. The TV was off, and if Lucy had her way, it was going to stay off.

"Because of Mrs. Pratt's murder we might be getting some media attention," she began.

"It's like being the Osbournes," said Elizabeth. "Except they keep showing Toby and our house. Why don't they show me? I'm the most photogenic."

Lucy's jaw dropped and Bill was speechless.

"You wouldn't like it so much if they did show you," said Toby, scowling.

"Will we get paid millions of dollars, like the Osbournes?" asked Sara.

"When is it my turn?" asked Zoe. "I think I'll wear my new pink shirt tomorrow, just in case they want to film me."

"Maybe I'll get discovered and get a modeling contract," mused Elizabeth.

"Uh, guys, I think you've got the wrong idea," said Bill. "This isn't 'The Osbournes'. It's more like 'Inside Edition' and we're the bad guys."

Now it was the kids' turn to drop their jaws in disbelief.

"We're the bad guys? That's crazy!" exclaimed Sara.

"We're nice!" exclaimed Zoe.

"It's all Toby's fault," grumbled Elizabeth. "Because of him fighting with Wesley."

"You better mind your own business," said Toby. "I'm not guilty, yet, for your information, and last I heard there's no law against defending yourself."

"Enough!" barked Bill.

"We're in this together," said Lucy, "and we're going to get through it together. And the way we're going to do that is we're going to go about our business, we're going to stick to our routines, and we're not going to answer any of their questions. Like the president coming back to Camp David, we're just going to keep on walking. That's what we're going to do."

"But Mom, this could be my big chance. I could talk to them about the weather or something. Just to introduce myself to the nation," said Elizabeth.

"I'm warning you, Elizabeth. Even something you think is harmless can be used against you. 'Neighbor's Daughter Sheds No Tears for Poor Pru.' You think you're making polite chit-chat and they make you out as a callous monster. I've seen it happen."

"You're a reporter," accused Toby, "you've probably done it."

"Watch your tongue, Toby," said Bill.

"Actually, I'm not a reporter any more."

They all looked at her.

"I quit my job today and I'm glad I did. I don't want to be part of the media anymore."

Chapter Seventeen

Lucy's opinion of her profession wasn't improved the next morning when Bill left for work only to stomp angrily back into the house, instructing her to look out the window. She was shocked to see a couple of vans and a handful of reporters parked on the grassy verge opposite the driveway.

"I don't believe this," she said, but Bill was busy dialing the phone.

"This is Bill Stone on Red Top Road," he said. "I want to complain about some reporters parked on the road outside my house."

Lucy assumed he was calling the police department. She didn't think he'd get very far.

"Well, no, they're not obstructing the road," he said. "They're not trespassing on my property, either. But they've got no business to be here. They're harassing my family—we have no privacy." He listened, growing redder in the face by the minute, until he snapped. "It's great to see my tax dollars at work!" he snarled, slamming down the phone.

"There's nothing they can do, right?"

"The road's open to everyone, it's public property," said Bill. "They're not even going to send a cruiser. Apparently, there's media all over town and everybody's calling and complaining. They don't have the manpower, she says."

"Bob warned us this might happen. He said we should just ignore them, but try to keep a pleasant expression. Try not to look guilty."

Bill looked at her. It wasn't a pleasant expression. Then he left.

When it was her turn to leave the house to take the girls to day camp, she promised herself she would follow Bob's advice. She'd stay cool, she wouldn't get rattled as she ran the press gauntlet. When she braked at the end of the driveway and signaled her turn onto the road, several reporters approached the Subaru, snapping photos and shouting questions.

"Did you hate Prudence Pratt?" "Have the police questioned you?" "Has your son been arrested?" "Will you make a statement?" "Can I interview you? We'll pay."

Trying not to look flustered, Lucy drove carefully and deliberately until she'd worked her way free of the reporters. She was breathing a sigh of relief when she spotted a couple of cars following her. She was being tailed!

"I can't believe this," she muttered.

"Believe what?" asked Zoe.

"Nothing," said Lucy, keeping an eye on the rearview mirror.

At least they couldn't follow her onto the camp property, and the drop-off area was at the far end of the parking lot, blocked from the road by bushes. Nonetheless, she felt uneasy as she let the girls out.

"Remember, don't talk to strangers. If you see anybody who shouldn't be on the camp property be sure to tell Melanie right away."

"Okay, Mom," grumbled Sara. "We get it."

Driving home, Lucy was tempted to stop the car at the driveway and tell those reporters the real story. About the lobster poaching and the way Pru Pratt had made enemies of everyone in town. She'd like to give them a piece of her mind. Then she remembered Ted, cackling merrily when a controversial story prompted a flurry of irate letters to the editor.

"It's a win-win situation," he'd told her. "We get 'em mad and they write us letters which get more people mad so we get more letters."

Yeah, she thought bitterly, it was a win-win situation for the media, but a lose-lose situation for her family. The only thing that would end it would be the discovery of the real murderer. Then this supposed feud would be quickly forgotten. Yesterday's news. The faster the better, she decided, resolving to do everything she could to speed the investigation along. Even if she had to solve the murder herself.

But how was she going to do that, she wondered, when she got back to the house. Her home was under siege by the media and she was followed whenever she left. How could she possibly investigate if she couldn't get out of the house?

She was pondering this problem when the phone rang. It was Sue.

"It's so great to hear a friendly voice," said Lucy, feeling as if Sue had thrown her a lifeline.

"What do you mean?"

"Didn't you see the news last night?"

"I never watch the news. It's depressing and it gives me frown lines. I figure I may not be well-informed, but I'm saving a ton on Botox."

"Oh." Sue's attitude was a revelation to Lucy. "Really?"

"Really. So what was on the news?"

"Toby. They made him out like the prime suspect in Pru Pratt's murder."

"That's ridiculous," said Sue.

It was like a breath of fresh air to Lucy. "You don't know how much it means to me to hear you say that."

"Right," said Sue, not getting it. "Listen, I have to do some shopping today and I was wondering if you'd come along and help me."

"You need help shopping?" This time Lucy didn't get it.

"It's not that kind of shopping," said Sue. "I'm organizing a Fourth of July picnic and I need to buy paper plates and stuff like that. I'm going to that warehouse store. It's a drive but I figure the savings are worth it. So, want to come along? I'll buy you a hot dog for lunch."

"Uh, sure," said Lucy. "But I'm kind of stuck in the house. There's a bunch of reporters on the road and I don't want to face them."

"No problem. I'll pick you up. See you in ten."

Sue was as good as her word and came barreling up the drive minutes later in her huge black SUV. She was dressed for action in a jaunty baseball cap, black shades and a shorts outfit styled like a track suit. Her slender arms and legs were perfectly tanned and gleaming with moisturizer; all that work on the sun deck had paid off.

When Lucy took her place in the passenger seat, well-protected by the rhino guard, she began to see the advantages of the gas-guzzling monster. For one thing, the rabble of reporters stood back respectfully as Sue made the turn onto the road. A few cars did attempt to follow them, but Sue quickly lost them by turning off the paved road onto one of the old logging roads that criss-crossed the region. Lucy hung on to the grab bar above the door for dear life as they bounced through ruts and pot holes.

"Yee-ha!" yodeled Sue as they became momentarily airborne, going over one of the humps in the road Lucy called "thank-you-ma'ams."

They were definitely more fun when you were a kid, thought Lucy, and didn't have to worry about the fillings in your teeth shaking loose. There was no sign of the followers, however, when they picked up the town road a few miles from the interstate.

"This picnic sounds like a great idea. Who's invited?" she asked.

"The whole town."

"You're kidding, right? I mean, that's a whole lot of paper plates."

"I'm figuring on a thousand people."

"Wow," said Lucy. "How are you paying for it?"

"I talked to Marge and she got the parade committee to give me their money. If there's no parade, they don't need it, right?"

"But what about the naturists?"

"What about 'em?"

"What if they come?"

"I hope they do. The more the merrier," said Sue.

Maybe that old saying was right, thought Lucy. Ignorance was bliss. She knew entirely too much about the naturists, the environmentalists, the fishermen, the Revelation Congregation and others pushing the anti-nudity bylaw. In her view the town was splitting apart, driven by these warring factions. Sue, on the other hand, didn't see the problem. The Fourth of July was days away and they had to have a celebration. If there couldn't be a parade, and there couldn't be fireworks, there was jolly well going to be a picnic. And if anyone could pull it off, it would be Sue.

"So tell me, who do you think killed Pru?" asked Sue, swerving suddenly and accelerating up the ramp to the interstate.

"My favorite suspect is Wesley," said Lucy, checking that her seatbelt was fastened. "After all, he was driving hell for leather down the road when he hit Kudo."

"You mean he ran his mother down with the truck and fled the scene?" Sue was doubtful. "His own mother?"

"I don't think it was a happy family," said Lucy, taking a peek at the speedometer. The needle was hovering around eighty. "The girls were over there and they heard Pru calling Wesley all sorts of bad names. And Wesley gave it right back."

"What were your girls doing visiting the Pratts?" Sue was rapidly gaining on a Mini Cooper, but couldn't pass because a tractor-trailer truck was in the fast lane. She slammed on the brake and flashed her lights, but the driver of the Mini continued at a stately pace.

"They were uninvited guests. They were upset

about the dog hearing so they wanted to find evidence that Pru mistreated her chickens."

The tractor-trailer advanced and Sue shot into the passing lane, apparently oblivious to a second tractor-trailer that was making the same move. Now the SUV didn't seem quite so large, sandwiched between the two trucks.

"Ooh, they are their mother's daughters, aren't they?" The first truck moved into the traveling lane and Sue shot ahead.

This time Lucy didn't want to see the speedometer; she didn't want to know how fast they were going. "Sometimes the end justifies the means," she said, checking her seatbelt. "But in this case, I don't think it helps. The cops say Pru died after ten and Wesley was long gone by then."

"I wouldn't give up on him, yet," said Sue, switching on the radio and searching for a station. "Those times of death are always pretty approximate, aren't they?"

A road sign warned of a steep incline ahead and urged reducing speed.

"I'll do the radio," she offered, nervously. "You watch the road."

"Calm down, Lucy. If this baby can tame the Kalahari it can certainly handle the Maine Pike."

Sue had found her favorite oldies station and was tapping the steering wheel, singing along with the BeeGees. "Who else is on the list?"

"Well, Cal, of course. Poor guy was probably the original hen-pecked husband."

"I know the husband's always the first suspect, but Cal? You've got to be kidding. He's afraid of his own shadow."

Sue was now weaving between lanes. Lucy wrapped her hand around the grab bar and tried to think of an appropriate prayer.

"They're the ones to watch out for," said Lucy, deciding to say something. "Are we in a big hurry or something? You're going awfully fast."

"It just seems like that," said Sue, hitting the brakes to avoid slamming into a horse trailer. "I don't know why they let these things on the road. And campers! Gosh, I hate those things! They're supposed to be seeing the country, but I don't think most of them ever get more than fifty miles from home, and it must take them two weeks considering how slow they go."

Well, she'd tried, thought Lucy, as Sue hit the accelerator and passed, only to swing abruptly onto the exit ramp.

"There was no love lost between Pru and the naturists. I suppose one of them could have done her in," speculated Lucy. "If they got rid of Pru they wouldn't have to worry about the bylaw. Chances are it would die with her."

"Are you serious? They seem pretty peace-loving to me."

"I'm not saying they did it as a group or anything like that. All it takes is one loony, somebody who feels threatened by the bylaw. And then there's the folks they attract. I've heard there have been some suspicious characters hanging around the pond."

"That's just local prejudice," exclaimed Sue, tapping the brake at the stop sign at the end of the exit ramp and zooming in front of a battered pickup truck. "Who else?"

"I have a theory," began Lucy. "You've heard about the lobster poaching, right? How everybody is convinced it's Calvin and Wesley?"

Sue nodded.

"Well, I have noticed that Pru and Wesley look an awful lot alike, especially from behind. If one of the fishermen came to even things up with Wesley he might have gone after Pru by mistake."

"That makes sense to me," said Sue, cutting off an oncoming station wagon and turning into the superstore parking lot. "Those fishermen have a code of their own when it comes to poaching. Whoever it was might have only wanted to scare Wesley, figuring he could jump out of the way, but Pru wasn't so quick and agile. It could have been some sort of tragic mistake."

"You don't like to admit that there could be a cold-blooded killer among us, do you?"

"No, I don't." Sue was cruising the lot, looking for a parking spot.

"What about Mel Dunwoodie? The guy with the campground? He had a lot to lose financially if Pru's bylaw went through. Maybe he did it."

"I don't think so," protested Sue, spotting a woman pushing a cart full of bags walking down one of the aisles between cars. Intent on her prey, she turned the SUV around and began a slow stalk.

"I'm adding him to the list. So far we've got Wesley Pratt, Calvin Pratt, a crazed naturist, an angry lobsterman and Mel Dunwoodie. Anybody else?"

"I can't think of anyone," said Sue, letting the car idle as she watched the woman load the shopping bags into her car. When she finished, she pushed the cart to one side and got in, taking her time starting the car. Sue drummed her fingers on the wheel impatiently.

"Finally!" she exclaimed when the woman backed out at a speed roughly that of a fresh bottle of ketchup. "Could she move any slower?"

When the car finally drove off, Sue hit the gas and promptly collided with the cart, which had rolled into the space.

"Shit!"

Lucy bit her lip and didn't say anything.

They'd just finished filling every inch of space inside the SUV with blocky cardboard boxes of paper goods and bags of red, white and blue party decorations when Sue suddenly asked, "What do we do now?"

"Try to get home alive so we can do this all over again and unload the stuff," said Lucy, pushing the cart back to the corral.

"No, silly. I mean about the murder," said Sue, following with the second cart. "How are you going to find out who did it?"

"Start asking questions," said Lucy, adding her cart to the line of linked carriages. "See what I can find out. I only wish there was some way I could find out more about the Pratt family. If they had some friends I could talk to them, but I don't think they had any."

"Pru belonged to the Revelation Congregation," said Sue, giving her cart a final little shove. "And so do my neighbors, the Wilsons. I could talk to them."

"That's a good idea."

"You'll have to pay me, though."

Trust Sue to extract her pound of flesh, thought Lucy. "Whatever you say."

"Ten pounds of potato salad, for the picnic."

"No problem." Lucy considered. "You've told Ted, right?"

"He's giving it front page coverage."

"That's good." For a minute Lucy wished she was back at the *Pennysaver*, writing up the story.

"His story won't be half as good as what you would have written," said Sue, patting her hand.

"You're right. He's probably missing me like crazy."

As she said it, Lucy was aware that she was voicing her own thoughts, not Ted's. She was already missing her job. She climbed up into the passenger seat and began fastening the seat belt. It didn't seem quite adequate; she wanted something sturdier for the trip home, like the harnesses they used in stunt aircraft. An ejection seat would be nice, too.

"Ready?" asked Sue, starting the engine and shifting into reverse.

"As ready as I'll ever be," said Lucy, resigned to her fate.

Chapter Eighteen

Lucy pondered her next move when Sue dropped her off at the house. Amazingly enough she was in one piece, but somewhat rattled by Sue's aggressive driving. She took a couple of aspirin for her tension headache and stood at the kitchen sink, drinking a glass of water and watching the watchers.

They were still there, which surprised her. You would think they would have something better to do than sit for hours in front of an empty house. Maybe, she thought, she could give them some help. Fearful that her Dutch courage would desert her, she placed her glass in the sink and marched out of the house and down the driveway, stopping at the road. Predictably, the reporters gathered around.

"This is off the record," she began, trying to ignore the cameras. "But I'm afraid you're missing the big story."

Now that she was actually face-to-face with them, the reporters looked very young. They were probably rookies, assigned to watch the house while their more experienced colleagues were attending news conferences and interviewing officials.

"What do you mean?" asked one, a freckle-faced kid with a crew cut.

"Well, you know, Blueberry Pond is just a bit down the road."

"So? What's Blueberry Pond?" This poor girl was camera-ready in a pastel polyester suit and Lucy knew she must be cooking in the heat.

"Haven't you heard about the nudists?" Lucy kept her voice neutral.

"Nudists?"

"Well, they prefer to be called naturists." Lucy dangled the bait. They were nibbling, but would they bite?

"Around here?" The kid with the crew cut was wary, sensing a trick.

"At Blueberry Pond. Some days there are hundreds over there. Sunning themselves and swimming. It's an official hot spot on the naturist Web site."

"That is interesting," began the girl, "but what's that got to do with the murder?"

"Oh, didn't you know? Prudence Pratt was very upset about all those naked people practically in her backyard. She was trying to get the town to pass an anti-nudity bylaw."

"At the very least it would be a photo op," said the photographer.

"And it might tie into the murder," said the girl.

"Thanks. Thanks a lot," said the kid with the crew cut.

"No problem," said Lucy, turning and strolling up the driveway. She turned back to look when she reached the porch and saw that the little caravan was departing.

Wasting no time she grabbed her purse and started the Subaru. Which way to go? She ran through her list of suspects and decided to head for the harbor, the scene of the most recent violence before the murder. She wanted to find out more about the lobster poaching and this was her chance, but only if the time and tide were right for the lobstermen to return to port.

Her heart sank when she turned into the harbor parking lot and discovered nearly all the berths were empty. If everybody was out fishing there wouldn't be anyone to talk to. Even the harbormaster's little shack was shut tight, with a handwritten sign indicating he would be back in two hours. Lucy wandered from one end of the pier to the other, looking for signs of life. All she found were seagulls perched on pilings, waiting for the boats to return with their dinner of bait bits and fish scraps.

She was about to give up when she heard a string of oaths, delivered by a gruff voice, coming from the Reine Marie, Beetle Bickham's boat. She went closer to investigate and noticed the hatch was open. She heard a series of clangs, followed by more profanity. Beetle was in the hold, working on his engine.

"Hi, down there!" she yelled.

"Hi, Lucy." Beetle's sweaty, red face appeared in the opening. "What's up?"

"Nothing much," she said, shrugging. "Do you have a minute to talk?"

"Sure. I'll be glad to take a break from this stubborn, hard-hearted old bitch of an engine. There's Cokes in the cooler."

He pulled himself up easily through the hatch with his powerful arms, strong from years of raising heavy lobster traps from the deep, and seated himself beside her on the locker. Lucy handed him a frosty can and he popped the top, downing most of the contents in one gulp.

"That is thirsty work." He looked down ruefully at his grease-stained hands and shirt.

"Sure is," said Lucy, sipping her drink. "Have you missed many days of fishing?"

"Naw. She just started acting up yesterday, when I was coming back in. And I made my quota anyway this week."

"Already?" Lucy was surprised since she'd heard that catches were low.

Beetle shrugged his shoulders. "Yeah. It's pretty good, much better than it was for a while there."

Lucy noticed that Calvin and Wesley's boat, Second Chance, was tied up at the dock, too.

"So you think the poachers have been busy with something else?"

His black eyes twinkled. "That might just be it."

Lucy took another sip. "You know, I've been wondering if whoever killed Pru Pratt might have mistaken her for Wesley. From the back, they looked a lot alike, you know?"

"She was a good woman, very religious, but not a womanly woman. You understand what I'm saying?" Beetle's hands were in motion, this was a subject he felt strongly about. "I used to make a little joke about her, eh? I'd sing that old song about skin and bones and a hank of hair. That's all she was." He paused, perhaps thinking of his own amply endowed wife and his curvaceous daughters, who had all inherited his sparkling black eyes. "But I heard she was a good cook, especially her chicken fricassee." He shook his head, pondering this incongruity.

"So do you think one of the lobstermen might have killed her by mistake, thinking she was Wesley? Were tempers running that high around here? Over the poaching, I mean?"

"It's hard to say," said Beetle. "Men get upset over a lot of things: women, money, politics. Lobsters, too." He glanced at the ramshackle Bilge, perched precariously on the hill overlooking the harbor. "Especially if they drink a little too much Pete's Wicked Ale, no?"

Lucy looked at him sharply. "Does anybody like that come to mind?"

Beetle raised his hands. "No, no. Nobody in particular. But the Bilge is a popular place. A lot of guys go there and drink, all night sometimes."

"All night? That's illegal," began Lucy, prompting a world-weary chuckle from Beetle. "Okay, I admit the Bilge is a law unto itself. So can you think of anybody who was especially upset by the poaching?"

"I'm sorry, Lucy, but I have to get back to work."

"I thought you said there was no rush."

"I need a part and I just remembered the boat-yard closes early today."

Lucy didn't believe it for a minute. She suspected Beetle didn't like the direction her questions were taking.

"Oh, I'm sorry." Lucy said slowly. "I didn't mean to keep you."

"No problem. You know I wish the best for Toby. He's a good kid."

"This has been hell for him, for all of us. If you could give me something to go on I'd be so grateful."

"I wish I could help you, Lucy." Beetle shook his head. "Say thanks to Ted for me, will you? I saw my letter in the paper."

She had to expect this, she realized. People didn't know she'd quit.

"I don't work there anymore."

"No?" Beetle's black eyebrows shot up in amazement.

"No. Ted says I can't be in the news and report it, too."

"He fired you? There was nothing else you could do there?"

"There was nothing I wanted to do, so I quit."

"Well, maybe you'll go back when this is all over."

Lucy gave him a tight little smile. "Maybe."

Maybe he was right, she thought, as she drove home. Maybe she would go back to the *Pennysaver* when this was all over. But right now it didn't seem as if it would ever be over unless Pru's killer was found. And that seemed extremely unlikely unless somebody talked. But if her conversation with Beetle was any indication, it wasn't going to be one of the lobstermen. They followed an unwritten code of loyalty, grown out of necessity. They depended on each other to help them if they ran into trouble on the water; it was expected that they would risk their own lives to save a fellow lobsterman.

The problem was that while most of the lobstermen were hard working and followed the law, a handful took advantage of the code of silence to supplement their incomes by scrubbing female lobsters of their eggs, a practice forbidden by law, or even to use their boats to smuggle illegal drugs, even cigarettes now that they were so highly taxed. If one of the lobstermen had killed Pru Pratt, it would be extremely difficult for her, or the police for that matter, to finger the culprit.

Lucy was thinking over this discouraging truth, when she spotted Ellie Sykes's "Fresh Eggs" sign. Remembering the ten pounds of potato salad she'd promised Sue, she slammed on the brakes, spun the Subaru into Ellie's driveway, bounced down the rutted dirt track and braked by the house.

The eggs were set out on a card table, underneath a huge shady maple tree, packed in recycled cartons from the supermarket. Lucy opened one of the boxes—these beauties were a far cry from supermarket eggs. The shells shone as if they'd been polished, gleaming globes of brown and blue and green, some even speckled. They were varying sizes, too, big jumbos for daddy and extra larges for mommy and even a few itty-bitty pullet eggs for baby.

Lucy was trying to decide how many dozen she needed when Ellie came out of the house.

"Can I help you?" she asked in her official egg-lady voice.

"I'm fine," said Lucy. "I'm just dithering, trying to decide how many to take."

"Hi, Lucy, I didn't realize it was you. The sun's in my eyes and you're in the shade."

"These are such beautiful eggs. I forgot how wonderful homegrown ones are, I've been buying those poor excuses the supermarket sells. I guess I got in the habit over the winter."

"My hens only lay enough for me in the winter," said Ellie, in a matter-of-fact voice. "I don't have enough to sell, so folks have to go to the store. It takes a while for people to find me again in the spring."

"Well, I'm glad I saw your sign. I need them for some potato salad I'm making for the town Fourth of July picnic. I guess you heard about it?"

"I think it's a great idea. Something to bring the whole town together."

"Not like the anti-nudity bylaw," ventured Lucy. "Do you think there's any hope for that now?"

Ellie shrugged. "Pru had drummed up quite a lot of support, before she was killed. I know the Revelation Congregation came out in force to demonstrate and I guess they'll carry on the fight." Ellie drew her brows together. "You know, these are yesterday's eggs. I can get you some fresher ones if you like. You can gather 'em yourself, for that matter."

"Really?" Lucy felt like a little kid. "From the hens?"

"Sure." Ellie grabbed a basket that was hanging on a handy hook. "Follow me."

They walked together to Ellie's chicken house, a neat little shed situated behind her house. An old apple tree partially shaded the fenced-in run, where a small flock of plump hens were busily engaged in preening their feathers and scratching at the pebbly soil.

"They're very handsome birds," said Lucy. "They look so healthy."

"Thanks," said Ellie. "Maybe this will be my big year, now that Pru's out of the picture."

"What do you mean?"

Ellie's nut-brown face reddened, and she looked embarrassed. "I didn't mean it the way it sounded. I'm sorry Pru is dead. Nobody should die like that. But the fact remains that she always got the blue ribbon at the county fair. Bitsy Parsons and I took turns getting second and third."

"Bitsy?"

"You know her. She has that little flower and egg stand on Newcomb Road."

Lucy nodded. "The snapdragon lady."

"And cosmos and zinnias and coneflowers and I don't know what all. She can make anything grow, claims it's the chicken manure. She's the sweetest thing, too, always giving away extra plants." Ellie waved a hand at the flowering border that ran along the front of her porch. "Most of my flowers came from her garden."

"I suppose the competition will be cutthroat now," said Lucy, entering the chicken house as Ellie held the door open for her.

"Not likely," laughed Ellie. "So what do you want? Colors? Jumbos? I bet we've got some double yolkers here."

Lucy reached into one of the straw-lined nesting boxes and found a warm egg. She liked the way it felt in her hand, she liked the smooth texture and the way it fit into her palm, and lifted it to her cheek.

"Don't you peck me," said Ellie, reaching under a sitting hen who glared at her with disapproving black-bead eyes.

"She wants to keep her eggs," said Lucy.

"Well, she's not going to," laughed Ellie. "If she gets a clutch and goes all broody, she'll stop laying."

"Do you eat them when they stop laying?" asked Lucy, tucking her egg into Ellie's basket.

"I do. It seems more respectful somehow, to me at least. Continuing the cycle of life."

Lucy knew that Ellie was part Metinnicut Indian and had a deep reverence for living things. She was certain that Ellie's chickens met a quick and merciful end on their way to the stew pot.

"So how many eggs do you want?' asked Ellie, breaking into her thoughts.

"Three dozen, I guess. And if I run out, I'll be back for more."

It was amazing, thought Lucy, how a simple change from the ordinary routine could make such a difference. You wouldn't think homegrown eggs would be that different from supermarket eggs, but somehow they were. She'd seen and touched the chickens and heard their throaty clucking, she'd gathered the eggs herself from their strawy nests, and she'd spoken with the woman who raised the chickens. It was a whole different experience from pushing a wire cart around a sterile supermarket and plucking a Styrofoam container from a chilly cooler. From now on, she decided, she was going to make a stop at Ellie's to buy eggs a regular part of her routine.

The route home took her past Mel Dunwoodie's campground where the "Nude is Not Lewd" banner was still flying high above the entrance. Workers were busy installing a stockade fence along the property line and Lucy wondered if Mel really intended to convert his campground into a nudist colony. It would be interesting to hear what the town's Planning Board would have to say about that, she thought, as she parked the car outside the office.

She hesitated for a moment outside the office, remembering her encounter with Mel at Blueberry Pond. She fervently hoped he would be wearing clothes, and breathed a sigh of relief when she saw him standing behind the counter. He was wearing a shirt, and although she couldn't see his lower half she assumed it was also decently covered.

"What brings you here?" he said, scowling at her.

"Are you upset with me about something?"

"I just don't need any more newspaper types nosing around here," he said.

"Well, you're safe from me. I'm not working for the *Pennysaver* anymore. And if there's any significance to that fence you're building, I could care less. I'm here to talk about Pru Pratt."

"Can't help you," said Mel. "You're not supposed to speak ill of the dead."

Lucy smiled at him. "I wasn't exactly a fan myself, and the police have been taking a very close look at my family, so I'd really appreciate any help you can give me. The sooner I can figure out who killed her the sooner we can all get back to normal."

"So you want to finger me?"

"No way," said Lucy. "I just thought you might be able to give me some leads. You must have gotten to know her pretty well. You were neighbors, for one thing. And you were on opposite sides of the bylaw issue, that would have brought you into contact at least."

"She was a sick woman," said Mel. "She said she was against nudity but she couldn't keep herself away from the pond. I think she was obsessed or something."

"You know, that doesn't surprise me," said Lucy. "I think a lot of people who vehemently reject some sort of behavior—say homosexuality for example—are actually fascinated by it. Sometimes they really are latent homosexuals themselves."

"I don't think she wanted to take off her clothes, but she didn't mind spying on people who did," said Mel, warming to his subject. "She'd sit there in a folding chair with binoculars and a paper and pencil, observing everyone and writing things down."

"She was observing and taking notes?"

"There's not much to observe, in spite of what her son said."

"Wesley? What did he say?"

"He tried to pick a fight with two of the guys one day. Claimed he'd seen them getting up to something in the woods."

"Does that happen?"

"No more than at a regular beach. I mean, I'm not gonna say it never happens. People have a way of. . . ." Mel shrugged. "You know. Sometimes they pair off. Sometimes something happens. It's normal human behavior." He scratched his chin. "Considering the situation here, with all the media and the bylaw and all, I think there's been very little of that sort of thing. Most of the naturists I've talked with feel a little bit uncomfortable, a little pressured."

Lucy nodded sympathetically. "I can relate to that." She paused. "Could you give me the names of the men who had the confrontation with Wesley?'

Mel shook his head. "I don't think so."

"It would be such a help."

"Sorry."

Lucy sighed. "Oh, well. Thanks anyway for taking time to talk to me. I know you must be very busy." She paused. "What time do you open in the morning? It must be pretty early, right?"

Mel grinned at her. "I suppose you want to know if I was here the morning Prudish Pru was killed?"

"You got me. I would like to know."

"Just like I told the cops, I was right here, checking out a family from Montreal. I've got the charge slips and paperwork to prove it."

"Lucky you," said Lucy.

Lucky for Mel, but a bad break for her. Not that she exactly wanted Mel to be guilty of murder, but she would like to feel she was making some progress on the case. But now as she headed for home she didn't feel any closer to figuring out who killed Pru than she had when she started. And if that weren't bad enough, when she passed the Pratts' place she noticed the press pack was back, with reinforcements, encamped opposite her driveway.

* * *

They were still there when Bill brought the girls home from day camp. When they went upstairs to wash up, he placed a small cardboard box on the kitchen table.

"Kudo's ashes," he said, in answer to Lucy's inquiring glance. "Shall I just bury them or . . . ?"

"I guess we should have some sort of ceremony," said Lucy. "He was a big part of our family for a long time."

After supper, Bill and Toby went out to dig a grave while she and the girls cleaned up the dinner dishes. Then they all gathered at the grave site underneath a gnarled old apple tree.

"Who will begin?" asked Lucy.

"I will," said Bill, kneeling down and carefully placing the box in the hole. He tossed a bone-shaped dog treat on top of it. "I had my differences with Kudo, but he won my respect when I saw him chase off a coyote one day when Zoe was playing outside all alone. He was absolutely fearless when it came to protecting her. I realized he wanted to protect my family just as much as I do. He was one tough dog and I hope they have room for him in doggy heaven."

"I'm sure he'll go to doggy heaven," said Zoe, "and there will be lots of rabbits to chase and big bowls of dog food and no fleas at all. Kudo deserves to go there because he saved me from the coyote, and he always warned us when somebody came to the house. He made me feel safe."

"He made me feel safe, too," said Lucy. "Especially if I was home alone at night. As long as he was snoozing I knew everything was okay. I think he knew when I needed a little extra security, because he always stuck very close to me when I was here alone. He kept me company, he was a good friend."

"I didn't like Kudo when Mom first brought him home," said Sara. "I thought he was smelly and scary and I was afraid of him. But after he'd been here awhile, one day he saw me and my friends playing soccer and he joined in. He was a really good soccer player; you couldn't get the ball past him."

The others all nodded, remembering.

"People at school who'd never noticed me before all wanted to come over and see my amazing dog. All of a sudden, I was popular, all because of my dog." She tossed a little plush dog toy shaped like a soccer ball into the grave. "Thanks, Kudo."

"I never told anybody this before," said Elizabeth, "but one time I came home from a date and it was a beautiful night and the guy suggested we lie down on the grass and look at the stars. We did that for a while but then the guy got a little pushy, if you know what I mean. He wanted me to do things I didn't want to do."

Lucy's and Bill's eyes met.

"He wouldn't stop and I started pushing him away and he started holding me tighter. I was really struggling when the door opened and Kudo came bounding out. He stuck his nose between me and this guy so I got a chance to break loose. Kudo didn't let the guy up, though. He put his paws on his chest and started growling at him. He did this for a minute or two and the guy started acting real scared, yelling at me to call the dog off.

I was on the porch then, so I called him and very slowly he backed away and came up and stood by me."

"What happened to the guy?' asked Sara.

Elizabeth smiled. "He ran away and I never heard from him again."

Lucy breathed a huge sigh.

Elizabeth tossed an old shoe into the grave. "Here you go, Kudo. You already chewed up one, now you can have the other."

Everybody laughed.

"What about you Toby?" asked Zoe. "Do you have a story about Kudo?"

Toby cleared his throat. "Kudo taught me an important lesson, that I've never forgotten. When I was in high school, there were a couple of guys that everyone was kind of scared of. They'd walk down the hall and everybody'd get out of their way, you kind of wanted to stay clear of them, didn't want to end up alone in a bathroom with them or anything like that. Sometimes I'd see 'em coming towards me and I'd almost feel sick. Sometimes I even dreamed about them. It was pretty weird. Anyway, one day I was in the yard, mowing the grass, and a couple of enormous German shepherds came down the driveway. Kudo had been sleeping under the apple tree, but he immediately woke up. He didn't stop to think or anything, he just started barking and headed straight for these dogs, teeth bared, hair on his back all bristly, he was ready for business. It was awesome, and the two German shepherds thought so, too, because they just turned tail and ran away as fast as they could, even though they were a lot bigger and probably could've beat him up pretty bad. So after that, whenever I saw those two bullies, I'd just stand up straight and stick my chest out and kind of show my teeth in a sort of half-smile and look those guys straight in the eye and walk right by them." He smiled and tossed two tiny ceramic figurines of German shepherd dogs into the grave, figures that Lucy had often seen on Toby's desk. "They never bothered me, ever again."

For a long minute they all stood silently, staring at the grave. Finally, Bill spoke.

"Good-bye, old pal," he said.

"Good-bye, old pal," they chorused in response.

"This service is now concluded," said Bill, pulling the shovel out of the mound of dirt and starting to fill in the grave.

Zoe was beginning to sniffle, so Lucy took her hand and led her away, towards the house.

"It's time for your bath," she said, "would you like to use some of my bubble bath?"

"Okay." Zoe wiped away her tears with the back of her hand.

"You know, it's really nice to know Kudo meant so much to all of us," said Lucy, as they walked through the firefly-lit twilight and mounted the porch steps. The screen door creaked as she pulled it open and they stepped inside. It was a comforting sound.

But later, as she filled the tub and watched the bubbles grow, Lucy felt prickings of worry. Bill's words about how Kudo protected the family played in her mind, as did Toby's story about learning to stand up for himself. Valuable lessons and laudable values, true enough, but they could be taken too far. She understood Toby's need for independence, but she wished he didn't have to be quite so private. She'd sure feel a lot better if she knew what he was up to these days.

Chapter Nineteen

Lucy was frying up some bacon and eggs for breakfast when the phone rang. It was Sue.

"Are you busy? Can you talk?"

"Talk away. I'm just cooking up some bacon and eggs."

"Are you trying to kill your family? Haven't you heard of cholesterol?"

"Oh, shut up. I haven't cooked a real breakfast for them in years. But now that I'm not working I have time to make things that take a little time and fussing. I think Sara was still in diapers the last time I made pancakes."

"Pancakes!"

"Tomorrow. If you're gonna do it, you might as well go all the way."

"That's the advice you give Elizabeth?"

"Not quite, but she doesn't listen to me anyway."

Sue chuckled. "That's so true. When Sidra was in college she'd smile and nod and agree with me. . . ."

"And then she'd go and do the exact opposite."

"Right!"

"Well, everything worked out for her," said Lucy. Sidra had a promising career in television in New York City and was happily married to her high school sweetheart, Geoff Dunford, who was a science teacher at the Bronx High School of Science.

"It will work out for Elizabeth, too," said Sue. "Listen, I had that talk with the Wilsons."

Lucy poked at the bacon with a fork, turning over a few pieces. "That's fast work. Did you learn anything?"

"Yes. It seems that, unfortunately, I am doomed to hell because I have not been born again."

"But you're such a nice person and you give lovely parties. I'm sure they'd love to have you in heaven."

"That's what I thought, too, but I was wrong. The important thing is being born again. You can be absolutely rotten, stinking with sin, but if you find Jesus and repent, you get to go to heaven."

"You mean heaven is full of crooks and thieves and murderers?"

"Reformed ones."

"They're the worst kind," said Lucy. "I'm not sure I want to go now. Especially if you're not going."

"Don't worry. Wherever we end up, we'll stick together."

"Good." Lucy lifted a piece of bacon with her fork and set it on a paper towel to drain. "There'll be all the fried chicken you want and you never gain any weight."

"Whipped cream?"

"Of course. The clouds are made of it." Lucy

smiled. "In Bill's heaven, the clouds will be made of beer foam."

"You're not going to be together?"

"Not all the time. How about you and Sid?"

"Well, you know how he hates shopping and there would have to be shopping, right?"

"Absolutely. Of course, maybe that would be your particular hell. Endless shopping, at full price, with your husband tagging along and complaining."

"Enough theology. I called to tell you what the Wilsons said about the Pratts." Sue paused for breath. "Apparently, many of the Revelation Congregation members considered Pru their cross to bear, if you know what I mean."

"Even those pious folk didn't like her?'

"Not much. She made a habit of pointing out other people's deficiencies, for example, she told Mrs. Wilson that her cakes were flat because she didn't have enough faith."

"Her baking powder's probably old."

"That's what I told her and it came as a great relief. Apparently Pru's accusation touched a nerve, because she was pretty upset about it. She also accused Mr. Wilson of lusting after other women because she saw him buying a *Playboy* at the Quik-Stop, but he insists it was only a gag gift for a friend at work."

"Likely story," scoffed Lucy.

"Well, whoever he was buying it for really wasn't any of Pru's business. She sounds like a real bully. Telling everyone how they ought to behave and pointing out their shortcomings. Especially Calvin's. The Wilsons said everybody felt sorry for him. She was constantly nagging him and belittling him in

front of other people. It was painful to watch, they
said. Everybody was waiting for the day when Calvin
would stick up for himself." Sue paused. "Do you
think he finally did? Maybe he snapped and ran
her down. You can just picture it: She's standing in
the driveway, giving him what for about buying a
Playboy or leaving the toilet seat up or not cleaning
out the gutters and he impulsively slams his foot
down on the gas. It's over before he has time for a
second thought."

"You think Calvin did it?" Lucy remembered her
encounter with him in the woods near Blueberry
Pond. Rather than speak to her, he had run away,
vanished into the woods. "He's afraid of his own
shadow."

"Those are the ones, Lucy. The quiet ones. Isn't
that what the neighbors of the murderer always
say. 'He was so quiet. He always kept to himself.' "

"I still think Wesley's a better candidate. He's
hot tempered, and then there's the incident with
Kudo. He was definitely running away from something that morning." She took the last pieces of
bacon out of the pan and flipped the eggs. "Which-
ever one it was, it's going to be awfully hard to
prove. If it were a stranger, there might be a foot-
print or some kind of physical evidence. But Wesley
and Calvin live there."

"What about damage to the truck?"

"He hit the dog right after. He could say the dog
caused the damage. If only I could talk to Calvin I
bet he would fold pretty quickly," said Lucy. "But
I'd have to catch him when Wesley isn't home, when
no reporters are around. We'll probably have a
solar eclipse before that happens."

"I have an idea," said Sue. "I could go to Pru's funeral. The Wilsons actually asked me if I was going."

"That's a great idea. Will you do it?"

"For you, sure. But in the meantime, since you're home anyway and enjoy cooking so much, do you think you could make *twenty* pounds of potato salad?'

Lucy's heart was bursting with gratitude. "Absolutely."

"And one other little thing?"

Lucy's grateful heart was shrinking; she was beginning to think the price of this particular favor was getting rather high. But what was she going to do? She couldn't go to the funeral herself without causing a scandal. "Whatever you say."

"Bake six dozen red, white and blue cupcakes. You don't have to make them from scratch—you can use a mix if you want."

"That's big of you," said Lucy.

"I know. I can't believe I'm not going to heaven."

"I can," said Lucy.

Lucy didn't really mind baking the cupcakes; she didn't really know what to do with herself now that she didn't have to go to work at the *Pennysaver*. She had a couple of boxes of cake mix in the pantry and it only took a few minutes to mix up a batch. While they were baking, she stirred up some brownies using her favorite recipe. She hadn't made it in a long time, and it reminded her of the days when the kids were small and she turned out a steady stream of baked goods for their lunch boxes and after-school snacks. Whatever happened to that recipe for peanut-butter bars, she wondered. That had been a favorite, with a thin coating of chocolate frosting.

She smiled when she took the cupcakes out of the oven, admiring the festive paper cups decorated with red and blue stars. She had found them in the pantry, tucked away with cupcake papers for every conceivable holiday: hearts for Valentine's Day, pastels for Easter, red and green bells for Christmas, little green shamrocks for Saint Patrick's Day. No holiday had gone unremarked when the kids were small.

Once she'd started working, however, that had changed. Dinner had to be something she could throw together quickly, and instead of baking treats she usually grabbed something from the store. These days they all seemed to be watching their weight anyway. More often than not they had fruit or frozen yogurt for dessert.

She sniffed the rich chocolate scent of the brownies baking in the oven and sighed. All that butter and sugar, not to mention the walnuts, they had to have tons of calories. But it would be worth it, just this once. A chocolate extravagance.

Maybe a bit too extravagant, she decided, taking the pan out of the oven and setting it on a rack to cool. It was a big recipe, making at least four dozen brownies. Elizabeth and Sara wouldn't touch them, Toby was hardly ever home, and Zoe shouldn't eat too many. Neither should she and Bill, considering their ongoing battle with middle-age spread.

She touched the brownies, waiting for the magic moment when they would be just the right temperature to cut. Too soon and she'd end up with a mess. Wait too long, and they'd be tough. She tapped the side of the pan with her knife.

Maybe she could take a few brownies into the *Pennysaver.* Phyllis loved her brownies and Ted would wolf down any food that came his way. It would be a good way to show there were no hard feelings, and maybe she'd even pick up some information about the murder investigation. She sank the knife into the brownies and drew it towards her in a straight line. Perfect.

Lucy was a bit surprised to see the little encampment opposite the driveway had disappeared when she left the house that afternoon. Maybe they were all at the funeral, or maybe they were busy chasing down nudists. Maybe the family feud was old news. She certainly hoped so. It felt great to go about her business unobserved.

The *Pennysaver* office hadn't changed a bit, she discovered, when she arrived carrying her plate of brownies, carefully covered with plastic wrap. The little bell on the door still jangled, the motes of dust danced in the sunlight that streamed through the venetian blinds, and Phyllis was still sitting behind the reception desk.

"Howdy, stranger," said Phyllis, beaming at her through her half-glasses. The rhinestones were gone, replaced by a pair with a garish abstract design inspired by Jackson Pollack.

"I like your glasses," said Lucy. "Wild."

"That's what I thought," said Phyllis, peering at the plate. "What have you got there?"

"Brownies. They're for you and Ted. Is he around?"

"Nope. He's covering the funeral." Phyllis picked

the largest brownie off the plate and took a bite, closing her eyes and moaning with pleasure. "These are fantastic. You really shouldn't have."

"I've got a lot of time on my hands these days."

"Ted doesn't, that's for sure," said Phyllis, her shoulders shaking with laughter. "I think he really misses you."

"Good," said Lucy. "You can tell him I'm enjoying this little vacation."

"I will." Phyllis eyed the plate. "I guess I better save some for him," she said, choosing a second brownie.

"It would be nice." Lucy glanced at her desk, which was covered with papers. "Whatcha doing?"

"Letters to the Editor." Phyllis sighed. "Between the nudists and the Fourth of July and the lichen, we're getting an awful lot of mail these days. Everybody's got something to say."

"Ted must be in seventh heaven," said Lucy, picking up a letter. "This one says the environmentalists are in league with the Communists."

"We've gotten a couple of those."

"This lady says she's glad there won't be any fireworks because they always used to upset her dog."

"Listen to this," said Phyllis, waving a sheet of paper with an impressive letterhead. "It's from the VFW. They say they've voted to oppose the antinudity bylaw because, and I quote, they 'fought for freedom, not for some petty-minded prudes to start telling people what they could do.' "

"Wow," said Lucy, taking the letter and examining it. "It gets better: 'A ridiculous attempt to legislate morality by a sexually repressed and unfulfilled woman who is attempting to impose her extreme religious beliefs on an entire town.' "

Phyllis raised an eyebrow. "Pretty strong language, especially about a dead woman."

Lucy checked the date. "It's dated the day she died."

"I'm behind in the mail," admitted Phyllis. "Who wrote it? The whole VFW?"

"It says they all voted on it, but the letter's written by Scratch Hallett."

"Sounds to me like he got a little personally involved."

The bell on the door jangled and Ted came in, accompanied by Mike Gold.

"Hi, Lucy!" he exclaimed, cheerfully. "Don't tell me you've reconsidered and you're here to help with the mail?"

"Not on your life, Ted," said Lucy, smiling sweetly. "But I did bring you some brownies, to help you keep your strength up."

"Your brownies? Your fabulous brownies?" Ted took one from the plate and passed it to Mike Gold. "You've got to try one. These are fabulous."

Lucy would have liked to ask Ted about the investigation but she knew she wouldn't get much out of him while Mike was around. Or even if he left, for that matter. She knew Ted well enough to know that he often used high spirits and jollity to block questions he didn't want to answer.

Mike had taken a brownie and was smiling as he bit into it. "Mmm. Real butter. You can always tell."

"Ah, so you're a connoisseur," said Lucy, wondering if he would be a better bet.

"More of a consumer, I'm afraid," said Gold,

patting his ample belly. He turned to Ted. "Do you have any more questions for me? I don't mean to rush you, but I've got another appointment. You said I could have some back issues. . . ."

"Oh, right." Ted disappeared into the morgue for a minute, returning with a handful of papers. "Here you go. Thanks for the interview."

"No problem. It was a pleasure," said Mike, opening the door.

"I'm going, too," said Lucy. "Mind if I walk with you?"

Ted's eyebrows shot up, but she was through the door before he could say anything.

"I'm Lucy Stone, by the way," she said, introducing herself.

"I know. I've seen you on TV." Gold's eyes twinkled mischievously.

Lucy rolled her eyes. "You can't believe everything you see on TV."

"You're telling me?"

They laughed together, walking down the street and stopping in front of the storefront the ANS was using as a temporary headquarters.

"I guess you're used to all the media attention," said Lucy.

"It's a constant battle for the organization," said Gold. "All we want is responsible, fair reporting but as soon as they realize who we are, they start to sensationalize our position. Basically, all we want is to be left alone to take our clothes off."

Lucy smiled sympathetically. "All I want is to find out who killed Pru Pratt so my family and I can get on with our lives." She sighed. "Do you mind if I ask you a few quick questions?"

Gold checked his watch. "Gotta be quick. I don't want to keep 'Inside Edition' waiting."

"Trust me, they'll wait for you," said Lucy. "I'm just curious about my neighbor, Mel Dunwoodie. Has he been involved with ANS for long?"

"Dunwoodie? The guy with the trailer park?"

Lucy nodded.

"I know he's a dues-paying member, and he's been real helpful to the organization. He's a member of the task force we organized to deal with the anti-nudity bylaw issue, but I don't really know anything about him personally." He paused. "He seems nice enough. He's a real hard worker."

"What about his relations with . . ."

"Sorry," said Gold, cutting her off. "I've got to go."

Lucy watched as one of the big white trucks with a satellite dish on top rolled up to the curb, then put on her sunglasses and quickly turned and walked down the street. She didn't want to risk any more media attention. Back in the car she considered her next step and decided she'd like to have a little chat with Scratch Hallett.

Driving through town to Hallett Plumbing & Heating, she remembered how angry he'd been at the selectmen's meetings when first the fireworks and then the parade had been cancelled. He'd been particularly angry about the parade, even blaming Pru for raising such a fuss over the nudists that organizers felt the parade had to be canceled. She wondered where all this anger was coming from, and if there was some long-standing grudge behind it.

Hallett Plumbing & Heating was located behind

Scratch's modest clapboard house, in a garage that had been enlarged throughout the years as the business grew. Scratch now employed five or six mechanics, and a small fleet of blue and white vans was parked every night on the blacktop outside the shop. Now, of course, the vans were gone as the crew of plumbers were out turning on the water in summer homes, repairing leaky faucets and replacing busted water heaters.

Lucy parked in the area reserved for customers and went in the office, pausing to admire a Rube Goldberg-like assemblage of pipes and plumbing fittings that was displayed in the window. Scratch himself was seated at an enormous gray steel desk dating from the fifties. A pinup calendar from a tool company, featuring a busty girl in a skimpy bikini holding a very large monkey wrench hung on the wall behind him.

"Lucy Stone! Are you here to interview me for the *Pennysaver?*"

"You know, I should. You're a real success story. What did you start with? A station wagon?"

"That's right. Back in '45. I got home from the war, married Mrs. Hallett and started the business, all in a couple of weeks. Didn't have time to waste after spending four years overseas in the Army Air Corps. Wasn't the Air Force then, it was still part of the Army."

"I guess you saw a lot of the world."

"I sure did. I crossed over on the *Queen Mary*, she was converted into a troop ship you know. We were stacked in bunks four or five high, and when your shift was done somebody else got your spot.

We was in England for a good while, then they sent us on to North Africa. I ended up in Italy, in Naples."

Lucy felt a twinge of envy; she'd never been to Europe. "Have you ever considered going back and visiting those places?"

"Nope. Once was enough," said Scratch. "So what can I do for you? I see you're not writing any of this down."

"No. I'm on a forced vacation. Ted says I'm too involved to work at the paper until this Pru Pratt thing is over."

Scratch raised an eyebrow. " 'Cause of the dog?"

"Well, that, and being neighbors and having differences with the Pratts. The whole package, I guess. The paper is supposed to be impartial and Ted's not convinced I can be objective," Lucy paused. "So I decided the sooner this thing is over, the sooner I can get back to work. The cops don't seem to be making much progress so I'm investigating on my own."

"Good for you!" said Scratch, leaning back in his chair and lighting his pipe. "So how's it going?"

"Not very well," admitted Lucy. "When you get right down to it, there are a whole lot of people who didn't like Pru Pratt."

"I suppose I'm one of 'em," said Scratch, pulling at his eyebrow. They had grown extremely bushy, as some men's do when they age. His were impressive, as was the white and wiry hair sprouting from his ears. "You probably think I could be the one who did the evil deed."

Lucy blushed. "I doubt that very much. But you've lived here your whole life. I bet you know a thing or two about the Pratts. For instance, was Pru always religious?"

Scratch laughed. "She was a real devil in high school. She was a couple of years ahead of my oldest and he used to say she was fast. Her father was a real mean one, rumor was he used to beat her." Scratch raised an eyebrow. "Mebbe even more, if you get my drift."

"Incest?"

"That's what some said. I don't put much stock in gossip meself, though."

"When did she change?"

"When that Revelation Congregation started, she was one of the first to sign up."

"Repenting for her sins?"

"That's prob'ly what she thought, but you ask me, those folks just replace their old sins with new ones. They're not fornicating so somehow that entitles 'em to go all intolerant. See what I mean? They start thinking they're better than everybody else."

"Pru was like that, that's for sure." Lucy paused. "What about Calvin? Did he grow up here?"

"Cowardly Calvin!" snorted Scratch. "That's what we used to call him. He kinda disappeared for a while during the Vietnam War, said he had business in Canada." He nodded at her. "When he came back, he came around here looking for work. I told him no way. No way I was going to hire a draft dodger. Not after what I saw in the war."

"I can understand that," said Lucy.

"A man's gotta do his duty," said Scratch. "It's the American way."

"The price of freedom," murmured Lucy.

Scratch was gazing into the distance. She wondered what he saw, what memories came to him.

"The *Queen Mary* hit a smaller ship when we made the crossing, you know. It felt like a bump, like she'd hit a log or something. Later I found out over three hundred British sailors died, went down in the cold dark Atlantic." He turned his bright blue eyes on her. "Beats me why Calvin Pratt thought his skinny little ass was worth more than those poor fellows' lives. They didn't try to get out of serving, most of 'em enlisted. That's what we did back then."

"I know," said Lucy, thinking of the dwindling ranks of veterans who showed up for Memorial Day and Veterans' Day observances. She could never get through one of those ceremonies without crying when the trumpeter played "Taps." "People forget. They can't even be bothered to vote."

"Not us vets," said Scratch. "We've got long memories."

"I bet you do," said Lucy, standing up. "It's been nice talking to you. Have a good day."

Going back to the car, Lucy felt terribly sad. Scratch had survived the war and come home to his sweetheart, but so many of the young men who had marched off to war with him never returned. She'd seen the photos of military cemeteries in Europe, row upon row of white crosses. And then there were the ones whose bodies were never even found, the missing in action. The prisoners of war. And the shell-shocked, who hadn't been able to forget the horrors they'd seen. The concentration camp liberators who turned to drink to get through the rest of their lives; the hollow-eyed survivors of the Bataan death march and D-Day invaders, who saw their comrades sink into the sea beside them.

She wondered about Scratch's wartime experiences. What had he seen? What had he done? She wondered if he'd been in battle, if he'd killed enemy soldiers. It was frightening to think of this white-haired old man taking a life, but she didn't doubt for a minute that he would have done his duty as a soldier. The question was whether he was still fighting the war, his own private war.

Chapter Twenty

Lost in her thoughts as she drove away from Scratch's, Lucy didn't notice the TV news van that was following her until she braked for a stop sign and checked her rear-view mirror. Curious to see if it was following her, she flipped on her turn signal. So did the van.

She'd enjoyed the break but she might as well face it: they were back. Noticing that several more vehicles had joined the line behind her, she decided that Pru Pratt's funeral must be over and the newshounds were sniffing out any possible leads. She decided to follow their example and head over to Sue's house to get a report on the funeral.

"I see the gang's all here," commented Sue, when she opened the door to Lucy.

Lucy paused and looked over her shoulder, straight into the lenses of several cameras.

"Darn!" she exclaimed, ducking into the shelter of the house. "I should know better by now. I suppose I'll look all furtive and guilty."

"Too bad your shirt is all scrunched up," said Sue, observing her coolly. "It makes your bum look bigger than it is. Of course, the baggy khaki shorts don't help."

"I didn't know I was going to be a cover girl when I got dressed this morning, now did I?" demanded Lucy.

"I think you should assume that somebody's going to be snapping your picture," said Sue. "I'd wear black if I were you. Maybe capris, they're slimming."

"Thanks for the fashion tip." Lucy's voice was dripping with sarcasm. "Like I've got time to go shopping. I'll put it on the 'to do' list, right after 'solve murder.' "

"Oooh, you are touchy, aren't you," said Sue, leading the way to the kitchen. "Would you like a glass of iced tea?"

"Yes, please," said Lucy, feeling like a scolded child. "It's just that I really thought the media had turned their attention elsewhere. I didn't think I was going to have to cope with this any more."

"I know," said Sue, setting a tall frosty glass in front of her. "It stinks. Lemon?"

"Please."

Lucy squeezed her lemon wedge into the tea and stirred it, then took a big swallow. "So how was the funeral?"

"Dry."

Lucy was puzzled. "Was rain forecast?"

Sue gave her a sharp look. "There was no booze. Not a drop. Not even that disgusting sweet sherry."

"What did you expect? The Revelation Congregation doesn't approve of alcohol."

Sue was doubtful. "Really?"

"Really. No drinking, no dancing, no card playing, no gambling."

"What do they do for fun?"

"I don't think they believe in it."

"That explains a lot," said Sue. "It was very somber. Definitely not Finnegan's wake."

"Who was there?"

"The entire congregation, I guess. There was a good turnout, but I didn't really know anybody, except my neighbors, the Wilsons. The hymns were all weird, too. I didn't know them, but everybody else did. They were in great voice, they sounded much better than the Methodists."

Considering that the Methodist congregation consisted of a handful of aged ladies, Lucy wasn't surprised.

"Did they have a reception afterwards?"

"In the church hall, not at the house." Sue considered. "The food was pretty good. They had little tiny egg-salad sandwiches with the crusts cut off, chicken salad, too. And cake and homemade cookies and deviled eggs and little cherry tomatoes stuffed with egg salad."

"You actually ate this stuff?" Lucy was doubtful; Sue was a career dieter.

"I did. There was nobody to talk to except my neighbors and they were busy with the food, and nothing to drink, so I ate." Sue patted her flat tummy. "I'll skip supper."

"You can send Sid over to my house—I'm grilling pizzas on the barbecue."

"Thanks, Lucy, but he's on duty at the fire station tonight."

Lucy nodded. She knew Sid was a volunteer fireman. "Did you overhear any interesting conversations?" she asked. "And how come they had so many egg dishes?"

Sue fluttered her beautifully manicured hand for emphasis. "I'm glad the great detective finally asked. That's a very interesting point. I asked Mrs. Wilson the very same question and she said all the eggs were donated by Bitsy Parsons, who apparently has been carrying a torch for Calvin. She thought it was very odd indeed that Bitsy wasn't there to comfort him in his time of trouble."

"And to remind him that she would be available to comfort him in the future?"

"Yes."

"It does seem funny that she would pass up the funeral," mused Lucy. "Maybe she didn't feel well."

"Maybe she was exhausted from cooking up all those eggs." Sue wrinkled her nose. "Faint from sulphur fumes."

"Maybe she was home, waiting, arranged attractively on the divan in hopes Calvin would show up after the funeral?"

"If she thought that, she miscalculated. I overheard Wesley saying that he and his dad were going fishing after the funeral. He said it's the only place they find any comfort."

"That's kind of fishy, isn't it? I mean, right after the funeral?"

"No puns allowed."

"Sorry. But they must have a reason for going out today, like they're meeting somebody or something."

"Like drug smugglers?'

"Or handing off poached lobsters." The wheels

were turning in Lucy's head. "I wish there was some way we could find out what they're doing."

"We could follow them in Pam's boat. She won't mind. She leaves it down at the harbor, you know."

"That's not a bad idea. What kind of boat is it?"

Sue was nonchalant. "A boat boat. I don't know. It floats."

Lucy got up and walked through the living room to the front window, where she peeked out through the blinds. "There's more of them now. How are we going to get down to the waterfront without being followed?"

Sue joined her and peered through the slats. "Good God! Don't they have anything better to do?"

"Apparently not."

"I could just go out and tell them you're not that interesting," offered Sue. "And certainly not a murderer."

"It's kind of you to offer, but they'd never believe you." Lucy tossed her hair. "I've become notorious."

"You know, J. Lo, I've got an idea. I bet Sid would drive down the street with his siren going and his light flashing."

"They'd all follow him! That's brilliant."

"I'll call."

Ten minutes later, Sue and Lucy heard Sid approaching, siren blaring. They watched out the window as he sped down the street in his shiny red pickup truck, with the light flashing. The reporters, who had been lounging against their vehicles, chatting in small groups, scattered and ran for their cars. They were all gone within seconds.

Minutes later, Lucy and Sue arrived unnoticed at the harbor, just in time to see Wesley and Calvin heading out to sea in their boat, Second Chance. They lost precious moments parking the SUV, then Sue led the way to the farthest end of the float where Pam's little runabout was bobbing in the water.

Lucy wasn't impressed with the little aluminum boat's seaworthiness.

"Pam doesn't go out of the cove in that thing, does she?" she asked.

"Sure." Sue eased herself into the boat and started fiddling with the engine. "Hop in! We're going to lose them."

"We'll never catch them in this thing," said Lucy, carefully lowering herself into the tippy little craft. In the distance she could see Second Chance rounding the point and heading out to the open sea.

"That's okay. We don't have to. We just want to keep an eye on her. The idea is to look like we're just out for some sun and fun on the water."

"You're wearing a little black dress," said Lucy.

"Perfect for any occasion," said Sue, slipping off her black slingbacks and rummaging in her over-sized designer purse. "Aha!" she exulted, producing a pair of miniature binoculars. "I knew they were in here."

"I'm not even going to ask," said Lucy, amazed.

"You keep an eye on them while I steer," ordered Sue, bringing the little boat neatly around the point.

"Aye-aye, Captain." Lucy squinted through the eye piece and fiddled with the adjustment knob. "I can barely make them out."

"You're looking through the wrong end."

"Oh." Lucy flipped the binoculars around. "That's

better. Oh no it isn't. They're looking right at us. They know we're following them."

"You're right. They're speeding up." Sue shaded her eyes with one hand, the other remained on the tiller. "That's a serious engine in that boat. Look how fast it's going."

"Especially considering how low it's sitting in the water. That boat is loaded with something."

"As long as we can keep them in sight, we're okay," said Sue, relaxing a bit. "Slow but steady wins the race, you know."

"It's a nice day for boating," said Lucy, settling in for the ride.

And truth be told, it was a nice day to be out on the water. The sun was strong and hot, but a gentle breeze cooled them. The sky was bright blue, broken only by the occasional soaring gull. The water was deep, deep blue and glassy with only the occasional little wave to lift them up and then gently set them back down.

"Too bad we don't have fishing rods," said Lucy.

Sue immediately began searching in her purse.

"Don't tell me you have a fishing rod in there?"

Sue raised her head. "No. Sunscreen. Put some on."

"Thanks." Lucy eyed the purse. "How about a sandwich? Or a candy bar?"

"Breath mints."

"I'll take one."

Lucy was placidly sucking on her mint when the engine sputtered.

"Oops."

"Don't panic. It's probably air in the line or something."

The engine sputtered again, then went dead.

"No big deal, right? It'll start right up."

"No." Sue was squinting at a little gauge. "We're out of gas."

"But there's a gas can, right?"

"I don't see one."

"You've got to be kidding."

"We were in a hurry, right? I didn't think to check."

"You've got your cell phone, though. We can call for help."

"No. It's on the kitchen counter, recharging. It's time to row."

At least the oars were in the boat, thought Lucy, as Sue moved from the rear of the boat to join her on the middle seat. They each took an oar.

"This is kind of like Girl Scout camp," said Sue, giggling.

"Yeah, except we're not in the middle of Lake Tiorati. We're in the middle of the North Atlantic."

"Not the middle, we're not even near Greenland, and there are no icebergs in sight," said Sue. "So don't start getting all dramatic on me."

"Well, how far do you think we are from shore?"

"Maybe a mile, certainly less than two."

Lucy looked around doubtfully. There was no sign of land. "We were going at a pretty good clip, you know. And I don't see land."

"That's 'cause of the fog," said Sue, rubbing her bare arms. "It's getting chilly."

"The sun's gone."

"It's definitely clouded over."

"Oh, shit. We could be rowing in the wrong direction."

"Don't panic," said Sue, her voice tight with nerves. "We'll put on life jackets and just sit tight. Somebody's bound to come along."

"That's the best thing," agreed Lucy, whose arms were tired from rowing. "And there's an air horn, right? We can let off a blast every five minutes or something."

"No air horn," admitted Sue, passing her a very small life jacket. "We'll have to yell."

"What is this thing?" demanded Lucy, who was having trouble fastening the straps.

"It's a kiddie-size. It was probably Adam's," said Sue, who was putting on an old-fashioned orange life preserver. "I'd give you this one, but it's pretty mildewed. It stinks."

"I can't believe this," said Lucy, her teeth chattering. "Doesn't Pam pay any attention to Coast Guard regulations? You're supposed to have . . ."

"I know. I know," snapped Sue, cutting her off. "But she's a free spirit. And all she uses the boat for is to putter around in the cove. I bet she never goes past the point."

"Still," fumed Lucy. "It's awfully irresponsible."

"She probably didn't realize we'd be borrowing her boat," said Sue, wrapping her arms around Lucy in an effort to stay warm.

"I know," said Lucy, slipping her arms around Sue's waist. "We'll be okay."

"I'm freezing." Sue's teeth were chattering.

"Me, too."

"We'll yell, on the count of three. Ahoy. Okay?"

They yelled, and then they listened. There was no sound except the lapping of the water against the side of the boat.

"At least it's calm," said Sue.

"There is that," agreed Lucy, shivering. "I'm starving. I didn't eat any lunch."

"Let's yell again," suggested Sue.

They yelled, but all around them there was nothing but silence. Lucy thought of the old sailor's prayer that was often printed on little wooden plaques and sold in gift shops: "Lord, thy sea is so great and my boat is so small . . ."

"I hear something," said Sue. "Listen!"

Lucy listened, then shook her head.

"No, really. It's a hum. A definite hum. Like an engine."

"Ahoy!!" yelled Lucy. "Mayday! Mayday!"

"Together!" ordered Sue, and they yelled together, at the top of their lungs. Lucy was starting to get hoarse when she finally heard the motor.

"It's coming closer!"

"We have to keep yelling." Sue counted off three on her fingers, and they both screamed.

Through the fog, they could just make out a dark shape.

"We see you!" yelled Sue.

The engine noise immediately grew quieter, as the boat cut its speed. Even so, it seemed to be coming awfully fast and the two women held on to their oars tightly, prepared to move quickly if they had to. There was no need, however, as the huge shape became clearer and glided towards them. It was the Carrie Ann.

"Mom!" exclaimed Toby. "What are you doing out here?"

Chuck maneuvered the larger boat carefully, bringing it close enough so that Toby could throw them a rope. Once the rowboat was tied fast, he helped them scramble aboard the larger lobster boat, where they were immediately wrapped in blankets and given hot coffee.

"Fog sneak up on you?" asked Chuck.

"You could say that," replied Sue.

"This is a real pea souper. You were lucky we found you."

Shivering, Lucy clutched her coffee in shaking hands. She didn't want to think about what might have been, but Toby wasn't going to let her off the hook.

"What were you thinking?" he demanded. "That's not a regulation life jacket. And where was your fog horn? What about a compass? Don't you have any navigational equipment?"

Sue pulled herself up to her full height and glared at him. "We had sunscreen," she said.

"That's something, I guess," grumbled Toby, reaching for the thermos and refilling their cups.

It was only when they were safely docked and alighting from the boat that Chuck mentioned Sue's outfit.

"Were you on your way to a funeral or something?" he asked.

"Actually," she said, "I went to one this morning." She paused. "Boy, that seems like a lifetime ago."

"Well, next time you take your boat out, make sure you've got the proper equipment. This could've been *your* funeral."

"I will," said Sue. "Thanks for everything." She turned to Lucy. "Are you coming?"

"No, I'll catch a ride with Toby," she said.

Toby didn't seem pleased with that idea. "It'll be a while, Mom," he said. "We've got a lot of work to do."

"I want to help," said Lucy, determined to make amends for her foolishness. "Just tell me what to do."

Chuck and Toby glanced at each other.

"Really," insisted Lucy. "I'm strong and capable. What do you want me to do?"

"Okay," said Chuck. "You can hose off the deck. There's a pipe stand and hose about halfway down the dock."

While Lucy went to get the hose, Chuck and Toby busied themselves unloading their haul. Each heavy box was hoisted out of the hold and onto the pier, then placed on a wheelbarrow to be taken to Chuck's pickup truck. Once the truck was full, he drove the short distance across the parking lot to the cooperative's refrigerated truck. When the day's catch was in, the truck took it to the fish markets in Boston and New York.

"Good haul?" she asked, as she began hosing down the fiberglass deck.

"Pretty good," said Chuck, grunting with the effort of lifting a plastic fish box filled with lobsters. "The catch has been up last few days."

"You know, I saw the Pratts' boat heading out to sea. It was sitting very low in the water."

Toby ducked and turned, suddenly very interested in getting the cover fastened tight on one of the plastic fish boxes.

"Maybe they haven't cleaned out the bilge for a

while," said Chuck, a smile curving his lips. "All it takes is a little leak, or maybe the pump's not working the way it should, and you can take on quite a bit of water. It's gradual, so you might not notice."

"Especially if you're kind of lazy to start with," added Toby, his shoulders shaking with suppressed laughter.

"Yeah," mused Chuck. "They're not exactly poster boys for good seamanship."

"Or maybe they've got a hold full of something they shouldn't have, like other people's lobsters," said Lucy.

"Or bales of marijuana," said Chuck, laughing. "It's been known to happen."

"Do you think that's what they're doing?"

"I don't know what they're doing and I don't care," said Chuck. He put his hands on his hips and surveyed the boat. "Nice job, Lucy. Thanks."

"No problem," said Lucy.

Chuck slapped Toby on the shoulder. "See you tomorrow, buddy."

"Right."

In Toby's Jeep, with the hot, asphalt-scented breeze whipping through the torn fabric roof and doors, Lucy soon discovered the tables had turned. This time it was her turn to get a scolding.

"Is that what you were doing? Following the Pratts? Why would you do that? Don't you know I've got this pretrial hearing coming up? This is the last thing I need. Believe me, I'm staying as clear of Wesley as I can and you should, too. For all I care, he can steal the whole damn town. I'm not saying a word."

"That's crazy, Toby. If he is doing something illegal and you knew about it and fought with him to get him to stop, well, that would be a mitigating circumstance."

"I'm listening to Mr. Goodman, Mom, and he said to mind my own business and stay out of trouble. And that's what I'm going to do." He gunned the motor as he turned onto Sue's street and parked behind Lucy's car. "And I wish you would, too."

"C'mon Toby, I know you've been up to something. You're never home. Where are you spending all your time?"

"Can't a guy have any privacy?"

Lucy exploded. "Sure, you can have all the privacy you want when you move into your own place. But while you're living in my house, I think I deserve some basic courtesy. Especially considering the fact you've got a court date coming up." Her voice softened. "Don't you understand? I worry about you."

Toby shifted in his seat and sighed. "Okay, Mom. You don't have to worry. I've been seeing somebody."

"Seeing somebody? Who?"

"A girl."

Lucy's jaw dropped. "Oh."

"Yeah."

"Do I know her?"

"Sure. It's Molly Moskowitz." He paused. "She's really cool."

"I'm sure she is," said Lucy, opening the car door and getting out. She leaned in through the window. "You should bring her around sometime, for dinner, maybe, so we can all meet her."

"Yeah, Mom." He tapped the accelerator, making the engine roar, and Lucy stepped back as he drove off.

So Toby had a girlfriend. That was a relief, she thought, as she started the Subaru. Or was it?

Chapter Twenty-one

W hen Lucy got home, she found trouble waiting in the form of a police cruiser parked in the driveway. Its arrival had not gone unnoticed by the newshounds, and the encampment had sprouted once again on the opposite side of the road, like a weed that had been pulled only to reappear a few days later, sturdier than ever.

As Lucy made her way down the driveway she saw Toby getting out of his Jeep. The waiting officer also got out of his cruiser and Lucy was relieved to recognize Barney. She hoped he was making a social call. Something to do with the picnic, maybe. She hurried to join them.

"Hi!" she greeted him with a big smile. "What brings you here?"

Barney's face was serious; he looked more than ever like a bloodhound, and Lucy's heart sank.

"Actually, Lucy, I'd like to have a word with Toby."

Lucy felt her back stiffen. "I'll call Bob Goodman. I don't think Toby should say anything without Bob."

"It's okay, Mom."

"Don't be foolish, Toby. You've got a lawyer, you should follow his advice."

"Let me find out what it's about before you go all hysterical," said Toby.

"I'm not hysterical," said Lucy, in a very controlled voice. "But there's no way I'm going to let him coax you into some kind of admission. . . ."

Barney looked hurt. "Lucy, you know me better than that."

Lucy immediately felt ashamed of her outburst. "I'm sorry, Barney. I'm a little irrational, I admit it. I've had a tough day."

"That's okay, then. Listen, both of you. The lab tests have come up clean on all your vehicles."

"That's a relief," said Lucy, stifling her impulse to hug Toby and do a little dance with him in the driveway.

"Same with Wesley Pratt's truck, too. They didn't find any human blood, just blood from the dog."

"So Wesley's in the clear?" Lucy tried not to sound disappointed.

"Looks that way." Barney's jowls quivered. "Calvin, too."

"So where's the investigation headed?"

"Nowhere fast," said Barney. "But there is something else I'd like to talk to Toby about." He gave Lucy a meaningful look.

"Right. I can take a hint. I've got to get supper started anyway," she muttered, heading for the house.

Once inside, she couldn't resist watching through the glass panel in the kitchen door. But they seemed to be having nothing more than a friendly chat. They even laughed together, before shaking hands and separating. Barney went back to his cruiser and drove sedately off; Toby came in the house, whistling.

"Did you tell him what he wanted to know?" she demanded, as soon as he was through the door.

"I did. And Barney said he'd be sure to put in a word for me with the DA's office."

"Really? Well, that's all right then," said Lucy, who was making a salad. "By the way, you don't need to mention my little adventure today to anyone, okay?"

Toby popped the top on a can of soda. "You mean Dad?" he asked, grinning mischievously.

"Dad, or anyone, for that matter."

"Okay, Mom." He took a long drink. "You don't need to mention that stuff I told you about Molly, either. Okay?"

He didn't wait for an answer but bounded up the stairs to his room, where he slammed the door.

After supper, Lucy and Bill settled down in the family room with their coffee to watch the news. "It's been more than a week since Prudence Pratt's lifeless body was found in her Tinker's Cove driveway and police are no closer to solving the mystery," began the announcer.

His face was bland and expressionless; it was all the same to him whether he was pitching Barbara Walter's next celebrity interview or announcing the end of the world. The report began with footage of the funeral, then turned to the "feud" between the two families. The network reran the same footage of the Stone family that had been aired so many times, ending with a new shot of the police cruiser in the driveway and Toby and Barney's conversation. In this context it didn't look like a friendly chat at all; the camera stopped running long before Barney and Toby laughed and shook hands.

Without saying a word, Bill got up and left the room.

Lucy reached for the remote, clicked off the TV and went into the kitchen. She had twenty pounds of potatoes to peel.

She set the bag on the floor next to the sink and rinsed off a few potatoes. She scraped furiously, making little bits of peel fly every which way. It just wasn't fair. Toby was no longer a suspect, the lab tests had cleared him, but that important piece of information hadn't made it into the evening news report. Probably because the police hadn't bothered to issue a statement to the press. And the media was so enraptured with the family feud story that they'd already convicted Toby without giving him the benefit of a trial.

She was so angry that the sink was filling fast with soaking potatoes. She transferred them to a pot to cook, and drained the sink, refilling it with fresh water. She was standing there, wishing the murderer's name would magically form in the water, when the phone rang.

It was Rachel Goodman, Bob's wife.

"Are you okay, Lucy? Sue told me what happened today. You two are lucky you made it home safely." She lowered her voice. "I can't believe Pam didn't have any safety equipment on that boat."

"She had life jackets."

"Come on, Lucy. Sue told me how you had to wear Adam's old kiddie-jacket."

Lucy groaned. She was never going to live this

down. "It wasn't Pam's fault. We were really stupid," she admitted. "I don't know what we were thinking. I haven't even told Bill."

"Is that wise? He's sure to find out anyway. Somebody's sure to tell him."

"The timing's not right. Bill's pretty upset about the TV news tonight. It showed Barney questioning Toby. It looked pretty incriminating."

"Oh, nobody pays attention to TV," said Rachel. "Don't let it upset you. You could try meditation, or yoga, to clear your mind."

"Actually, I'm peeling twenty pounds of potatoes. It's remarkably soothing."

"Twenty pounds! Whatever for?"

"The picnic. Sue asked me to make twenty pounds of potato salad."

"That's a lot."

"I know. I never made so much before."

"You'll need to be very careful, you know. Did you hear about that church in Gilead? Practically the whole congregation got food poisoning at a potluck supper. It was traced back to some strawberries that weren't properly washed."

Lucy glanced at the stove where two kettles full of potatoes were bubbling merrily.

"Mayonnaise," she said, groaning.

"If I were you, I'd make sure the potatoes were good and cold before I added the mayo. The eggs, too. And keep it in flat pans in the refrigerator, instead of a bowl. That way it will stay colder. And make sure it's kept on ice at the picnic."

"I will," promised Lucy. "Thanks for the advice. We don't want any more deaths in Tinker's Cove."

Chapter Twenty-two

After thinking over Rachel's warning, Lucy decided the safest course of action would be to cook the potatoes, slice them, toss them with a bit of olive oil and vinegar and chill them thoroughly in the refrigerator in a couple of plastic containers she'd bought just for the purpose. She would add the mayonnaise and hard-boiled eggs at the last minute. It would mean leaving the ball game and dashing home just before the picnic, but she wasn't going to risk the possibility of contamination. As it was, she planned to set the trays of potato salad in a bed of ice, considering the forecast of sunny skies and ninety degree temperatures.

The cupcakes were another matter. They were so full of sugar and cake-mix preservatives that she didn't have to worry about them spoiling. She brought them along when the family arrived at the softball field behind the Tinker's Cove High School. The others went ahead while she took the cupcakes over to the long tables covered with red-and-white check tablecloths set up in the shade of the building and she added them to the mouth-watering array of brownies and cookies. Several large watermelons were cooling in a tub of ice water.

Members of the volunteer fire department were already firing up the huge grills constructed out of fifty-five-gallon steel drums and the sharp chemical scent of charcoal starter filled the air. A small refrigerator had been set up temporarily behind the tables to hold hot dogs and hamburgers but there was no room for salads. A cluster of Crock-Pots filled with fragrant molasses-baked beans were connected to a power source by a spider's web of extension cords. It was going to be quite a feast.

"Where's your potato salad?" demanded Sue, planting herself in front of Lucy.

"At home. I'll get it at the top of the ninth, I promise," said Lucy, aware that she was babbling. "Rachel's got me terrified about food poisoning."

"I didn't know you murder suspects were so picky," said Sue. She was dressed for the occasion in a red-and-white striped T-shirt and a blue denim mini skirt and had added a red, white and blue ribbon to her straw hat.

"Ha, ha," replied Lucy, scowling. "I was going to tell you what a fantastic job you've done organizing all this but now I don't think I will."

"It's pretty amazing, if I do say so myself," said Sue. "I've even arranged for some surprises."

"Like what?"

"Wait and see," said Sue.

The sun was shining, balloons were bobbing in the breeze and the discordant notes of the high school band tuning their instruments were heard as Lucy made her way to the packed bleachers where Bill was saving a seat for her. Some of the players, including Toby, were out on the field, warming up, stretching their muscles and tossing balls back and forth. Groups of teenage girls clustered near the dugouts, arranging themselves to advantage in the midriff-baring outfits that were currently the rage. Younger kids were chasing each other, playing endless games of tag. The very youngest, the babies, were tucked in backpacks and strollers, or were napping on blankets spread out on the grass under the trees. It looked to Lucy like a Norman Rockwell painting.

"Who's got the best team?" she asked Bill, taking her seat beside him. "Should I root for the Bait Buckets or the Nail Bangers?"

"It's hard to say," he said, watching the Bait Bucket's pitcher warming up. "Jeff Sprague was named to the state all-star team when he was in high school, but the Nail Bangers have some solid hitters."

"I guess I'll cheer for everybody," she said, shifting over to make room for Elizabeth, who had climbed up the bleachers to join them.

"Don't bother, Mom," she said. "I'm sitting with Molly. I just want to use your sunscreen. Did you bring any?"

"Sunscreen?" This was the last thing Lucy had expected.

"Yeah, Mom. You can't be too careful. Sun causes wrinkles, you know, and I sure don't want to end up looking like you."

"Heaven forbid," said Lucy, rummaging in her bag. "Isn't Molly the girl that Toby's seeing?"

"Yeah. That's her talking to him."

Lucy abandoned her task and checked the field, where a petite blond in a pink halter top was standing beside Toby. She was shifting her weight from one side to the other, moving her hips provocatively, and had her hand on his arm.

"I work with her at the inn," continued Elizabeth. "They hooked up a few weeks ago."

"Hooked up?"

"Yeah, you know, Mom. They're, uh, a couple now."

Lucy looked at Bill, who was nodding approvingly at his son's choice. He was also smirking.

"Do you mean they're . . . ?" Lucy's eyebrows shot up. "Is that where he's been spending the night?"

"Yeah, Mom. He's twenty-one, you know."

Lucy watched as Toby and Molly parted with a kiss, he to join his teammates in the dugout and she taking a seat in the stands.

"Sunscreen, Mom?"

"Oh, right." A bit dazed, Lucy resumed her search and found the tube.

"Thanks, Mom."

Elizabeth skipped down the bleacher steps and Lucy turned to Bill.

"Did you know about this? What do you think? Isn't he awfully young?"

"Had to happen sooner or later." He shrugged philosophically and stood up as the VFW color guard began marching onto the field.

Lucy was watching Molly, but she couldn't really learn much from the back of the girl's head. She turned instead to the color guard, who looked especially sharp as they wen ough their paces, following Scratch Hallett's b d orders. The high school band took their places behind the color guard and then a group of singers filed onto the field.

"Who are they?' asked the woman next to Lucy. "I don't recognize them."

"Oh my goodness," said Lucy, recognizing Mike Gold's curly head of hair. "I think it's the naturists."

"At least they're wearing clothes," fumed the woman.

"They are indeed," said Lucy, placing her hand over her heart as they began singing the National Anthem.

As she sang, Lucy's eyes drifted over the scene: the brightly colored flags snapping in the breeze, the aged members of the color guard standing at attention, the red faces of the high school band members whose uniforms were too warm for the weather and the earnest faces of the chorus. Tears sprang to her eyes as they always did when she heard the Star-Spangled Banner and she was glad she was wearing sunglasses.

The singers belted out the last words of the song—"and the home of the free"—and everyone cheered and clapped and whistled as the town's oldest resident, Miss Julia Ward Howe Tilley, was driven onto the field in a red mustang convertible. The car circled the playing field and Miss Tilley waved to everyone, her pleasantly pink face wreathed with an aureole of fluffy white hair. The car stopped at home plate and she was helped from the back seat and led to a spot about fifteen feet from home plate. There Howard White presented her with a brand new ball.

"This ought to be good," muttered Bill. "I'll bet she can't throw it four feet."

"You might be in for a surprise," said Lucy.

Miss Tilley bounced the ball a few times in her age-spotted hands, leaned forward, winked at the pitcher and hurled it straight into the glove.

Everyone cheered and clapped enthusiastically as she made her way to the seat of honor behind home plate.

"Play ball!" yelled the umpire, and the game began.

First up to bat for the Nail Bangers was Eddie Culpepper, Barney's son. He was the same age as Toby and Lucy remembered the days when they were on the same Little League team. Quite a few players from that team were playing today: Tim Robbins was playing, as well as Ted's son Adam. Not Richie Goodman, he was spending the summer in Greece studying ancient ceramics. And come to think of it, Wesley Pratt had been a member of that team, too, though Lucy remembered he rarely showed up for practices. She scanned the field and the bench, but there was no sign of him.

Hearing a solid thwack she looked up just in time to see Eddie send up a high fly, which was neatly caught by Chuck Swift. That's how the first half of the inning went, with the Nail Bangers getting some promising hits, but no runs thanks to the Bait Buckets' competent fielding. After the third out the Nail Bangers took the field, with Eddie pitching. He had quite an arm, but Tim Robbins had been an all-star player when he was in high school. He sent the ball speeding through first and second base and past the fence, rounding the bases to applause and groans.

After a while Lucy lost interest in the game, simply enjoying sitting in the sun and people watching. Maybe she was crazy, but it looked to her as if folks were a little more prosperous these days. A lot of the kids had new summer clothes instead of thrift shop shorts and tees, she'd noticed some new trucks in the parking lot, and a lot of the young wives had frosted their hair—at ten dollars a foil, that was something that tended to get skipped when money was tight.

"Those naturists have really given the local economy a boost," she said.

"Why do you say that?" asked Bill.

"People have got money again. Just look around. And it can't be the lobsters, so it must be the influx of naturists."

"That, or the fireworks," said Bill, groaning as Toby hit a low ball directly to the first baseman who easily caught it.

"But there aren't any fireworks," said Lucy, puzzled.

"I mean the smuggling."

"Smuggling?"

"A lot of the lobstermen have been buying fireworks in Canada and New Hampshire and taking them down to Massachusetts. They're illegal there, they don't sell them in stores and people will pay a lot of money for them."

Lucy was horrified. "They should be illegal everywhere, you know. They're dangerous. Are Chuck and Toby doing that?"

"Have to ask them," said Bill, narrowing his eyes

and watching closely as the next runner made it to first, by a hair.

"I will," said Lucy, her eyes returning to a certain blond head of hair, "I have a lot of questions for Toby. But first I have to go get the potato salad."

Bill was on his feet, cheering as Tim Robbins whacked another homer high above the scoreboard.

Driving home, Lucy's emotions were in turmoil. Her little boy wasn't a little boy any more. He was practically setting up housekeeping with that girl. And smuggling! She hoped he wasn't involved with that. She remembered the blown-out watermelon, she believed fireworks were dangerous, you didn't have to convince her. How many people would get hurt because of the illegal fireworks the fishermen were smuggling? Kids could lose fingers, even eyes, or be horribly burned, but that didn't dissuade these fishermen from making a quick buck.

Though she had to admit, fireworks were legal in lots of places. And to be fair to the fishermen, they worked hard trying to make an honest living, but were constantly frustrated by fisheries' regulations, unpredictable weather and dramatic fluctuations in fish and shellfish populations due to disease, pollution and even natural causes. There was also a long tradition in Tinker's Cove of making money whenever and however you could, dating back to eighteenth-century mooncussers.

No wonder she couldn't make much headway in this murder investigation. Folks in this town were slippery and devious. They all had secrets. Here she'd lived next to the Pratts for years and she had no idea what their family life was really like. Had Calvin lived in terror of Pru? Had Wesley grown up simmering with resentment, even hatred for his mother? It certainly seemed likely, but she hadn't known about it. But the more she thought about it, the surer she was that Pru had been killed by either her husband or her son, or perhaps both of them working together. Just how she was going to prove this, though, was one detail she hadn't worked out yet.

Checking her watch, Lucy discovered it had only taken five minutes to make the drive from town. She'd be back in plenty of time for the picnic. She hurried into the house and went straight to the refrigerator, taking out the trays of cooked potatoes, the jars of mayonnaise and, well, where were those eggs?

She'd left an entire dozen, hard-boiled, in a bowl with a little note on top that said "NO!" in capital letters. Such notes had been Lucy's solution to the problem of snacking husbands and children, who were continually on the watch for anything edible. They had learned over the years to respect these notes, or risk incurring Lucy's wrath. That wrath was building, as she scrabbled around the shelves, shoving pickle jars and plastic containers aside in a frantic search for the eggs. All she turned up, was the note, which had landed on top of the crisper.

What was she going to do? She was known for her potato salad, everybody loved it. And it always had eggs. The eggs gave it a lovely golden tint, and added a nice flavor note. Damn it! She wanted the eggs.

She looked at the clock. She had time, if she hurried. But where could she get eggs? The stores were closed for the holiday, everybody was at the game, including Ellie. But not Bitsy Parsons, she realized. Members of the Revelation Congregation didn't celebrate holidays. Maybe she could call Bitsy and ask her to get a dozen eggs cooking. They'd probably be almost done by the time she got there. It was worth a try, she thought, consulting the phone book. But when she dialed, there was no answer.

No matter, she decided. Bitsy was probably outside tending to her little flower and egg stand. She'd leave a message. It was worth a try, anyway, she decided, packing up the trays of undressed potato salad. If worse came to worst, she could serve one tray plain while she cooked up the eggs in the home ec room at the school and dressed the second tray.

She was not going to get frantic about this, she told herself as she headed over to Bitsy's. It was only potato salad. It wasn't a life and death situation. And the drive to Bitsy's was beautiful, taking her along Shore Road with its incredible ocean views. Bitsy had certainly lucked out when she came into possession of the family property. It was perched on a rocky bluff high above the water and she had been heard to joke that on a clear day she could see straight to England. She couldn't, of course, but on certain crystal-clear days it seemed a distinct possibility.

Lucy took a deep breath of the ozone-scented air when she got out of the car, then leaned back in and honked the horn.

"Coming, coming!" called Bitsy, hurrying out of the house and drying her hands on a dish towel. She stopped in her tracks when she saw Lucy.

"Did you get my message?" asked Lucy, running towards her.

Bitsy stepped back. "Message?"

"On your answering machine," said Lucy, impatiently.

"No. I didn't notice," said Bitsy, blinking nervously.

"Well, I need eggs and I need 'em fast. Any chance you could hard-boil a dozen for me, while I wait?"

Bitsy looked puzzled. "Are you really here for eggs, Lucy Stone?"

"Of course," said Lucy, growing frustrated at Bitsy's dallying. "Why do you think I came all the way out here on the Fourth of July?" Then Lucy remembered that Bitsy was reputed to have a crush on Calvin Pratt. Could he possibly be paying her a call? Is that why Bitsy seemed so nervous? "Listen," said Lucy, "I know all about . . ."

"I'll get the water started," said Bitsy, cutting her off. "You go on and get the eggs."

That was all Lucy had to hear, she was off and running for the hen house. She yanked the door open, startling a few chickens who rushed out the little door for the safety of the run. Only one or two stubbornly broody hens remained on their nests and Lucy decided she would avoid them. There were plenty of eggs in the other nesting boxes. One on the bottom, in fact, seemed to have nearly a dozen. She bent down, not looking up when she heard Bitsy enter.

"Are you finding enough?" asked Bitsy.

Lucy turned to answer, but never had a chance to speak. She was out like a light before she knew what hit her.

Chapter Twenty-three

Lucy didn't want to wake up, so she kept her eyes screwed tight shut. She had a pounding headache and if she could only go back to sleep she wouldn't have to deal with it. Or the pain in her shoulders and arms. The arm she was lying on was asleep and if she moved it, if she rolled over onto her other side, she might be able to get back to sleep. But she couldn't move her arms. That's when she realized she was tied up.

Eyes wide open, she discovered she was lying in the sawdust litter on the floor of Bitsy's chicken house. The chickens didn't seem to mind this strange creature in their midst; one was perching on her foot. Lucy shook her foot as well as she could, considering a rope was neatly looped around both ankles and dislodged the bird, who ruffled its feathers in protest before hopping up onto a perch. The occasional clucks of the chickens had an oddly soothing effect, but Lucy didn't want to be soothed. She needed to get out of there before whoever did this to her came back to finish the job.

Who had done it? Had Bitsy conked her on the head and tied her up? It seemed impossible. Bitsy

was a little homebody who loved her chickens. She
was a faithful member of the Revelation Congregation, a sect that Lucy did not necessarily agree with
on doctrinal points but which held its members to
the highest standards of conduct. Members didn't
smoke, drink, dance or play cards, but they apparently did conk people on the head and tie them
up. Lucy couldn't believe it. Just thinking about it
made her headache worse.

She had to get out of here and figure out what
was going on. Maybe it wasn't Bitsy who had tied
her up; maybe it was Calvin or Wesley, or some ma-
niacal stranger who might also have attacked Bitsy.
Who might even be doing awful things to Bitsy at
this very moment. And who might be saving her
for last.

Lucy struggled against the ropes, straining against
them in hopes of loosening the knots. She couldn't
tie a knot to save her soul, not one that would actually hold against persistent pressure, and she
hoped whoever had trussed her up like this was
similarly challenged. It hurt her sore muscles to
tense them and her efforts to twist loose from the
ropes around her wrists seemed only to have the
opposite effect of tightening them, and rubbing
her skin raw. She let out a huge sigh of frustration
and realized her mistake when a cloud of sawdust
rose and settled back on her face, causing her to
sneeze furiously. She knew she had to get control
of herself, so she concentrated on her breathing
and gradually her heart stopped racing and the
sneezing was replaced with persistently running
eyes and nose she could do nothing about.

When she heard the door opening her heart
began pounding with fear, a reaction that didn't

subside when she recognized Bitsy, holding an evil little hatchet. It was so sharp that the edge gleamed, despite the deepening gloom. How long had she been here, she wondered. From the lengthening shadows she guessed it must be close to seven o'clock.

"Oh, dear," said Bitsy, standing before her and waving the hatchet. "Oh, dear. Oh, dear."

"Could you do something for me?" asked Lucy, struggling to keep her voice conversational. "Could you untie me?"

"Oh, silly me," exlaimed Bitsy. "What was I thinking?"

She immediately fell to her knees and began sawing away at the ropes. Lucy sat up, wiggling her toes and turning her feet in circles to restore the circulation and gently rubbing her tender wrists. She wanted to question Bitsy about what happened but hesitated for fear of setting off some sort of psychological fit. She was beginning to doubt Bitsy's sanity. And she still had that hatchet.

"I'm terribly sorry, Lucy. This was a terrible thing to do," said Bitsy. "I just panicked when I saw you, but now I see the error of my ways. I spent the afternoon praying and God has told me what I must do."

"And what's that?" asked Lucy in a small voice, keeping a wary eye on that hatchet.

"I have to accept responsibility for what I did. I have to go to the police and confess. Will you take me, Lucy?"

"Take you to the police station? That's not necessary, Bitsy," babbled Lucy, giddy with relief. "We all make mistakes. I'm perfectly happy to forget about this. I don't want to press charges."

"You didn't know?" asked Bitsy, looking down at the blade. "You didn't figure it out?"

"I just came for some eggs," said Lucy. "Figure what out?"

"That I killed Prudence Pratt."

The confession hit Lucy like a sledgehammer.

"*You* killed Pru?" she stammered.

Bitsy fell to her knees, facing Lucy, and letting the hatchet drop to the floor beside her. "If only I could do it over and take it all back," she said, sobbing. "I just lost my temper—I literally saw red—and when it was over, Prudence was lying there in the driveway. Dead."

Lucy reached out and patted her hand. "I'm sure it wasn't entirely your fault. Pru had a way of upsetting people."

"Oh, I was upset. I've struggled with this for years, you know, and I've struggled to forgive her. Sometimes I even thought I was making progress. I'd see her and Calvin sitting together in church and I'd say to myself, well she's the one he chose. He married her, not me, and that's the way it is. There was absolutely nothing I could do about it, even though it was very painful to see the way she treated him. But he chose her and they were married and marriage is forever in the sight of the Lord and that's all there is to it. So I prayed and prayed for acceptance and to make my life worthy in other ways. Without Calvin. And one day when I was praying it came to me, a revelation, that I should raise chickens. I should forget about pining for Calvin who I could never have and raise chickens instead. So I did. I took all the love I had for Calvin and poured it out into my chickens. My beautiful chickens."

Bitsy gestured with her hand and oddly enough, Lucy saw that at least half a dozen of the birds had gathered around Bitsy, as if listening to every word.

"They're amazing chickens," said Lucy.

"Oh, thank you, Lucy. I certainly think so." Bitsy patted the nearest chicken on the head, and stroked its feathery breast. "People tend to underrate chickens, but I've found that my birds are quite intelligent and, well, empathetic. They seem to sense when I'm troubled and try to comfort me. They'll lay extra big eggs, for example. And that clucking noise they make is so lovely. I've tape recorded it and play it when I have trouble sleeping."

"What a good idea," said Lucy, utterly convinced that Bitsy had lost her marbles. Every single one.

"I've always fed my chickens extremely well. Not just feed from the store but cracked grains for variety and lots of greens. They love them and it makes the egg yolks so yellow, and keeps the birds healthy, too. Some friends told me I should enter them in the county fair, so a few years ago, I did. And one of my birds won second place. And I really tried to be happy with second place even though Prudence's chicken won first place. I know envy is wrong, we're not supposed to covet our neighbor's chickens and I didn't. I honestly didn't because Pru's chickens are mean and don't have the same loving personalities that my chickens have. And I'd rather have a sensitive second-place chicken than a mean first-place chicken that pecks at all the other chickens."

"Absolutely right," agreed Lucy, observing the

little group of chickens that were clustered around Bitsy. A couple were even sitting in her lap.

"Then last year, one of my hens produced a clutch of chicks, and one of them was really eye-catching right from the beginning. She was a Buff Orpington, and that's a handsome breed to start with. They're kind of strawberry blond. Very pretty chickies. And this one was really kind of a Miss America of chickens. Just perfect. Everything you want in a Buff Orpington. Breasty and fluffy and pretty, with clear, bright eyes and a curvaceous beak and a coquettish little comb. So pretty. I named her Mildred, after my cousin who was a Miss Maine runner-up in 1982."

Lucy looked around the hen house, trying to identify Mildred, but in the growing gloom all the chickens looked pretty much the same to her.

"Now I know that saying about not counting your chickens before they're hatched and I believe it, I mean, there's a lot that can happen to a chicken. Dogs. Skunks. Raccoons. Disease. But I must say that Mildred seemed to thrive. She was a delight, and I was beginning to hope that she'd win the blue ribbon at the fair. I was just hoping, you understand, and taking good care of her. And praying. Not that she would win, because that would be wrong, but only that she'd have a happy, fulfilling life."

"Which one is Mildred?" asked Lucy.

"Bitsy's face whitened and she pressed her lips together. "She's gone."

"I'm so sorry," said Lucy.

"Prudence stole her. I didn't notice she was gone right away, because I was out all morning getting names on the petition about those nudists and then I stayed in town for the noontime prayer service. I had some nice salad greens for the hens—Dot Kirwan has the produce man at the market save them for me—so I went out to give them their treat and that's when I discovered Mildred was gone. I went over to my neighbors to ask if she'd seen anyone and she described Prudence's car, and then I remembered she left the petition drive when I got there and she wasn't at noontime prayer either. So I went over to her house and challenged her and she didn't even bother to deny it. She just looked at me in that mean way she has and asked if I'd like to have some lunch. She'd just cooked up some chicken fricassee, she said, and I knew she was referring to Mildred."

"Oh, dear."

"That's when I saw red. Everything went red. And I got in my truck and she was standing there in front of me, smacking her lips over the chicken hash and I just put my foot down on the pedal and the truck vroomed ahead and she was there and then she wasn't."

Lucy didn't know what to say so she simply reached out her hand to pat Bitsy's knee.

"Will you take me to the police station now, Lucy?"

"Whenever you're ready."

"I'm ready," said Bitsy.

Chapter Twenty-four

Bitsy seemed perfectly at peace sitting in the passenger seat but Lucy's mind was a whirl of ifs, buts and maybes. Maybe Bitsy didn't really kill Pru, maybe it had all been an insane delusion. Perhaps she'd wished so hard for it to happen that she'd actually convinced herself she'd done it. Some sort of guilt process. Lucy didn't know much about psychology but she knew even the soundest mind could play tricks. And she wasn't convinced that Bitsy was actually sane. Maybe she could plead insanity and go away for a nice, long rest somewhere.

It was amazing the stuff a good lawyer could come up with. She'd have to make sure Bitsy had a lawyer. Somebody who'd really fight for her. Who knows, maybe she could avoid a trial altogether by pleading guilty to a reduced charge of manslaughter? Or maybe she could get off entirely by arguing that it was justifiable homicide, considering the callous way Pru had murdered Mildred. It was just one of many mean things Pru had done and there were plenty of people in town who could testify to similar incidents. Bitsy was popular, too, and could certainly produce plenty of character witnesses.

"Try not to worry," said Lucy. "I'm sure things will work out."

"I'm not worried," said Bitsy. "I know that whatever happens the good Lord will take care of me. I'm truly sorry for what I did and I know he'll forgive me and that's all that really matters."

"Right," said Lucy, wondering if Bitsy had actually ever seen the inside of the women's wing at the county jail and if she knew what was in store for here there. Lucy had visited on several occasions and she'd found the experience difficult. There was something terrifying about the way everyone was treated so impersonally. "Processed" they called it, whether you were being admitted as an inmate or a visitor. Though it was infinitely better to be processed as a visitor because that only involved a quick pat down, a walk through a scanner and a handbag search instead of a humiliating full-body examination. That and the fact that even though all the doors closed with a final-sounding clang, you knew you'd be able to leave.

Lucy felt absolutely horrible when they reached the police station and she turned into the parking lot. She hoped Bitsy wouldn't have to spend time in the county jail—maybe they would release her on bail or even her own personal recognizance. She was certainly no threat to the community and wasn't a flight risk, either. On the contrary, she seemed eager to confess and receive her punishment.

"Thank you, Lucy," she said, her face radiant in the glow of the street lamp. "I'm sorry for any distress I caused you and I want you to know that today you were truly God's instrument."

Somehow that didn't make Lucy feel any better

as she accompanied Bitsy into the police station lobby. A uniformed officer she didn't recognize was sitting behind a counter, protected by a thick sheet of Plexiglas with a small opening that allowed a visitor to present documents or identification. The only access from the lobby to the offices beyond was through a forbidding, metal-plated door. It had always irritated Lucy, who wondered exactly what threat the Tinker's Cove police department believed required such an extreme level of security.

"What can I do for you ladies?" asked the officer, speaking through a microphone. His voice echoed.

"I'm here to make a confession," whispered Bitsy. "I murdered Prudence Pratt."

"You'll have to speak up," said the officer, looking like a goldfish in a tank.

"I murdered Prudence Pratt," yelled Bitsy. "I want to turn myself in."

"Sure you do," said the officer, looking extremely doubtful. "Tell you what, we're kind of busy right now with some holiday merry-makers, so why don't you go on home and come back tomorrow?"

"I'm a murderer," said Bitsy, indignantly. "I'm not leaving until I talk to somebody. I should be locked up."

"If you say so," replied the officer, yawning. "You can take a seat on the bench there but I can't guarantee anybody will get to you anytime soon."

"That's all right," said Bitsy. "We'll wait."

Once they sat down, however, Bitsy's resolve seemed to crumple. She began crying quietly, carrying on a whispered, prayerful dialog with God. Lucy felt excluded and useless, unable to offer comfort, but didn't want to leave Bitsy all alone, ei-

ther. She shifted restlessly on her chair, worried
that Bill and the kids would be missing her. She
checked the clock on the wall and discovered with
a shock that it was almost eight o'clock. Poor Bill
must be frantic with worry. She wanted to get out
of there and rejoin her family.

Suddenly ashamed of her selfishness, she patted
Bitsy's hand.

"Do you have someone to take care of your
chickens? Do you want me to do it?"

"That's sweet of you, Lucy, but Ellie Sykes said
she'd do it."

"Ellie? When did you talk to Ellie?"

"It was the last thing I did before I went out to
the coop and untied you." Bitsy paused. "I know I
apologized before, but I'm so sorry I hit you on
the head like that. There was no excuse for it,
truly. I don't know what I was thinking. And tying
you up like that. It must have been horribly uncomfortable. And the hatchet. I can understand
why you were so frightened, though of course I
only intended to use it to cut the ropes. I never
meant to harm you."

Lucy happened to glance at the officer, noticing
his surprised expression. He was talking on the
phone.

"I think the detective is free to talk to you now,"
he said. "Come on through."

A buzzer sounded and Lucy was able to open
the heavy metal door leading to the bowels of the
station. The officer met them on the other side.

"One at a time," he said, pointing to Lucy. "You
can wait outside."

Then, before she could even wish Bitsy luck, the
door slammed in her face.

Lucy hesitated a minute, standing uncertainly in the lobby, then decided to make her escape while she could. If the cops wanted to talk to her they knew where she lived. She was going to salvage what she could of the holiday.

A pungent smell assailed her when she opened the car doors—the potatoes. Sitting in the hot car at Bitsy's, not to mention the long wait at the police station, hadn't done them a bit of good. There was nothing to do but throw them out, all twenty pounds. Lucy drove the car over to the dumpster and chucked them in, then opened all the doors and windows to let the car air out. While she waited she called home on her cell phone. There was no answer—everyone must still be at the picnic.

The party was still going strong when Lucy arrived at the field overlooking the harbor. A local rock group was in the bandstand playing oldies. Some people were dancing, especially the kids, while others sat on lawn chairs and blankets listening to the music. Lucy spotted Bill chatting with Rachel and Bob, but before she could join them she was confronted by Sue.

"Lucy Stone, you promised me twenty pounds of potato salad. What happened?"

"I got tied up, solving the murder," said Lucy. "It was Bitsy."

"Right," laughed Sue. "Tell me another."

"Later," said Lucy, spotting Bill coming towards her. "I've got some explaining to do to my husband."

She ran up to Bill and threw her arms around him, practically knocking him off his feet.

"Whoa, Lucy," he said. "What's this all about."

"I'm safe. Everything's okay."

Bill looked at her sideways. "Of course you are."

"Don't tell me you didn't realize I was gone?"

"I thought you were helping out in the kitchen."

Lucy was indignant. "I was held captive in a chicken coop."

Bill was starting to speak when a huge explosion seemed to rock the very earth they were standing on. It was followed by shrieking rockets that soared high into the sky before exploding into streams of shimmering light. Shock quickly turned to delight and everyone cheered as dazzling chrysanthemum bursts of red and yellow filled the sky. They oohed and aahed as showers of whirling pinwheels danced high above their heads. The explosions came faster and faster, filling the sky with one beautiful display after another. It was the best fireworks show anyone had ever seen. It was incredible and it went on and on until Lucy began to wonder if it would ever stop.

"I didn't think they were going to have fireworks this year," said Bill, when the last rocket fizzled out and the sky was once again dark.

"They weren't," said Lucy, wondering exactly who had set them off and what the repercussions would be.

It wouldn't take long—police sirens could already be heard.

Chapter Twenty-five

The phone was ringing when they got home and Lucy was pretty sure she knew who it was. Her hunch was confirmed when she picked up the receiver.

"This is Lieutenant Horowitz," began the deep voice at the other end of the line. "I understand you were the victim of an assault earlier today and I'd like to talk to you about it as soon as possible, preferably tonight."

"Uh, sure," began Lucy, aware of her civic duty.

"I can be there in ten minutes."

"Uh, I don't think so," said Lucy, having second thoughts. She didn't want to add to Bitsy's woes. "I don't want to be interviewed."

"Bitsy Howell has confessed to assaulting you in her chicken coop."

"There must be some misunderstanding," said Lucy, firmly. "There was no assault."

"Ms. Howell claims she hit you on the head with a feed bucket rendering you unconscious. She then proceeded to tie you up and left you unattended for several hours, according to her statement, given

willingly and freely and under no duress whatso-
ever."

"I can't imagine why she's saying that."

"Mrs. Stone, I'd like to remind you that it is your
duty as a citizen to report a crime to the proper au-
thorities."

"I understand that."

"If you refuse to press charges we will be unable
to prosecute this case. Have you thought of that?"

"Actually, I have."

"Am I to understand that you are refusing to
press charges?"

"That's right," said Lucy, smiling as she hung up
the receiver.

The phone rang again almost immediately. It
was Ted.

"Lucy, can you come back to the paper and
write a first-hand account of how you solved the
murder? And don't forget to include Bitsy's attack
in the chicken house."

Lucy considered. She wanted to get back to
work, but there was no way she was going to go
public about the episode in the chicken house.
She knew all too well what it was like to be the subject of media scrutiny and she wasn't going to in-
flict that on Bitsy. She didn't want to add fuel to
the prosecutor's case, either. She wouldn't lie
under oath, if it came to that, but she wasn't going
to volunteer damaging information. Pru Pratt had
caused enough grief in Tinker's Cove and Lucy
was determined to end it.

"I'll come back, but I won't write about Bitsy."

There was a long pause.

"That's okay," said Ted, "There's plenty of other

stuff you can work on like the big fireworks explosion on Calvin's boat."

"The fireworks were from Calvin's boat?"

"Yeah," said Ted, chuckling. "He was desperate to get them to Massachusetts before the holiday so he and Wesley left yesterday as soon as the funeral was over. They only got a few miles before the bilge pump conked out and the engine was flooded. The current was pretty strong and pushed them back towards the cove, which was the last thing they wanted, of course. They were trying to solder a connection in the pump when they set off the fireworks by mistake. It was a heck of a show."

"People were saying it was the best they'd ever seen," said Lucy.

"Well, it looks as if they wiped out the purple-spotted lichen. The boat was just off the point when the fireworks started going off. Calvin and Wesley are in big trouble. The state environmental police are pressing charges and I'll bet Franke and the APTC are going to sue them, too."

"That doesn't seem fair. A lot of people are probably going to be grateful to Calvin and Wesley."

"What do you mean?"

"Well, if the lichen's gone, there's no reason the town can't have fireworks next year."

"That's right," said Ted.

"It gets better," said Lucy. "If the Quisset Point colony is gone, that means the only remaining lichen is at Blueberry Pond, and that means APTC will be making sure the naturists don't disturb it. At this rate, Calvin and Wesley will probably be named grand marshalls of the parade next year."

"I wouldn't count on that, Lucy. Don't forget

Wesley is still facing assault charges and Calvin has confessed to killing his wife."

"Calvin's confessed? But what about Bitsy?"

"That's exactly it. Barney told me that when Calvin heard about Bitsy's confession he went crazy, jumping up and down and screaming that he did it. And people say chivalry is dead."

"So who are they going to charge?"

"It's anybody's guess right now. But I can tell you that Horowitz is fit to be tied. It doesn't look as if he's going to be able to make a case against either of them." Ted paused. "There's a lot going on Lucy. I really need you. Will you come back?"

"See you tomorrow, Ted," she said.

"Don't be late."

Lucy smiled to herself. Some things never changed.

She was rinsing off the glasses and mugs that had collected in the kitchen sink when Toby came in the kitchen and opened the refrigerator, looking for a snack.

"Toby, I heard Calvin and Wesley had some trouble with their bilge pump. Do you know anything about it?"

"Poor maintenance, Mom," he said, lips twitching as he reached for the orange juice. "It's amazing how something like that can blow up in your face."

"Very funny," said Lucy, shaking her head.

She went into the family room to join Bill, who was watching the holiday shows on TV with Sara and Zoe. They were all sitting on the couch, and Lucy squeezed in between the girls just as the Boston Pops began playing the final section of the "1812 Overture" complete with church bells ringing and howitzers firing. The music ended and the fireworks were beginning when Elizabeth came in the room.

"Shut off the TV," she said. "I've got a surprise."

Bill clicked the remote and the TV fell silent.

"Promise you'll keep your voices low and soft. No shrieking, okay? He's little and his ears are sensitive."

"Whose ears?" asked Lucy, but Elizabeth had dashed out of the room.

When she returned she was accompanied by Toby and Molly. Molly was holding a squirming bundle wrapped in a towel.

"Mom, Dad, everybody," said Toby, "this is Molly. She's got something for you."

Molly placed the towel in Lucy's lap and unfolded it, revealing a wiggly little chocolate lab puppy.

"My dog had puppies a couple of months ago. When I heard about Kudo I told Toby you could have one, if you want it that is."

"We made sure it was a boy, like Kudo," said Elizabeth. "We thought you'd like that best."

"He's adorable," cooed Lucy as the puppy squirmed against her and licked her face. "What a cutie. Of course we want him."

"That's a cute puppy, sure enough," said Bill, "but it's no he."

Lucy lifted the dog up to see for herself. Bill was right.

"Goodness, Elizabeth. All the time you've been spending down at the pond with the naturists, and you still can't tell the difference?"

Epilogue

Things hadn't been going well on the home-front, that was for sure. For one thing, Mom just hadn't been her sweet self lately. Instead of settling down with the family and opening the milk bar, the way she used to, she'd suddenly become restless. Up and down. A pup would no sooner find her spot and start snacking when Mom would be up and on the move, leaving her and the others to dangle hopefully for a minute or two before tumbling to the floor with a thud. And there'd been no restorative, healing licks, either. Mom was too busy pawing at the door, demanding freedom, to attend to the puppies' needs.

It was nothing at all like those first blissful days when they all curled up together for endless naps and cuddles with plenty of rich, warm milk to drink. Now, even if Mom did decide to catch a rare nap things had suddenly gotten very crowded in-deed. And the competition was fierce with every-body pushing and shoving and nipping at each other. No, things had definitely changed.

In some ways, it was probably better. It was fun to chase her own tail and even more fun to chase somebody else's tail. And then there was wrestling, rolling around with her brothers and sisters and attempting to pin the other one down. Though even if she succeeded she only had the advantage for a moment before they were off and running again.

She'd finally gotten used to the routine—naps and meals and playtime—when it all changed again. She was plucked out of the pen, taken away from the gang. Without any warning, she found herself held tightly by one of those large, noisy, pink creatures. Its voice was so loud and piercing it hurt her ears. And then she was stuck in a box, all by herself. It was very upsetting and she'd started to cry.

That's when they had all descended on her—a whole litter of the huge, hairless beasts. All talking and passing her back and forth like she was a hot potato. And when she'd had that little accident, oh, the shrieks! All she wanted was to go back to Mom and the gang.

She was resigned to misery when she was picked up again and carried to one of the enormous creatures. This one was different. She felt soft, kind of like Mom. And her voice was quiet. She didn't shriek. Maybe there'd be milk, she thought, licking hopefully at the creature's face. There wasn't, but it was all right. Suddenly tired, she yawned, then curled up in the creature's lap and went to sleep.

Libby, Liberty, had found her new home.

Please turn the page for
an exciting sneak peek of
Leslie Meier's next
Lucy Stone mystery—
NEW YEAR'S EVE MURDER,
coming in hardcover in November 2005!

Chapter 1

WIN A WINTER MAKE-OVER for YOU and YOUR MOM!

A solid month of baking and chasing bargains and wrapping and decorating and secret keeping and it all came down to this: a pile of torn wrapping paper under the Christmas tree, holiday plates scattered with crumbs and half-eaten cookies, punch cups filmed with egg nog, and sitting on one end table, a candy dish holding a pristine and untouched pyramid of ribbon candy. And then there was that awful letter. Why did it have to come on Christmas Eve, just in time to cast a pall over the holiday?

Lucy Stone shook out a plastic trash bag and bent down to scoop up the torn paper, only to discover the family's pet puppy, Libby, had made herself a nest of Christmas wrap and was curled up, sound asleep. No wonder. With all the excitement of opening presents, tantalizing cooking smells, and people coming and going, it had been an exhausting day for her.

Lucy stroked the little Lab's silky head and decided to leave the mess a bit longer. Best to let sleeping dogs lie, especially if the sleeping dog in question happened to be seven months old and increasingly given to bouts of manic activity, which included chewing shoes and furniture. She turned instead to the coffee table and started stacking plates and cups, then sat down on the sofa as a wave of exhaustion overtook her. It had been a long day. Zoe, her youngest at only eight years old, had awoken early and roused the rest of the house. Sara, fourteen, hadn't minded, but their older sister, Elizabeth, protested the early hour. She was home for Christmas break from Chamberlain College in Boston, where she was a sophomore, and had stayed out late on Christmas Eve catching up with her old high school friends.

She had finally given in and gotten out of bed after a half-hour of coaxing, and the Christmas morning orgy of exchanging presents had begun. What had they been thinking, wondered Lucy, dreading the credit card bills that would arrive as certainly as snow in January. She and Bill had really gone overboard this year, buying skis for Elizabeth and high-tech ice skates for Sara and Zoe. When their oldest child, Toby, arrived later in the day with his fiancée Molly, they had presented him with a snow board and her with a luxurious cashmere sweater. And those were only the big presents. There had been all the budget-busting books, CDs, video games, sweaters, and pajamas, right on down to the chocolate oranges and lip balm tucked in the toe of each bulging Christmas stocking.

It all must have cost a fortune, guessed Lucy, who had lost track of the actual total sometime around December 18. Oh, sure, it had been great fun for the hour or two it took to open all the presents, but those credit card balances would linger for months. And what was she going to do about the letter? It was from the financial aid office at Chamberlain College advising her that they had reviewed the family's finances and had cut Elizabeth's aid package by ten thousand dollars. That meant they had to come up with the money or Elizabeth would have to leave school.

She guiltily fingered the diamond studs Bill had surprised her with, saying they were a reward for all the Christmases he was only able to give her a handmade coupon book of promises after they finished buying presents for the kids. It was a lovely gesture, but she knew they couldn't really afford it. She wasn't even sure he had work lined up for the winter. The economy was supposed to be recovering, but like many in the little town of Tinker's Cove, Maine, Bill was self-employed. Over the years he had built a solid reputation as a restoration carpenter, renovating rundown older homes for city folks who wanted a vacation home by the store. Last year, when the stock market was soaring he had made plenty of money, which was probably why the financial aid office had decided they could afford to pay more. But even last year, Bill's best year ever, they had struggled to meet Elizabeth's college expenses. Now that the Dow was hovering well below its former dizzying heights, Bill's earnings had dropped dramatically. The economists called it a "correction" but it had been a disaster for vacation communities like Tinker's Cove as the big city lawyers and bankers and stockbrokers who were the mainstay of the second home market found themselves without the fat bonus checks they were counting on.

The sensible course would be to return the earrings to the store for a refund, but that was out of

the question. She remembered how excited Bill
had been when he gave her the little box and how
pleased he'd been at her surprised reaction when
she opened it and found the sparkling earrings.
All she'd hoped for, really, was a new flannel night-
gown. But now she had diamond earrings. He'd
also written a private note, apologizing for all the
years he'd taken her for granted, like one of the
kids. But they had surprised her, too, with their
presents. Toby and Molly had given her a pair of
buttery soft kid gloves, Elizabeth had presented
her with a jar of luxurious lavender body lotion from
a trendy Newbury Street shop, Sara had put together
a tape of her favorite songs to play in the car and
Zoe had found a calendar with photos of Labrador
puppies—all presents that had delighted her because they showed a lot of thought.

So how was she repaying them for all their love
and thoughtfulness? In just a short while she was
going off to New York City with Elizabeth and leaving the rest of the family to fend for themselves.
Really abandoning them for their entire Christmas
vacation. The bags were packed and standing ready
in the hallway; they would leave as soon as Elizabeth
returned from saying good-bye to her friends.

She had been thrilled when Elizabeth announced
she had entered a *Jolie* magazine contest and won
winter makeovers for herself and her mother. Not
only was she enormously proud of her clever daughter but at first she was excited at the prospect of
the makeover itself. What working mother wouldn't
enjoy a few days of luxurious pampering? But now
she wished she could convert the prize into cash.
Besides, how would Bill manage without her? What

would Zoe and Sara do all day? Watch TV? That was no way to spend a week-long holiday from school.

Also, worried Lucy, checking to make sure the earrings were still firmly in place, what if the supposedly "all-expense paid" makeover wasn't quite as "all-expense paid" as promised? Traveling was expensive—there were always those little incidentals, like tips and magazines and mints and even airplane meals now that you had to buy them, that added up. What if it turned out to be like those "free" facials at the make-up counter where the sales associates pressured you to buy a lot of expensive products that you would never use again?

Lucy sighed. To tell the truth, she was a little uneasy about the whole concept of being made-over. There was nothing the matter with her. She stood up and looked at her reflection in the mirror that hung over the couch. She looked fine. Not perfect, of course. She was getting a few crow's-feet, there were a few gray hairs and that stubborn five pounds she couldn't seem to lose, but she was neat and trim and could still fit in the sparkly Christmas sweatshirt the kids had given her years ago. And since she only wore it a few times a year it still looked as festive as ever.

Now that she was actually giving it a critical eye, she could understand why her friend Sue always teased her about the sweatshirt. It was boxy and didn't do a thing for her figure. Furthermore, it was the height of kitsch, featuring a bright green Christmas tree decorated with sequins, beads, and bows. Not the least bit sophisticated.

She sighed. She hadn't always been a country mouse; she'd grown up in a suburb of the city and had made frequent forays with her mother, and later with her friends, to shop, see a show, or visit a museum. It would be fun to go back to New York, especially since she hadn't been in years. And she was looking forward to a reunion with her old college buddy, Samantha Blackwell. They had been faithful correspondents through the years, apparently both stuck in the days when people wrote letters, but had never gotten in the habit of telephoning each other. Caught in busy lives with numerous responsibilities, they'd never been able to visit each other, despite numerous attempts. Lucy had married right out of college and moved to Maine, where she started a family and worked as a part-time reporter for the local weekly newspaper. Sam had been one of a handful of pioneering women accepted to study for the ministry at Union Theological Seminary and had promptly fulfilled the reluctant admission officer's misgivings by promptly dropping out when she met her lawyer husband, Brad. She now worked for the International AIDS Foundation, and Lucy couldn't wait to see her and renew their friendship.

Which reminded her, she hadn't had a chance yet today to call her friends to wish them a Merry Christmas. That was one holiday tradition she really enjoyed. She sat back down on the couch and reached for the phone, dialing Sue Finch's number.

"Are you all ready for the trip?" asked Sue, after they'd gotten the formalities out.

"All packed and ready to go."

"I hope you left room in your suitcase so you can take advantage of the after-Christmas sales. Sidra says they're fabulous." Sidra, Sue's daughter, lived in New York with her husband, Geoff Rumford, and was an assistant producer of the *Norah!* TV show.

"No sales for me." Lucy didn't want the whole town to know about the family's finances, so she prevaricated. "I think I'll be too busy."

"They can't keep you busy every minute."

"I think they intend to. We're catching the ten o'clock flight out of Portland tonight so we can make a fashion show breakfast first thing tomorrow morning, then there are numerous expert consultations, a spa afternoon, photo sessions and interviews, I'm worried I won't even have time to see Sam." She paused. "And if I do have some free time, I'm planning to visit some museums like the Met and MOMA. . . ."

Sue, who lived to shop, couldn't believe this heresy. "But what about Bloomingdale's?"

"I've spent quite enough on Christmas as it is," said Lucy. "I've got to economize."

"Sure," acknowledged Sue, "but you have to spend money to save it."

It was exactly this sort of logic that had led her into spending too much on Christmas in the first place, thought Lucy, but she wasn't about to argue. "If you say so," she laughed. "I've got to go. Someone's on call waiting."

It was Rachel Goodman, another member of the group of four that met for breakfast each week at Jake's Donut Shack.

"Did Santa bring you anything special?" asked Rachel.

Something in her tone made Lucy suspicious. "How did you know?"

"Bill asked me to help pick them out. Do you like them?"

"I love them, but he shouldn't have spent so much."

"I told him you'd be happy with pearls," said Rachel, "but he insisted on the diamonds. He was really cute about it. He said he wanted you to wear them in New York."

This was a whole new side of Bill that Lucy wasn't familiar with. She wasn't sure she could get used to this sensitive, considerate Bill. She wondered fleetingly if he was having some sort of midlife crisis.

"Aw, gee, you know I'm really having second thoughts about this trip."

"Of course you are."

Lucy wondered if Rachel knew more than she was letting on. "What do you mean?"

"Haven't you heard? There's this awful flu going around."

"What flu?"

"It's an epidemic. I read about it in the *New York Times*. They're advising everyone to avoid crowds and wash their hands frequently."

"How do you avoid crowds in a city?"

"I don't know, but I think you should try. Flu can be serious. It kills thousands of people every year."

"That was 1918," scoffed Lucy.

"Laugh if you want. I'm only trying to help."

Lucy immediately felt terrible for hurting Rachel's feelings. "I know, and I appreciate it. I really do."

"Promise you'll take precautions?"

"Sure. And thanks for the warning."

She was wondering whether she should buy some disinfectant wipes as she dialed Pam's number. Pam, also a member of the breakfast group, was married to Lucy's boss at the newspaper, Ted

Stillings, and was a great believer in natural remedies.

"Disinfectant wipes? Are you crazy? That sort of thing just weakens your immune system."

"Rachel says there's a flu epidemic and I have to watch out for germs."

"How are you supposed to do that? The world is full of millions, billions, zillions of germs that are invisible to the human eye. If Mother Nature intended us to watch out for them, don't you think she would have made them bigger, like mosquitoes or spiders?"

It was a frightening picture. "I never thought of that."

"Well, trust me, Mother Nature did. She gave you a fabulous immune system to protect the Good Body." That's how Pam pronounced it, with capital letter emphasis. "Your immune system worries about the germs so you don't have to."

"If that's true, how come so many people get sick?"

"People get sick because they abuse their bodies. They pollute their Good Bodies with empty calories and preservatives instead of natural whole foods, they don't get enough sleep, they don't take care of themselves." Pam huffed. "You have to help Mother Nature. She can't do it all, you know."

"Okay. How do I help her?"

"One thing you can do is take vitamin C. It gives the immune system a boost. That's what I'd do if I were you, especially since you're going into a new environment that might stress your organic equilibrium."

Lucy was picturing a dusty brown bottle in the back of the medicine cabinet. "You know, I think

I've got some. Now I just have to remember to take it. It looks like we're going to be pretty busy with this makeover."

"Don't let them go crazy with eye shadow and stuff," advised Pam.

"Is it bad for you?"

"It's probably a germ farm, especially if they use it on more than one person, but that isn't what I was thinking about." She paused, choosing her words. "You're beautiful already. You don't need that stuff."

"Why, thanks, Pam," said Lucy, surprised at the compliment.

"I mean it. Beauty comes from inside. It doesn't come from lipstick and stuff."

"That's the way it ought to be," said Lucy, "but lately I've been noticing some wrinkles and gray hairs, and I don't like them. Maybe they'll have some ideas that can help."

"Those things are signs of character. You've earned those wrinkles and gray hairs!"

"And the mommy tummy, too, but I'm not crazy about it."

"Don't even think about liposuction," warned Pam, horrified. "Promise?"

"Believe me, it's not an option," said Lucy, hearing Bill's footsteps in the kitchen. "I've got to go."

When she looked up he was standing in the doorway, dressed in his Christmas red plaid flannel shirt and new corduroy pants. He was holding a small box wrapped with a red bow, and her heart sank. "Not another present!"

"It's something special I picked up for you."

Lucy couldn't hide her dismay. "But we've spent so much already. We'll be lucky to get this year's bills paid off before next Christmas!" She paused, considering. There was no sense in putting it off any longer. "And Elizabeth's tuition bill came yesterday. Chamberlain College wants sixteen thousand dollars by January 6. That's ten thousand more than we were expecting to pay. Ten thousand more than we have."

He sat down next to her on the couch. "It's not the end of the world, Lucy. She can take a year off and work."

"At what? There are no good jobs around here."

"She could work in Boston."

"She'd be lucky to earn enough to cover her rent! She'd never be able to save."

Bill sighed. "I know giving the kids college educations is important to you, Lucy, but I don't see what it did for us. I'm not convinced it really is a good investment—not at these prices."

Lucy had heard him say the same thing many times, and it always made her angry.

"That's a cop-out, and you know it. It's our responsibility as parents to give our kids every opportunity we can." She sighed. "I admit it doesn't always work out. Toby hated college; it wasn't for him. And that's okay. But Elizabeth's been doing so well. It makes me sick to think she'll have to drop out."

Bill put his arm around her shoulder. "We'll figure something out . . . or we won't. There's nothing we can do about it right now. Open your present."

Lucy's eyes met his, and something inside her began to melt. She reached up and stroked his beard. "You've given me too much already."

"It's all right, really," said Bill, placing the little box in her hand. "Trust me."

"Okay." Lucy prepared herself to accept another lavish gift, promising herself that she would quietly return it for a refund when she got back from New York. What could it be? A diamond pendant to match the earrings? A gold bangle? What had he gone and done? She set the box in her lap and pulled the ends of the red satin bow. She took a deep breath and lifted the top, then pushed the cotton batting aside.

"Oh my goodness," she said, discovering a bright red plastic watch wrapped in cellophane. "It's got lobster hands."

"That's because it's a lobster watch," said Bill. "They gave them out at the hardware store. Do you like it?"

"Like it? I love it," she said. "I think it makes quite a fashion statement."

"And it tells time," said Bill, pulling her close.

Lucy took a second look at the watch. "Was it really free?"

"Absolutely. Positively. Completely."

"I'll wear it the whole time I'm away," said Lucy. "I'll be counting the minutes until I get home."

"That's the idea," said Bill, nuzzling her neck.

The wrapping paper underneath the tree crinkled and rustled as Libby rolled over. Instinctively, just as they had when they'd briefly shared their bedroom with the newest baby, they held their breaths, afraid she would wake up. They waited until she let out a big doggy sigh and her breathing became deep and regular, then they tiptoed out of the living room.

As they joined Sara and Zoe in the family room, where they were watching a "A Christmas Story,"

Lucy resolved to enjoy the few remaining hours of Christmas. She'd have plenty of time on the plane to break the news to Elizabeth and to try to come up with a solution. A ten thousand dollar solution.

ABOUT THE AUTHOR

Leslie Meier lives with her family in Massachusetts. Her newest Lucy Stone mystery, NEW YEAR'S EVE MURDER, will be published in hardcover in November 2005. Leslie loves to hear from her readers and you may write to her c/o Kensington Publishing. Please include a self-addressed stamped envelope if you wish a response.

Grab These
Kensington Mysteries

Mischief, Murder &
Mayhem – Grab These
Kensington Mysteries

More Mischief, Murder
& Mayhem in These
Kensington Mysteries